"Gracious me, Abby, did you see that? We have to turn off the TV."

I nearly choked on my chicken. "Excuse me?"

"Didn't you see that strip along the bottom of the screen?"

"No, I was looking at my plate. What was it? A tornado watch?" Houses in Charleston sit only a few feet above sea level so there are no basements. We don't often get tornado watches, but when we do, Mama insists that we repair to her closet, where there is another television.

"It's about some woman—"

"Don't tell me Cher's on yet another farewell tour."

Mama patted her pearls indignantly. "I wouldn't interrupt my Holy Hour (she actually calls it that) for Cher. The woman on the news bulletin was found in Charleston Harbor wrapped in a carpet."

A gaggle of geese waddled over my grave. "Was she dead?"

"Of course, dear. It said some tourist found her floating next to the seawall near the Charleston Yacht Club.

"Mama, I think I know who it is!"

Den of Antiquity Mysteries by
Tamar Myers

TAMAR MYERS

Death OF A Rug Lord

A DEN OF ANTIQUITY MYSTERY

AVON

An Imprint of HarperCollinsPublishers

This is a work of fiction. Names, characters, places, and incidents are drawn from the author's imagination or are used fictitiously and are not to be construed as real. Any resemblance to actual events, locales, organizations, or persons, living or dead, is entirely coincidental.

AVON BOOKS
An Imprint of HarperCollins*Publishers*
195 Broadway
New York, NY 10007

Copyright © 2008 by Tamar Myers
ISBN 978-0-06-084659-6
www.avonmystery.com

First Avon Books paperback printing: June 2008

Avon Trademark Reg. U.S. Pat. Off. and in Other Countries, Marca Registrada, Hecho en U.S.A.
HarperCollins® is a registered trademark of HarperCollins Publishers.

Printed in the U.S.A.

10 9 8 7 6 5 4 3

To the highly esteemed and prestigious Charleston Authors Society, of which I am proud to be a member.

Death
OF A
Rug Lord

1

When I looked the gift horse in the mouth, it was clear that she'd been drinking. I couldn't help but take a step back. She, alas, took two steps forward.

"Aren't you Abigail Timberlake?" she said.

"Guilty."

"You own the Den of Antiquity down on King Street, right?"

"Right as rain in November."

"I've been in your shop dozens of times."

I smiled quickly over clenched teeth. I'm a tiny woman, just four-foot-nine. One good whiff of her breath could send my alcohol level over the moon.

"So you saw my ad on TV, huh?"

It was either give up on sobriety or appear to be rude. "Yes, ma'am," I said, "I've seen your ads, and I couldn't believe my ears. And now I can't believe my eyes. How can y'all afford to price these Oriental rugs so low?"

Gwen—that's what was printed on her badge— glanced around the crowded room. "I believe it's something to do with high volume."

"Yes, but y'all have got to be selling these *way* below cost. Even if y'all sold a million, y'all still won't turn a profit."

She shrugged. "Yeah, well, go figure."

"Take this one for example," I said. "It's a Persian from Tabriz, right? The traditional *mahi*, or fish, design."

Gwen had to flip three corners over before she found the tag, which was sewn on the back. "You're good. Mrs. Timberlake."

"Actually it's Washburn."

"Huh?"

"The 'Missus' part. I keep the Timberlake for business reasons."

"You related to Justin?"

"Not that we know of. But you see, Timberlake is also a married name— Never mind, it's a long story. Now about this price, there has got to be a zero missing, right?"

"No, it's correct."

"But it says 695. Even wholesale, it's worth twice that."

"Maybe." She tossed her head to get some irksome hair out of her face. Her amber mane was thick and waist length, truly worthy of being envied. "But like they say," she continued, "don't kiss a gift horse on the mouth."

I stifled an impulse to snicker. "Still, this has to be a mistake. May I speak to the manager, please?"

"Uh . . . I am the manager."

"You are? I mean, of course you are." Funny, but I was sure the manager of Pasha's Palace was a man. Gary something or other.

A mind as small as mine is easily read. "Gary quit last month. I'm Gwendolyn Spears, his replacement."

"Oh, but then surely you must know that these rugs are underpriced."

Gwen's eyes locked on mine. "Didn't I read in the paper about your brother getting married recently?"

"Yes." Where could she possibly be going with this? Could she be hoping for a similar discount at my shop? Well, that just wasn't possible; I price my merchandise fairly, but I don't give it away.

"Then it's a wedding present for him and his lucky bride."

"*Excuse* me?"

"Here." She expertly rolled the rug and slung it over her shoulder. "I'll walk you to your car."

"But you can't." My protest was sincere, although a part of me was excited about acquiring such a beautiful work of art.

"I can, and I will," Gwendolyn Spears said.

My full name is Abigail Louise Timberlake Washburn. My first husband, Buford Timberlake, was more of a timber snake, and we divorced after he traded me in for a woman half my age. My second, and last, husband is Greg Washburn, a retired detective from Charlotte. Greg is now half owner of a shrimp boat in Mount Pleasant, South Carolina.

We are S.O.B.'s, and proud of it. Our lovely home is *south of Broad* Street in historic Charleston, South Carolina. My widowed mother, Mozella Wiggins, lives with us, as does Dmitri, an orange tabby that tips the scale at sixteen pounds. I have two grown children, Susan

3

and Charlie: the former lives in New York, where she works as a legal secretary; the latter in Paris, where he supports himself by cleaning chimneys (Charlie's ambition is to be a painter).

Most of us are happy—at least some of the time—so one might conclude that life at 7 Squiggle Lane proceeds on a fairly even keel. But if that is what one concludes, then one would be wrong. Murder and mayhem follow me around like sin chases after televangelists. On the plus side, I never have time to be bored. But then neither do I have much time in which to relax.

One of these rare moments of leisure found me sitting in my favorite chair whilst watching *All My Children* and eating lunch. I will confess right now that during the commercials, I cast admiring glances at that glorious Persian rug from Tabriz. I know, it was supposed to be a wedding present for my brother, Toy, and his wife, C.J. But they lived all the way up in Sewanee, Tennessee, and I wasn't scheduled to see them for a couple of weeks. Besides, the rug was already old and used. If I derived joy from it in the meantime, who could it possibly hurt?

Mama is also addicted to AMC, the finest soap opera on network television, and it is she who encourages me to leave my shop, on a daily basis, in the hands of my very capable assistant, and join her for lunch. Since Mama can cook up a storm (all the while looking like Donna Reed, replete with pearls and starchy crinolines), I'd say I have it pretty good. While normally Mama can chatter a magpie into submission, during AMC she insists on total silence. The occasional gasp is permitted—as surprises in the story line unfold—but words are never allowed. *Ever.*

I was quite enjoying my chicken salad sandwich and fresh fruit plate when I heard the unimaginable.

"Gracious me, Abby, did you see that? We have to turn off the TV."

I nearly choked on my chicken. "Excuse me?"

"Didn't you see that strip along the bottom of the screen?"

"No, I was looking at my plate. What was it? A tornado watch?" Houses in Charleston sit only a few feet above sea level, so there are no basements. We don't often get tornado watches, but when we do, Mama insists that we repair to her closet, where there is another television. Someday, perhaps, we'll be watching Erica Kane fool Jackson Montgomery into marrying her yet again, while we sail off to Oz.

"It's about some woman—"

"Hillary?" Mama is a huge fan of Barack Obama and takes it as a personal affront when his rivals are in town.

"No, Abby. This woman—"

"Don't tell me Cher's on yet another farewell tour."

Mama patted her pearls indignantly. "I wouldn't interrupt my Holy Hour"—she actually calls it that—"for Cher. The woman on the news bulletin was found in Charleston Harbor wrapped in a carpet."

A gaggle of geese waddled over my grave. "Was she dead?"

"Of course, dear. It said some tourist found her floating next to the seawall near the Charleston Yacht Club.

"Mama, I think I know who it is!"

5

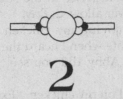

2

I couldn't get Greg on the phone, which probably meant he was too far out at sea. Sometimes when the shrimping isn't good, he and his cousin, Booger Boy, head out do to some deepwater fishing. As long as I don't have to skin or scale what he catches, I'm fine with the way he spends his days. After all, it's not like we need the money.

Plan B was to make a beeline to the harbor before the police had a chance to seal off East Bay Street—if they hadn't already. Unfortunately I was a few seconds too late, and even then I had to park my car in someone's driveway along Zigzag Alley. From there to the sidewalk that traces the harbor, I had to slip through (and even under) a tangle of tourist bodies. That's the downside of getting pulled from Charleston Harbor in April: your friends will have to work very hard to watch them drag your waterlogged body out of the drink.

I got trapped in a forest of polyester-clad legs belonging to a group of women trying to get back to their cruise ship. The forest was anything but enchanted.

6

"What the heck was that thing?" a woman from one of the square states said.

"I heard someone say it's a mermaid," her companion said.

"Mermaids don't exist," the first woman said.

"Then maybe it's a manatee."

"It's a woman, for crying out loud," I said.

"You know they're not going to let us back on the ship for another couple of hours. We may as well return to the market and kill time there. I saw a coral bracelet in one of the booths that was really nice. I'd like to get it for Cindy."

"Cindy! After what she did to you?"

"Ladies, please," I said, "I need to get through."

"Don't be so pushy." The speaker shoved me hard enough to knock me off my feet. Fortunately I landed on someone's feet, instead of the hard concrete walkway.

Strong arms jerked me to a standing position. "You children need to larn ya manners," their owner said. "Hey, you ain't no child; you're a woman. Full growed and mighty purty too."

"Thank you."

"Where ya trying ta get to, little lady?"

"The woman they pulled out of the harbor—I know her."

"Ya wanna get up close? That it?"

"Yes, sir."

"Then as we say where I come from, no prob, Bob." Without further ado he gripped my waist with one massive hand, grabbed my ankles with the other, and hoisted me straight up into the air as if I was a flag and he was a member of the color guard. My first thought was: thank goodness I'd worn jeans that day, and not the skirt I usually wore to work.

Big Bob—or whatever his name was—was truly a godsend. Despite some rather audible grumbling from the crowd, I was soon deposited gently on the seawall, just inside the yellow crime zone tape.

"Thanks," I whispered.

"My pleasure, little lady."

But before I'd taken one step in the recovered body's direction, someone else tapped me rudely on the shoulder. "Oh no you don't, Timberlake."

I turned slowly, knowing I would find myself eye-to-bosom with the very unpleasant Detective Tweedledee of the Charleston Police Department. What can I say, except that the woman just plain doesn't like me? Okay, so perhaps there's a bit more to the story.

For some bizarre reason the universe insists on throwing the corpses of murder victims into my path. It's as if I'm walking in the shadow of Jessica Fletcher—although given my size, it would have to be her noon shadow. At any rate, almost invariably it's Detective Tweedledee who becomes involved in these cases, and not with the best results. Usually her poor performances stem from the fact that I solve the crimes first. It's not that I simply want to; I *have* to, in order to stay alive.

I'm sure it should be remembered that Detective Esmeralda Tweedledee is some mother's daughter. She might even mean well—in her own sort of way. That said, she is so stupid, bless her heart, that she couldn't pour water out of her boots, even if the instructions were written on the heels. She's also as ornery as a snake, possesses a memory like an elephant's, and jumps to conclusions faster than my friend Magdalena Yoder who lives up in Pennsylvania.

"I know this woman," I said, infusing my voice with enough respect to soothe the savage breast of a third world dictator.

"How do you know it's a she?"

"Because her blouse is thin and I can see the outline of her bra—because I recognize her, that's why." I was, in fact, not ten yards from the body. Although Gwen's face was turned away from me, her long amber hair was a dead giveaway.

"What's her name?"

"Gwendolyn Spears. She is—was—the manager of Pasha's Palace."

"That rug warehouse?"

"Yes."

"I know you're making this up, Timberlake, because Gary's the manager. 'It's not scary, when you buy from Gary. Au contraire . . . ' I've seen the ads on TV." Although she didn't touch me, she still managed to push me back behind the yellow tape. I'm not sure how that happened—perhaps she moved inside a bubble of anger that had its own force field.

"Gary quit last month."

"Yeah? Says who?"

"The woman rolled in the rug. She told me herself last week."

"We'll see." She stomped off and made a couple of calls. Upon her return she looked even more cross. "How do you know so much about the deceased?"

"She sold me a carpet. We had a brief conversation."

"Is that the only time you spoke to her?"

"Yes."

"Maybe."

"What is that supposed to mean?"

"So which is the right word? Rug, or carpet?"

"They're pretty much interchangeable, although more often the larger ones are referred to as carpets, and the small ones are called rugs."

She must have found that not only immensely interesting, but worthy of extensive commentary. Knowing her as well as I did, I waited patiently while she filled several pages on a metal clipboard in the loopy handwriting reminiscent of a teenybopper. Finally, sighing from her efforts, she looked up.

"You still work at the Den of Iniquity on King Street?"

"Den of Antiquity—yes."

"That's what I said."

"May I pay my respects to Ms. Spears?"

"You mean get closer?"

"Yes."

"Now why would you want to do that? You didn't even know the woman; you only had one brief conversation with her. Said so yourself not a minute ago."

"Okay, Detective Tweedle*doo*," I said, deliberating mispronouncing her name, "I confess. I have no interest in seeing the corpse of someone I've only just met. However, I am interested—"

"It's Tweedle*dee*."

"What?"

"My name, you idiot. That's how it's pronounced."

"Are you sure? I have a friend up in Charlotte who pronounces her name *doo*. Jasmine Tweedledoo. Do you think the two of you could be related?"

"Timberlake, get to your dang point! Why do you want to get closer to the recovered body?"

"I want to see if the rug is the genuine thing, or a reproduction."

"Hmm." Her eyes rolled back slightly as she cogitated on the pros and cons of granting me my desire. Perhaps she'd gone to another time and place altogether. In fact, no telling where she may have wandered, lost in thought, had we not been interrupted by the forensic photographer.

"Ma'am," he said, "I'm all done. Shall I tell the morgue they can haul her away now?"

"Haul?" I said. "She's not a load of cargo!"

Tweedledee snapped back to the here and now. "Wait a minute. This woman from the Den of Inequality wants to get a close look at the rug. Who knows, she might even have something useful to tell us."

"Thank you, Detective Twaddledee," I said, and strode in Gwen's direction as fast as my short legs could carry me.

"Well?" the detective demanded. "What'd you make out? Is it the real McCoy or not?"

"It's a genuine, handmade, Oriental rug."

"How do you know?"

"There are inconsistencies in the pattern. These often—but not necessarily—show up in the corners."

"You mean mistakes?"

"More likely the weaver misjudged the amount of

yarn needed in a particular color, or was bored. A machine-made carpet would likely be symmetrical."

"Anything else?"

"Look here—at the back. This is the warp, and these are the wefts. They're the grid, if you will. In this case it's kind of wobbly."

"Yeah, but these things make it less valuable, don't they?"

"Oh, not at all. If you want a machine-made carpet, then go to Home Depot or Lowe's. There you can buy a mass-produced one for as little as three hundred dollars. If you want a handmade one, you have to go to a carpet store. Some of the best will cost tens of thousands of dollars, depending on the materials and the craftsmanship. And, of course, size."

"Maybe."

I turned away from the sanctity of Gwen's body before raising my voice in frustration. "There you go again, Detective Tiddlywinks! I know what I'm talking about."

"If this one had any value at all, why would someone wrap a dead woman in it?"

"Isn't that your job to find out?"

"I'm warning you, Timberlake. I've had all the attitude from you I can take. Do you hear me?"

I slipped under the crime scene tape.

"Do you *hear* me?" she shouted.

"Yes, ma'am."

I tried slipping back into the crowd. One of the few advantages of being my height is that anonymity can usually be achieved in a matter of seconds. This time I was not so lucky.

"I'm coming with you," a voice from on high said.

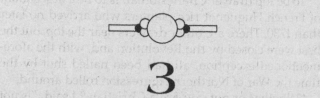

3

It was Big Bob again—or whoever the stranger was. It certainly was not God.

"Uh . . . sir, I really appreciate what you did before, but this time it feels like you're stalking me."

"No, ma'am, I ain't doing no such thing. It's just that you being a Charlestonian—well, I was wondering if you could show me some of the sights. And I mean that totally legit, ma'am, I assure you. I am a Christian, born and bred."

A Charlestonian! Ha, I wish. While I happened to live in Charleston, I was by no means a Charlestonian. To be a Charlestonian, one's forbears must have arrived on the scene before the Late Unpleasantness, and if you had to ask when that was, you were automatically disqualified. Although there is one very prominent family residing in the area—which I shall not name—that arrived a tad after the Late Unpleasantness, and which tries very hard to get around this very basic qualification by getting as many things stamped with the family name as possible. But, to paraphrase the Bard, a rose is just a rose is just a rose.

To be top drawer Charlestonian is to be a descendant of French Huguenot rice planters who arrived no later than 1730. There are other drawers near the top, but the best were closed by the Revolution and, with the afore-mentioned exception, all had been nailed shut by the time the War of Northern Aggression rolled around.

"Whether or not you are a Christian," I said, "is not a concern of mine. One of my best friends is Jewish and he is no more, nor less, upstanding than my Christian friends. The thing is, I am not a tour guide; I am an antiques dealer. The City of Charleston has one of the best tourist offices of any city its size. I'd be happy to drop you off there if you like."

"Ma'am, I'd be much beholden."

Beholden? Who the heck talked like that these days? The giant who'd come to my rescue was certainly charming, I'd give him that. What harm could there possibly be in driving him a couple of blocks north to the tourist center?

"Sure thing," I said. "I'm parked over there along the Battery. And just so you know, my husband, Greg, used to be a detective for the city of Charlotte."

He laughed loudly and, frankly, far too long. "Is that so? Can't say as I blame you for saying that, seeing how you're just an itty-bitty thing."

"Yeah, well some days I feel ittier than others, and this just happens to be one of those days."

"Good one, Abby."

"Wait a minute! How did you know my first name?"

"Detective Tweedledork used it."

"That would be funny—if she had. But she didn't. She never uses my first name, because that would be

showing me a modicum of respect. Detective Tweedledee lives to humiliate me."

"Okay, Abby, you busted me. My name is— Excuse
me, ma'am." With that, he leaped into the street and
began chasing a slow moving tourist bus.

What a peculiar way of running he had. I'd never
seen anything like it—except perhaps on *National Geographic*. That's it! He loped; he didn't run. He loped like
a giraffe.

"Geez, what a weirdo."

I whirled. Normally I don't allow judgmental state-
ments like that to go unchallenged, but it was my dear
friend Bob Steuben who was doing the judging. He
kissed me on both cheeks.

"The new manager of Pasha's Palace was found
dead in the harbor," I said.

"I heard; your mom just called. Is it true that she
was wrapped in a rug?"

"Unfortunately, Mama wasn't blowing smoke rings
this time. Anyway, that evil Detective Tweedledee let
me go right up to Miss Spears so I could examine the
rug; my thinking was that it might hold a clue as to
who killed the poor woman, and why."

"*And?*"

"And I'll never get used to death, that's what; it
makes you sick to your stomach every time. This girl
was so young—barely more than a college student.
Plus she looked so pale, especially with that long
amber hair—Bob, if I tell you a secret, you've got to
swear you won't tell anyone."

"Of course I won't tell anyone, Abby. You insult
me."

"Sorry. Anyway, the rug was an Ispahan—*silk*."

"No way."

"Yes, way. Even soaked with seawater, it is probably the most beautiful carpet I have ever seen."

"But that doesn't make sense."

"Go see for yourself, if you don't believe me. Good luck, however, dealing with Detective Tweedledee."

Bob blanched. If there is one person in Charleston that the detective dislikes more than me, it is the gay antiques dealer from Toledo.

"Abby, I believe that it is what you say it is: a silk Ispahan carpet from Persia. I'm just saying it doesn't make sense to throw something that valuable away. So how much is it worth? Thirty thousand?"

"This one had to be worth twice that—maybe as much as seventy thousand. No, I can think of at least two clients right off the bat that would pay upwards of eighty for that rug in excellent condition. In exceptional condition . . . shoot, I wouldn't feel bad asking a hundred grand for it."

He nodded. "Well, it's obviously murder. Did you see any blood on the carpet? That could explain why the killer—or killers—dumped it into the harbor, along with Gwendolyn Spear's body."

"No. But I only examined one corner. I couldn't bring myself to look at Miss Spears, even though I'd only met her once, and that was at the Palace."

"I don't blame you," he said, and put his arms around me. We stood embracing for several long minutes. Perhaps we gave the impression of lovers caught up in a May/September romance (I being the Virgo), but I didn't care. He was the first to let go.

"Abby, if you have a second, I need to talk to you about Rob's mother."

"Sure. What's up?"

"I have a plan for how to get rid of her."

"Finally!"

"It's not going to be pretty."

I giggled. "The uglier the better."

Mama's been frozen in a time warp since July 4, 1958. (That's the day Daddy died in a boat accident that involved a sea gull with a brain tumor the size of a walnut.) Mama, who at five feet is three inches taller than I, is a miniature June Cleaver. She wears only dresses with cinched waists and full skirts; her feet are always clad in pumps, even at home; and she feels utterly naked without a string of pearls around her still slender neck. But although she's as odd as a three dollar bill, she's not senile. Not by any means.

"Abby, sit down!"

"In a minute, Mama. I want to put away my purse and grab a soda first."

"Darling, those things can wait; this can't."

She sounded too ebullient for it to be bad news, so I obediently walked over to the nearest chair, which just happened to be a Louis XIV—a *real* Louis XIV, by the way, one that had remarkably never been recovered. His Majesty's royal bottom had actually connected with the yellowed silk fabric. Perhaps His Majesty had even—

"Abby, are you even listening?"

"Of course, Mama."

"Then what did I say?"

"It didn't have anything to do with Louis XIV farting, did it?"

"Why Abigail Louise Wiggins Timberlake Washburn! You know how I hate the F word."

"Mama, everyone does it."

"Not *everyone*, Abby."

"Yes, Mama, even Daddy did it." Over the years my daddy's pedestal has grown so tall that were he ever to resurrect—even just for a second—he would be overcome by vertigo, fall off, and die all over again.

"Abby, I will not allow you to drag your father's name through the mud. Your father was as close to a saint as ever walked this earth, and that's the end of this conversation. Besides, you're ruining my surprise."

"Sorry, Mama." I meant it too.

"So guess what I'm going to be doing Saturday night?"

"It's something to do with church, right?"

"Wrong!" Mama sounded positively giddy.

"Don't tell me! You and Connie Beth have finally got up the nerve to visit that new biker bar up in Myrtle Beach. Mama, please don't. It may be called Arnold's, but it's not *Happy Days*. That was only a television show. Not every biker is as sweet as Fonzie."

"Abby, you must think I've got a head full of stump water. I have no intention of *really* going into a biker bar; I just like to talk about it. No, what I'm doing Saturday is quite the opposite. I'm getting presented to royalty."

We both waited patiently while this sunk in. There are many reasons to visit Charleston: it is beautiful, historic, the winters are mild. But even taking those factors into consideration, it seems to get more than its fair share of aristocratic visitors. Mama and I had been residents for only three years, and even we lowly peasants from "off" (anyplace other than Charleston) had already been invited to several functions where the guests of honor were in possession of titles. (Although to be honest, the last big reception was thrown by a "Scottish Lady" who'd bought one cubic foot of land over the Internet for ten thousand dollars, and with it, the right to put on airs.)

"Who is it this time?" I asked.

"The Duke and Duchess of Malberry," Mama said. "He's eighty-seventh in line to the throne."

"Which throne?"

"I don't know; she didn't she say. England, I should imagine."

"Who is *she*?"

"Kitty Bohring. She's a cousin of a cousin of a cousin of one of the duke's stable hands, so you see, Abby, she's *practically* kissing cousins with the queen herself."

Using Mama's logic, since I enjoy watching Colin Farrell movies, and there aren't even any pesky cousins to come between us, he and I are practically having an affair. And along those lines, I own a coffee mug that once belonged to Truman Capote. I bought it at the celebrity gift store at MGM Studios in Disney World. Everytime that hot coffee passes over the rim and through my lips, I like to imagine that fame and fortune does as well; I certainly couldn't expect any infusion of the writing muse. When you think about it, Truman and I had a lot of things in common: we both grew into diminutive adults; we both were nurtured by the South; and both our mothers—

"Abby, there you go again; you're off your own little world."

"Mama, I'm trying to work up enthusiasm, for your sake, I really am. But a distant cousin of a stable boy is hardly royalty. Why would a duke be visiting Miss Bohring?"

Mama glanced around the room, and seeing no one, not even my cat Dmitri, lowered her voice anyway. "You know."

"Because she's richer than God?"

Mama giggled. "Abby that's awful, but it might be true."

Kitty Bohring, and I hesitate to speak ill of the dead (which she is from the neck up), is Charleston's most ambitious social climber. She blew into town shortly after Hurricane Hugo, purchased a heavily damaged mansion for a song, and then poured a large fortune into refurbishing it. Because Kitty was scrupulous in following the historical guidelines, no one could find fault with the finished product. What had been an eyesore was now a local showpiece. She then furnished the house with as many pieces made by local artisans as she could, before going abroad to get the rest.

In addition to the money she pumped into the economy through jobs, Kitty donated staggering amounts of cash to every charitable organization she saw listed in the yellow pages and a dozen others that crept out of the woodwork. Suddenly she was everybody's darling, as well as everyone's favorite person to hate.

I didn't hate her, mind you. In fact, I was very pleased when she purchased a rice planter bed in my shop. I will, however, admit it annoys me that she honestly believes she can buy social standing in this town simply because of her vast resources, that she can be the one exception. And no, not for a second do I believe that the fact she is from Michigan—well above the Mason Dixon line—will have anything to do with her ultimate rejection.

The highest tiers of Charleston society are forever closed to unmarried persons from "off," divorced Charlestonians, and of course Charlestonians who are decidedly of the other color (a few venerable families are known to sport deep tans the year round, but as they are truly old families, no one dares question their status).

African Americans from "off" are usually surprised to discover that Charleston African Americans maintain their own multitiered society that is as rigid as white society. Their cotillions are every bit as elegant, and take up just as much room on the society page of the *Post and Courier*, as do those of white Charleston. Black Charlestonians are expected to attend church on Sundays. The uniform for men is dark suits; for women it is white dresses and elaborate white hats, referred to fondly as crowns of glory. The services last for at least three hours, sometimes four, and are followed by a promenade down to the Battery.

"*Abby!*"

"What, Mama?"

"You've been sitting there in a daze. Are you going to answer my question or not?"

"Thirty-six."

"Dear, that answer might work on some, but I was there when you were born, remember? You are forty-six, and not a day younger." She shook her head. "But how I can be your mother and still not be fifty? Now *that's* a miracle. My question, however, is what on earth am I going to wear Saturday night?"

"How about that yellow dress with the cap sleeves and bell skirt you like so much?"

"Well, I *did* like it until Denise Ayerston told me I looked like a tulip."

"I know it's a little late in the year to be wearing velvet, but that midnight blue gown you wore to meet the Contessa d'Porquesville was gorgeous. You got a million compliments."

"Yes, but Jonathan Dearborn said that I looked like a drag queen doing Liza Minnelli—a *bad* Liza Minnelli."

"Jonathan only wishes he could do half as good a job."

"Abby!"

"Sorry, Mama. How about we go shopping for something new?"

"Can we go now?"

"Mama, I've got to get to my own shop and check on Wynnell. Besides, don't you even want to know about the body in the rug?"

My minimadre patted her pearls. "Of course, dear. I've merely been trying to stall the unpleasant. Did you really know her?"

"Yes, I'm afraid so. You did as well; it was Gwendolyn Spears, the lady from Pasha's Palace."

The pearls began a slow rotation. "Oh my! And you said she was such a nice young lady, even though she did reek of alcohol."

"Yes, and that's not all. The rug she sold me for C.J. and Toy's wedding was worth ten times what I paid for it."

"Do you think she was trying to tell you something?"

"It would appear that way."

The pearls twirled until they were a blur. "Abby, you're going to involve yourself in another murder investigation, aren't you?"

"I haven't decided yet, Mama. And I don't mean to get you upset; I'm just trying to be honest. Last time, you complained that I didn't trust you enough to confide in you."

"No, you're doing the right thing," Mama hastened to assure me. "Have you called Greg?"

"Mama, you know he's such a worrywart. He'll tell me to mind my own business. Then he'll have the police put a tail on me which, in the end, won't do any good. Instead, it will tip off whomever I'm investigating, only making it that much more dangerous for me."

"You get your stubbornness from your daddy's side of the family, you know."

"There was never any doubt."

She nodded, bravely accepting the inevitable. "Well," she said at last, "I suppose I could resurrect that beige jacket dress I wore to Mindy Coatweiler's coming-out party last year."

"I hadn't a clue she was a lesbian. But now that I think of it, I do remember her giving me a very thorough once-over in the locker room at the club."

"She came out *socially* at a cotillion, dear."

"Oops."

"Abby, so now we know what I'm going to wear, but what about you?"

"*Me?* Oh, Mama, it's so sweet of you to bring me along as your date, but it's really not necessary. You know what they say: when you've met one pseudo-royal, you've met them all."

"Who says that?"

"Folks."

"Which folks?"

"Folks who've met them, of course." I tossed back my head and attempted a royal, yet casual, laugh. It was something the queen might do while on a family picnic. Unfortunately, I sounded more like a very small member of the parrot family whose foot had been stepped on by a water buffalo.

Mama took no notice of the strange sound I'd produced. She reached under her seat cushion and withdrew a thick, cream-colored envelope with scalloped edges. It smelled cloyingly of musk, with undercurrents of cardamom and sage.

"Then I suppose you want me to toss this in the rubbish bin?"

"Rubbish bin? Since when did you turn British? Oh my stars! Is that—it *isn't*, is it?"

Mama was on her feet. She didn't have to answer. We held hands and like fools jumped around the room shrieking. Then, when we'd calmed down enough so I could drive, we drove around Charleston in a frenzy until we'd both gotten ourselves new outfits for the biggest night on our social horizon.

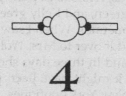

4

Rob Goldburg, who is the second most handsome man in all of Charleston, was my date that night. Meanwhile, *the* most handsome man, my darling husband, Greg, was stuck on his shrimp boat along with Booger Boy, due to a faulty engine. As for Mama's date, he was due to show up any minute.

Mama and I had been surprisingly successful with our dress hunt. Right off the bat Mama stumbled upon a rack of vintage dresses in petite sizes, including one "exactly like the one worn by Lucille Ball on the *I Love Lucy Show*." Of course that show was filmed in black and white, so Mama can't be sure of the color, but in any case, hers is buttercup yellow. I, on the other hand, was not *quite* so lucky. At four-foot-nine, I am almost never able to find a dress straight off the rack that doesn't need altering. But I was quite successful in finding the perfect bolt of cloth.

Emerald green is Greg's favorite color, and over the years it has become mine as well. Recently the stores have been swamped with the bluish shades of aqua green and springlike yellow greens that Greg, never

25

one to mince words, refers to as puke green. But emerald green, forest green, and Kelly green, are all as rare as real, flawless emeralds. When I saw that bolt of perfect green I hefted it over to Mrs. Wolfowitz, my Russian seamstress, and in three days she created a dress that looked as if it might have been purchased from one of the finest New York boutiques.

"Abby, you look stunning," Mama said.

"So do you, Mama."

"You really think so? I thought maybe it needed another crinoline." Already her voluminous skirts stuck straight out like a beach umbrella.

"Mozella," Rob said, "if you gild that lily any more, I shall be forced to turn hetero, sweep you into my arms and kiss the living daylights out of you. Who knows, perhaps even I might be so overcome that I find myself losing control altogether and making mad passionate love to you. Think of the ammunition that would give the Bible thumpers."

Mama giggled flirtatiously. "Oh Rob, you can be so naughty. I say let's give the Bible thumpers what they want: a little show. I'm reading this romance called *Patty Needs a Plumber*. We could reenact the cover. Abby, do you have a toolbox? Robby, dear, take off your tux jacket and your shirt, and tuck a wrench in your cummerbund. Then—"

She was beginning to flush with excitement; it was time to put a stop to the nonsense. "Mama, Rob is interested in *out*side plumbing, not *in*side. Remember?"

"A girl can dream, can't she?"

Fortunately for all of us the doorbell rang, but when I opened it, I nearly keeled over backward with surprise. The man on the porch grabbed my wrist and steadied me.

"Howdy ma'am. Fancy meetin' you here—except that we already done met."

"Big Larry?" Mama trilled. "Is that you?"

Big Larry? Big *Scary* was more like it. Where on earth did my social-climbing mother, bless her heart, meet someone as uncultivated as the giant who'd literally plucked me from the crowd by the harbor?

Mama tried to push me aside with her slips, but I stood my ground. "Actually, we haven't met. You skedaddled before we had a chance to formally introduce ourselves. I'm Abigail Washburn."

"Abigail *Wiggins* Washburn," Mama said over my shoulder. "Abby's my little girl."

"I'm Big Larry McNamara."

"The Big is really part of his name," Mama said, "on account of he weighed fifteen pounds at birth."

"Which is what Abby weighs now," Rob said from over Mama's shoulder.

Big Larry emitted a laugh that no woman should be forced to listen to while sober, but trapped between two loved ones and a behemoth, what was I to do? Make myself faint? I'd only been able to do that once. That was the time my first mother-in-law forced me to listen to a family history she'd written, beginning with Great-great-great-grandpa Titus Beauchamp Timberlake. I held my breath when, by page thirty-seven, she'd only reached the patriarch's birth.

When Big Larry was finally through braying I piped up immediately. "Mr. McNamara," I said, "I'd invite you in, but we were just about to step out."

"I know, ma'am; I'm your little mama's escort for the evenin'."

I wiggled into an about-face. "'Lucy, you have some 'splaining to do.'"

Mama giggled. "I know, dear. I'll give you one minute in the powder room. Then it's off to meet their royal highnies."

I grabbed both her hands, and pushing past Rob, half dragged her into my downstairs hall bath. I was able to slam the door behind me with a dyed-to-match emerald green pump.

"Mama, have you been drinking?"

"You poured the glass of wine yourself, and I only had a few sips."

"That's it?"

"You know I don't drink; it gives me migraines."

"Then why are you acting so giddy? Giggling all the time? And where did you meet Goliath?"

"Abby, don't be rude. His name is Big Larry. We met three weeks ago, if you must know, at the Shepherd's Center. He was giving a program on torturing trees."

"What?"

"You know. Like the Japanese do."

"It's an *art* called bonsai, Mama; it's not torture."

"Have you ever seen it done? Big Larry brought in this shrub he'd bought at Home Depot and set it on a table. Then he lopped off half the branches. As for the others, he twisted them like pretzels after wrapping them in wire. And that's not all; he sawed away a good chunk of the root ball and crammed the remainder into a pot so small it made me wince. It was like watching a Chinese lady get her feet bound."

"How many times have you done that, Mama?"

"You know what I mean."

"Well, for the record, the Chinese no longer do that. But with your graphic description of bonsai techniques, you've totally diverted the story away from Larry. Mama, you really are a pro."

"Thank you, dear."

"I'm not sure you're welcome."

We stepped back into the living room, and even though the men appeared not to have moved, I swear I saw Big Larry's left ear retract like a telescope being closed. At any rate, he soon made it clear that he'd overheard our conversation.

"Mozella's right," he boomed, "it is kinda like torture—funny, but I ain't never thought about it that way. Ya cut, and ya snip, and ya twist—it shore ain't natural, and all so that something young will look old. That ain't the way of things normally."

"It may not be one of our traditions, sir, but it's long been respected in the East."

"Right you are, Abby. May I call you that?"

"Must you?"

"Abby!" Mama snapped.

"Very well then," I said, "if you *must*." I snatched my Moo Moo pocketbook from the bench by the door, grabbed Rob's jacket sleeves, and somehow managed to maneuver him outside.

Kitty Bohring lives along White Point Gardens, which is an easy walk from my house. The trick at night is to avoid stepping on the palmetto bugs that scurry across the sidewalks from every direction. Don't let their exotic name fool you: they are nothing more than palm-dwelling roaches. *Enormous* roaches. (I have heard that New Yorkers run screaming in terror when they first see them.) Palmetto bugs are so big, in fact, that by strapping two of these creatures to each shoe, one might expect to be propelled by a new means of locomotion—except for one thing: they are reportedly darn hard to steer. At any rate, I sure as shooting wasn't going to ride, or walk, with Big Larry.

"Abby!" Rob called, running to catch up. He too sounded reproachful.

"What?"

"Why were you so rude to that man?"

"Because he infuriates me, that's why."

"In what way specifically?"

"That's just it; I don't know. Earlier this week he was so helpful. He literally picked me up and then set me down on the business side of a police barricade. But he's conning us—he's conning Mama. That accent! Have you heard anything so awful since Gomer Pyle went off the air?"

I was born and raised in Rock Hill, South Carolina, up in the Piedmont. Rob was born and raised in Charlotte, not thirty miles from me, and this was all the way back in the days when Charlotte still had a recognizable Southern accent. Neither of us, however, talked like we had a mouth full of marbles.

"It is pretty bad," Rob agreed. "Where did he say he was from?"

"He didn't—not to me. I never gave him a chance. You know me and my big mouth."

"But a very shapely mouth."

"Thank you. Is Bob hurt because I invited you to fill in for Greg, instead of him? And please be honest."

"You really want honesty?"

"Absolutely."

"Well, uh, both Bob and I received our own invitations, so Bob, figuring you'd get one too, decided to take a mercy date to the big doings."

"A *mercy* date? Who?"

"But you can't breathe a word of this. Promise?"

"Cross my heart and hope to die, stick a needle in my eye."

"Wynnell."

"*My* Wynnell?"

"Do you know another?"

"But what if I *hadn't* gotten invited?"

"Believe me, Abby, we would've known. All of Charleston would have known."

"Touché."

We walked in silence, enjoying an evening fit for the gods. If there is a place on earth more beautiful than Charleston in early April, then the person who has seen it is very lucky, for he, or she, has survived a near-death experience.

For it is in this short span of just three weeks (the last two weeks of March, and the first week of April) when the best of nature's blessings are bestowed upon this city by the sea. The last of the camellias have yet to fade, the azaleas are in full flush, the jasmine adds its perfume to the gentle sea breeze, the wisteria swings from the trees like Japanese lanterns, and the bright yellow Carolina jessamine tumbles over courtyard walls and fences, illuminating the dark corners of secret gardens and knitting together hundreds of years of history.

Light spilled from every window of Kitty Bohring's vast mansion, and the sounds of a full orchestra flowed through the open French doors that led to the balcony off the second floor ballroom. Anyone who was *anyone* in Charleston—in fact all of the Lowcountry—was queuing up to get past the two burly security guards posted at the wrought-iron front gates. Anyone who was *not* anyone watched enviously behind a velvet rope.

Every now and then one of the unlucky hoi polloi—usually a tourist—would try to bluff his, or her, way into the royal reception, only to be bodily carried into the street by another two security guards. The crowd would cheer or boo, depending on how vigorously the manhandled person struggled.

In front of us in line was an Olympic gold medal figure skater who lives on nearby Kiawah Island. She had brought her mother, and both were pleasant enough. Standing in line three couples behind us was a movie star who is not from anywhere near the Southeast coast, nor does he own a home here to my knowledge. But this wasn't just any old movie star; he was also a director, and a writer, and who knows what else.

"Rob, bend down so I can tell you something."

Rob bent, but he kept his eyes on the burly guard at the left gate. "Yes madam?"

"You're never going to believe who's behind you."

"It's who's in front of me that has me intrigued."

"Stop it, Rob; you're a happily married man."

"I look but I don't touch—and that's more than I can say for a lot of straight people. So, who's the star?"

"Let's just hope he doesn't hand Kitty Bohring a bag of poop."

Rob swiveled long enough to draw the same conclusion I had. "Abby, darling, this can't be good."

"But this evening might be dreadfully amusing after all," I said in an English accent.

Little did I know.

33

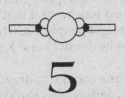

5

The burly guard didn't even ask to see my invitation. He merely put his hand on Rob's arm and mumbled a few words.

"What did he say?" I shouted as we stepped through the gates.

Rob did a good job of pretending not to hear me, so I repeated the question several times as we climbed the white marble steps up to the portico. He finally answered, just as we stepped over the threshold and into the throng of well-connected somebodies.

"He said he gets off at midnight, and to meet him at the back gate."

"You *won't*, will you?"

"No—not that it's really your business."

"But you and Bob are both among my closest friends. What am I talking about? You *are* my closest friends."

"Then you should respect our privacy."

"You're right."

My face stung with shame, and it was probably scarlet as well. No doubt Rob, being the dear friend that he was, could read me like a book: a very small diary, to be sure.

"Hey," he shouted, "enough seriousness for tonight. Have you ever seen a reception hall this large?"

Looking around me didn't do much good, but I allowed my gaze to travel upward to admire a pair of six-foot alabaster vases mounted on black marble pedestals. Above these exquisite white containers rode a crest of red Oriental poppies; this added another six feet of height. It was a simple arrangement, but all the more breathtaking for its simplicity.

Another ten feet above the flowers soared a stamped tin ceiling that was said to be original to the house, which was built in 1817. The great hall was rectangular and three stories high, the rooms all arranged around the reception area. Some of the earliest guests had already given themselves over to gay abandonment (those were Rob's words, by the way, not mine).

Leaning over the mahogany balustrades, champagne glasses in hand, they called merry greetings down to us.

The invitation read that there was a receiving line in Parlor One. Although Charlestonians are a genteel lot, nonetheless, I could detect a decidedly strong current heading toward the far left corner of the reception hall. All I had to do was lift up my feet and let it carry me along. Suddenly, the river of well-heeled humanity came to an abrupt halt as women (who had no business doing so) tried their hand curtsying, while their husbands whispered business proposals in a bored duke's ear (as if they foolishly expected something would actually come of this).

Suddenly Kitty Bohring's meaty hands grabbed mine and she swung me high up into in the air, bringing me in for an uncertain landing directly in front of the duchess. "Your Graces," she intoned, "this is my very dear friend, Her Royal Highness, Princess Abigail Strugendorf of Weisbladderbadden."

At some point during the day I must have eaten fish, a.k.a. the brain food, because it took me just two seconds to figure out what she was up to. I flashed her a look, telling Kitty that it would cost her, but of course I was more than willing to play along.

The first move was not to move. As a royal princess, I was a couple of notches above a nonroyal duke and duchess, so I most certainly would not curtsy. Of course I would shake hands—if one was offered. But only then.

"Ah, one of the *Continental* royals," the Duchess of Malberry said. She made the C word sound as distasteful as cod liver oil.

Thank heavens I'd been raised on *Hogan's Heroes*. A bad German accent is exactly what we speak in Weisbladderbadden.

"Ya, my family tree, she goes back to Charlemagne. Und yours? No? I didn't tink so; I tink mebbe you are recent marriage into zee nobililty."

"Whatever makes you think that?"

"Because a longtime duchess, ya, she vould know dat eet eez alvays coostamary to make curtsy to zee direct descendents of Charlemagne."

The duchess glanced at her husband, who was still being hypnotized by a hopeful businessman. Then, much to my continued amazement, she dropped a quick curtsy.

"I have much to learn from you, Princess Strugendorf." Then she spotted Rob, and was halfway through her next curtsy when the meaty hand of Kitty yanked her back to parade position.

"This man is of no account," Kitty said. "He's only the princess's bodyguard."

The duchess frowned, but managed to wrest her husband away from the overzealous entrepreneur. She whispered something in his ear, whereupon he snatched up my hand, kissed it with lips as dry as packaged figs, all the while bowing deeply from the waist.

"I am honored, Your Royal Highness," he rasped in a smoker's voice.

"Und eet eez a playzure to meet you, sir," I said.

"Don't bother about the man with her," the duchess said. "He's just her bodyguard."

"But a very good one, ya?" I said. "Last veek der vas an attempt on my life—surely you read about eet in dee interpalace circular. Anyvay, Freddy here literally caught zee grenade weez his ties." I pointed to my thighs for clarity. "Fortunately eet vas a dud."

"Or I would be singing soprano," Freddy said. "If at all."

Their graces chuckled agreeably, but I silenced them by shooting Freddy a stern look. "Really, Freddy, how many times must I tell you to shpeak only vhen shpoken to?"

"Thirty-six times."

"Dat vas a rhetorical question," I snapped. I flashed their royal highnesses my trademark smile, which has graced the front page of newspapers as well as gossip rags around the world. "Vell, I shall move along now, but I hope dat next time you are anyvhere near Weis-bladderbadden, you vill shtop in at zee castle. Hans is eager to go shnicklehobblezeeben mitt you again. He says there is room for one more shnicklehobble over zee fireplace in zee north tower. Men!"

We all laughed.

I winked at the duchess. "Und vile zee men point der big bad guns at zee vilde gammenhuben, vee vill strumenabben our dingleberries in zee pies mitt glee. Ya?"

"It sounds absolutely lovely, dear." She gave me a peck on both cheeks before curtsying again.

"What the hell was that all about?" Rob demanded.

"Please, dear, watch your language. You're speaking to a royal princess."

"Princess, my ass—"

"Phalt." I managed to pull Rob into a nook behind a statue of a Greek with very small genitals. "Kitty smells a rat."

"*Excuse* me?"

"She suspects that their graces are not who they say they are, and she's asked me to perform background checks on them."

"Oh, come on, Abby, don't give me that crap. I was standing right behind you, remember? Kitty didn't even speak to you. Instead, she handed you over to the duchess like you were the pawn in some private game. I was amazed that you actually played along."

My sigh was so hard and prolonged that it must have ruffled the sails of boats in the harbor. "Think about it, Rob. There were other people listening to

Kitty's introduction—which, by the way, she made with a straight face. For a social climber, that's serious stuff."

"Yes, but nobody believed her."

"Her guests of honor did. Did you see the duchess's face when I told her that I outranked her?"

"Okay, so the duchess did look like she'd eaten some bad shrimp. But if Kitty Bohring suspected she had some bogus nobility mooching off her, it would have been pretty easy to check that out before now. With the Internet being at everyone's disposal, private investigators are a dime a dozen these days. And heck, all Kitty had to do was google them."

"For all we know, Kitty has been watched for every second of the day for the past couple of weeks. This party could be one big scam, like, say, a jewelry heist. Or not. Maybe on some level Kitty suspected there was something fishy going on with those two, but something happened in the receiving line tonight that made her *so* sure that she risked public humiliation to act on her hunch. What you saw as a game, I saw as a desperate plea for help. And just so you don't get all bent out of shape, the only reason she picked me, and not you, is because I'm married to a real-life detective. She probably thinks some of it rubbed off on me."

"You sure have an active imagination, Abby, I'll give you that. You ever think of writing mysteries?"

"I never even read fiction, Rob, you know that. I mean, what's the point? It's all made up."

"Ha ha, not funny. So now what do you plan to do?"

"Find someplace to google, just like you said."

"I suppose it wouldn't hurt."

"Famous last words."

Holding hands, so as not to lose each other, Rob and I snaked through the thickening crowd until we found a room on the third floor that appeared to be an office. It was, however, quite occupied. The fainting couch, in particular, appeared to be taken.

"Get out!" It was the woman occupant who saw us first, and pushed her unsuspecting lover to the floor.

"Dang it, Mrs. Knopfsky," the boy said. "You don't have to be so rude."

Rob cleared his throat. "Never mind us. We just want to use the computer."

"You young people and your computer games," the woman railed, shaking a liver-spotted fist at us.

The boy turned his head. "Dang it again! I had no idea that Mrs. Knopfsky was so old."

"Just like I'm sure she had no idea that you're so young. By the way, just how young are you?" Rob said.

"Twenty-three."

"And I'm forty-six," Mrs. Knopfsky said.

Rob snorted. "Is that so, Mrs. Robinson?"

"I age poorly—it's the Charleston sun. That and the fact that I'm a heavy smoker. Besides, we wouldn't even be having this conversation if I was a forty-six-year-old man and he was a twenty-three-year-old woman."

"Except that if you were the forty-six-year-old man," I said, "you'd really be a *sixty-six*-year-old man, given that you belong to my mother's parlor game club. 'Clueless,' I believe it's called."

The boy's clothes were across the room, but he'd been trying—somewhat unsuccessfully—to cover himself with his hands. Suddenly that became unnecessary because he had less to hide, comparatively speaking, than even the Greek statute.

"Dude—I mean, Mrs. Knopfsky—you used to be a man?"

"He's not the brightest of lads, is he?" Rob said.

"Look, not-so-lady and not-so-gentleman," I said, "were it not for the fact that you, Mrs. K, are a widow with certain healthy needs, and you, young man, yada yada yada—well, it's like this: we'll be back in two minutes. By then you'll have your clothes back on, *capisce*?"

The boy waved his arm furiously. "Is that like spinach pie?"

"Yes, and you'll eat it with a smile on your face."

"But I don't like spinach."

"Tough cookies," I said.

"Now where was I? Oh yes, then we come inside, and you wait out there and stand guard. If anyone tries to come in, stop them. Don't even let them come close."

"So you two are gonna do it, huh?"

Rob answered him with a neat clip to the left jaw.

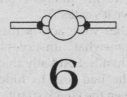

6

It took us less than a minute to google the Duke and Duchess of Malberry; there were no listings. We did searches on both the royal and noble houses of Europe, but found no trace of them. Of course there were other avenues to explore, but the odds were that Kitty's hunch was a sound one.

"Now what?" Rob said. "You say 'I told you so'?"

"No. I say 'a hunch from a woman is worth two facts from a man.'"

"Stop gloating. When do we call the police?"

"We don't. We cause a major distraction of some sort, and then drag Kitty's butt out of there. Then we ask her what tipped her off."

"I suppose I get to do the dragging because I'm the man."

"No. You get to do it because you've always been quite good at dragging."

"That's good enough for me; I'll take compliments whenever I can get them."

We logged off the Internet, but we didn't even get as far as the door when the sound of raised voices—one of them far too familiar for comfort—announced that a roadblock had been thrown up in our way. I glanced desperately around for places to hide; there were none. *Unless*. As it was the third floor, a small trapdoor in the ceiling gave access to electrical and cable wires, but it was doubtful Rob could squeeze through the opening. And even though it was pleasant outside, we would be so close to the roof that we'd undoubtedly steam to our deaths within a few minutes. If not literally, we would at least look as if we had been steamed, which for some of us is just as bad.

My heart skipped *three* beats as the door opened just enough to allow Mrs. Knopfsky to slip in. "It's your mama, Abby. She swears she saw you go in here. She was on the other side of the atrium and couldn't get here any faster. I told her I'd just come out of this room and it was empty, and she accused me of calling her a liar. She's going to barge in here at any second. What shall I do?"

"Give me ten more of those seconds and your tryst with Oliver Twist is history—assuming he really *is* twenty-three."

"He is. I know his parents; his daddy is my pastor. You're welcome to check him out."

"Okay, I believe you."

The hard part was getting Rob to believe he could fit through the access hole. I finally got him to imagine it as a rabbit hole in reverse, and me as Alice, but not with a second to spare.

"Abby, I know you're up there!" Mama shouted, "There's no place else you could be. Big Larry," she said to her gentle giant, "if you scoot that chair over . . . "

43

She let her voice trail off, not needing to waste words on a fait accompli.

But they weren't destined to breach our defenses quite so easily. Rob passed me up through the trapdoor first. Upon entering the hot dark space, I bonked my head on a lightbulb so small it would have gone unnoticed on a Christmas wreath. There was just enough illumination for me to spot a loose plank, which we set about jamming under the eave, over the door, and under a bowed area on the nearest truss. A team of gentle giants wasn't going budge that door up even a fraction of an inch.

"Mozella," Big Larry said between pants, "I think it's nailed shut."

"Fiddlesticks," Mama said. "Didn't you think I can recognize my own daughter?"

"I didn't say that. But you know how it is."

"I'm afraid I don't; how *is* it?"

"At a certain age—I mean at the end of the day—one's eyes can play tricks on them."

The steam from Mama's nostrils was making the torrid little space even more unbearable. "I'll have you know that I am *not* that certain age! And even if I was mistaken about Abby, what are the odds I'd be mistaken about Rob too?"

"That handsome fellow she was with?"

"He's not that handsome, by the way; he just thinks he is."

Rob needlessly gasped, and I went light-headed from lack of oxygen. The next thing I know, he was prodding me with his not so handsome index finger.

"It's your turn, Abby."

"Turn to do what?"

"You have to name your favorite male vocalist?"

"Isn't that taking a risk?" I whispered. "They might hear us and never leave."

"Geez, you really are getting loopy. They've already left. We decided to wait an extra ten minutes to make sure it's not a trap. Now hurry up before I pass out as well."

"Russell Watkins."

"How about Josh Groban?"

"Yeah, him too."

"Best female vocalist?"

"I'm still going with Barbra Streisand."

"Are you sure that you're not a gay man in a woman's body?"

"I'm fairly certain. Would you like to check to make sure?"

"No. We did that when you were between husbands, remember?"

"Oh, yeah. During the ice storm when we lost power for three days."

"Then we both ran from the house screaming, but at least I knew I'd taken the right path at age fourteen."

"And I learned that the old saying, 'If you've seen one, you've seen them all,' is simply not true."

"I choose to take that as a compliment."

We waited a few minutes longer, and then I waited a lifetime longer than that while Rob struggled to dislodge the plank he'd jammed into place. At last it popped free, sending my buddy sprawling backward into a pile of insulation. Once we were down, Rob insisted on being the one who scoped the hallway for lurking mamas. I was beginning to feel like a cat with only six full lifetimes remaining by the time he gave the all clear.

"Stick right by my side," he said.

"*Au contraire,* you contrary one. I'm the one with the distraction plan, remember?" I kicked him in the shins and zipped ahead.

Much to my relief, the reception line was still going strong. The only thing that had changed was Kitty's complexion. Instead of an expensive man-made "peaches and cream," it was the lackluster grit gray that can only come from excessive perspiration coupled with fear. Her face glowed feebly, and only for a second, when she saw us. Their Gracious Frauds were occupied deceiving someone else at the moment, so I winked broadly.

Gathering my wits and my skirts about me, I strode up to the duke and slapped him hard across the left cheek. Unfortunately, I had to jump to reach his face, so I didn't connect nearly as hard as I would have liked.

"You bashtard!" Before anyone had a chance to react, I whirled and faced any would-be judgers. "Dis man eez a fraud und I can prove eet!"

"I don't know what's she's talking about," the duke said. He actually had the gall to sound calm.

"Your Royal Highness," the duchess said, "please, can we talk about this in private."

"Een *private*? Ha! Dis eez vhere eet happen—een private." I rubbed my belly, which was extended as far as it could go. "Dis man impregernate me und now he vant dat I should haf an abortion."

46

Her grace turned ricotta white. "Bruiser, is this true?"

Bruiser? Now we were getting somewhere!

"Babe, it's all lies, I swear."

"Dis man he lies all right. Before he ask me to have abortion, I ask him to marry me." Despite hundreds of gasps, I plunged ahead. "I do dis because he say dis voman, dis so-called duchess, is really not his wife. He call her strumpet. I tell him that by marry me, he can become a royal prince—Prince Christian Frederick Alfred von Strugendorf of Weisbladderbadden. Is not such an easy ting, you know, because the voman's title does not automatically transfer to her consort, but I have so much moneys, I can buy anyting—even a title, ha ha. But no need to buy title, because I am legitimate descendant of Charlemagne, ya? Is most powerful kind of royal in dee vorld. I tell him I have so much moneys I can never spend it all. For his love I could buy him a hundred Lamborghinis—vhatever he vants. But vhat does he say? He say no!"

The duke, obviously given to drama, threw himself down on one knee. Unfortunately, his thoughts took a while to catch up with him. Either that or he was waiting for a prompt from off stage.

"I did not refuse to marry you," he finally cried. "You never asked. I would have said yes. Ask! Ask me now!"

Suddenly the duchess was all over me like white on rice. "You little bitch! I should wipe the floor with you. Don't think you can get away with this just because you're a real princess. I'm going to sue your Stroganoff-Wise-Bladder-Bag-Ass until you don't have a euro left."

"Whatever," I said. That word, by the way, has been voted by POST NASAL DRIPS (Parents of Snotty Teens Needing Assistance Since Adolescence Leads to Divorce Rapidly in Parenting Studies) as *the* single most irritating word in the English language.

"Wait," a woman in the crowd shouted. There was some buzz and a bit of mayhem among the onlookers, but the amazing thing is that the bogus duke and duchess actually did just stand there like characters in a high school play who'd forgotten their cues. Even Kitty Bohring appeared under a spell of some sort. Then again, stress can distort time—so can hunger, and I had been fasting all day in order to stuff myself with the inevitable goodies available at a Charleston gala of this magnitude.

Time started moving again when I realized that the woman who had stopped it was none other than Mama. Of course, that made perfect sense. According to Aunt Marilyn, my mother was in labor with me for eight hours (the time it took Aunt Marilyn to drive from Savannah to Rock Hill before there were interstate highways). Over the years, the woman who endured the pain has tripled that time, halved it, and once even quadrupled it—depending on the audience and her mood on the day she tells the story.

"You can't sue this princess," Mama said, shaking a dainty and well-manicured finger at Yours Truly, "because she isn't one; in fact, she's just as common as the next woman."

"Thanks, Mama—I think."

"Abby, where have you been? I've been looking all over."

"Not now, Mama."

"Don't you tell me when to be quiet, dear. I suffered forty-eight hours of excruciating labor to bring you into this world. I've earned the right to speak whenever I want."

There was a smattering of applause, most of it from Mama's behemoth of a sidekick, who was just now catching up. "You should always respect your mama," he echoed.

"You stay out of this," Her Bogus Graciousness said before turning to Kitty. "I can't believe you're putting up with this. Send these people home."

Kitty, who was no small woman to begin with, expanded her chest like a puffer fish. "It's *you* who should leave," she snapped.

The dummy duchess reared back in surprise. "*Ex-ca-use* me!"

"Certainly. Now out you go."

The crowd, which was just now catching on, murmured their appreciation for a first-rate drama.

The so-called Malberrys, however, were not amused.

"We're not budging," the dastardly duke said. "We are the guests of honor, and as such, we intend to stay until the bitter end."

"Then this *is* the end," Kitty said. She clapped her hands. "Attention please. May I have your attention?"

The woman meant well, but she was clearly not quite in touch with reality. The odds of a woman in her sixties (with a quavering voice) garnering the attention of two hundred people scattered about on three floors were about as good as being able to sit through a feature-length movie and not have the person behind you kick your seat—not even *once,*

I cupped my hands to my mouth. "People! Listen up. Your hostess has something to say."

Mama's new beau didn't cotton to folks giving ladies the deaf ear treatment. *"Give them your attention, dang it all!"*

Suddenly it was so quiet in the great hall that you could have heard a June bug hatch. "Ladies and gentlemen," Kitty said as she added extra syllables to each word in a pitiful attempt to make them sound Southern, "although it has been a pleasure—"

"You might want to speed things up," I whispered. "It's like holding back a leak in the dam."

"The party is now over."

Instantly the dam sprung myriad leaks. "What do you mean it's over" was the most common refrain.

"Shut yer pie holes fer a minute and she'll tell ya!"

Although Big Larry's voice came dangerously close to stripping the mansion of its wallpaper, the second time around seemed to do the charm. The great house fell silent, and remained so, as the dispirited citizens of Charleston filed out.

When the only ones remaining were three fake heads of European nations I'd never heard of until a week before, one sheepish social climber, a woman with a fifties fetish, a mysterious giant with quite flexible grammar styles, and a handsome antiques dealer from "off," I decided it was high time to get down to business.

7

"**K**itty, dear."

"Yes, Abby?"

"Are those your goons, out front?"

"In a manner of speaking. Funny, you should refer to them as that; they're listed in the phone book, under security, as 'Goons for Tycoons.' I couldn't resist."

"Très droll," Rob said, without being the least bit sarcastic.

"Kitty," I said, "how did you meet these two sorry characters?"

"Hey, watch what you say," the phony duchess said. "We commoners have feelings too."

"Abby," our hostess said, "do you mind if I sit first before I answer your questions? It seems as if I've been on my feet for hours."

"No, that'd be fine. Why don't I just call your goons, while you watch this diabolical duo—"

"You can't prevent us from leaving," Bruiser growled. "We got rights, you know?"

Big Larry smacked a bowling ball size fist into a dinner-plate-size palm. "I'll watch 'em fer ya, little lady."

"Thanks—I think."

"Abby! Be grateful."

"Yes, Mama. Thank you very much, Big Larry."

"My pleasure, ma'am."

And it was his pleasure to fix both Kitty and I plates of food before ushering us into the downstairs conservatory. The room was wallpapered in cherry red; housed two concert grand pianos, both white, and a gold harp. Each instrument was flanked by a semicircle of side chairs, which were painted white and gold in the old French style.

On the floor, connecting everything, spread an enormous Savonnerie carpet from seventeenth century France. At perhaps eighteen by fourteen feet, it was the largest carpet of its kind I had ever seen in a private home. The pattern—multicolored floral on dark cream—was pretty enough. However, the border, a garland of cheery blossoms that beautifully echoed the wall, *really* made it "pop."

Mama and Rob had thoughtfully remained behind, so only Kitty saw and heard my reaction.

"You like?" she said.

"It's awesome! Where did you get it?"

"Once upon a time I had the pleasure of living in Paris—when I was younger, and not quite so foolish."

"Please, Kitty, don't put yourself down. Those two are con men. Sooner or later we all get had by the likes of them. Tell me, how did it begin?"

"I found them on the Internet. I was looking for a title to buy?"

"Like a car title?"

"I wish it was as normal as that. No, there are actually

sites where, for enough money, you can purchase titles of nobility. That's how Zsa Zsa Gabor's husband became a prince; he paid a German princess to adopt him. I thought their graces, the Duke and Duchess of Malberry, might create a position of honor for me in their court if I helped keep their struggling little corner of the world afloat."

"And which corner would that be?"

"The ancient Kingdom of Malberry, of course. Where *else*?"

Where else indeed? In school I stunk at math, was pretty good in English, and enjoyed geography (which is different from being good at it). Still, I don't remember studying about a kingdom named "Bad"-berry, as it would translate, if one read the first syllable as if it were from the Latin.

"Where is Malberry located? Next to which other countries?" I dipped a shrimp into cocktail sauce and bit it off at the tail.

"Well, I'm not exactly sure—but it's one of those countries where English is spoken."

I swallowed before speaking. "I see. How much would your title cost?"

"I didn't say I was going to actually *buy* a title, now did I?"

"But you *were* going to do just that, am I right?"

She looked miserably down at her plate. "Okay, so you found me out. He was only a duke—not even a royal one—so the best he could come with was the title of countess in my own right. In other words, I don't have to be married to a count to be called a countess. The title alone was a quarter of a million U.S. dollars. The title plus the crest, and the ancestral home

53

was 4.5 million dollars. But first I had to pass a very stringent test."

The two best ways to close a gaping mouth are: to either push it shut with a closed fist, or tempt it shut with tasty food. I popped in another shrimp that was dripping with sauce. Unfortunately I am not the neatest thing since toothpicks, and a very teensy, weensy, tiny, minuscule bit of sauce didn't quite make it into my mouth. Perhaps it would even be more accurate to say that it ended up on the Savonnerie carpet.

"I'm so sorry," I said, and in the process may have drooled a mite more of the sauce on that colossal work of art.

I must give credit where credit is due. Although she was clearly nouveau riche, Kitty showed the restraint of a true queen. "Oh, that old thing," she twittered, although her face was as white as a sushi roll.

You can bet that I did my best to undo the damage. First I soaked the surface sauce up with one of the thick, soft paper napkins Big Larry had handed me along with my plate. Meanwhile I sent Kitty in search of club soda and a roll of plain paper towels. Not only did she return with the requested items, but she had Mama, the aforementioned giant, and Rob with her as well.

"Oy vey," Rob said when he me saw trying to remove a red stain on a four-hundred-year-old masterpiece.

"Don't worry," Mama said. "My Abby has had a lot of practice at this."

"Thanks, Mama—I think."

The secret to cleaning just about anything is to blot, blot, and blot some more. Whatever you do, use white paper towels, not the fancy designer towels that fea-

ture drawings of kitchen implements or silly rendi-
tions of geese with bows tied around their necks. The
ink from these printed towels can transfer to the object
one is trying to clean. White cotton cloth—never use
polyester, or even a blend—is also good for blotting,
but the cloth must be dry in order to wick up the
liquid, and one can go easily go through more cloth
than one has on hand. That is why it pays to always
keep rolls ands rolls of plain paper towels on hand.

Rob, ever the good friend, joined me on his hands
and knees. "Dear sweet Abby, whatever are we going
to do with you?"

"Put me in a pumpkin shell, there to keep me very
well?"

"I thought of that, but your skin tone doesn't lend
itself to orange. To watermelon maybe. Do they grow
watermelons as big as giant—"

"Rob, look," I whispered

"Believe me, dear, I am looking. Fortunately, we've
managed to lighten the ketchup stain enough to
where—"

"No, *really* look. At the carpet. And keep your voice
down."

"What am I looking for?" he asked in an exaggerated whisper. "Does it do tricks?"

"Rob!" If there had been an S in his name, I would
have hissed.

"Okay, I'll behave. I was just trying to make you feel
better by employing a little humor."

"How about you employ your diagnostic skills instead?" I ran my index finger along a line of pale green
stitches. "Do these look hand-stitched to you?"

"Uh—no."

"And these? Or these? Or any of these?"

"Holy guacamole, Abby! This thing's a fake!"

"Well, genuine facsimile of an original sounds a little kinder."

"Rack of lamb sounds nicer than ribs of a dead baby sheep, but that doesn't change what it is. Does Kitty Bohring know what she has?"

"I don't think so."

"Are you going to tell her?"

"I don't know; I guess I'm going to play it by ear."

We worked in silence until the stain was barely visible to the naked eye. After Rob helped me to my feet, we flipped the carpet back until the damp area was exposed to the air.

"Just leave it dry like that overnight," I said to Kitty. "Tomorrow morning I'm sending Charleston's best carpet cleaners over to finish the job."

My announcement seemed to startle her. "What? I mean, there's really no need to do that. I can't even see where the sauce was anymore."

"I can," Mama said.

"Mama, *please*."

"Well, I can. Abby, you never could understand why I made you rewash half the dishes when it was your night to wash them. But honestly, dear, if you'd have scraped off all the food you left clinging to those plates before you stuck them in the soapy water, you'd have solved the issue of world hunger. No doubt they would have awarded you the Nobel Prize."

I flashed Mama a look that I knew would be wasted. "Anyway," I said, turning back to Kitty, "I insist that this is professionally cleaned, and I'm footing the bill."

"That's very nice of you, Abby," Kitty said, "but after tonight—I just don't want intrusions for a while. I'll call somebody on my own when I'm ready. But thank for you for your kind gesture."

"Okay, but then I still owe you one free cleaning, good for whenever the mood strikes you. By the way," I said, as I slid into my most casual voice, "it's none of my business, so please feel free to tell me to mind my own business, but seeing as how I *am* in the business—"

"She wants to know how much you paid for that rug," Mama said.

"Mama!"

"Well, it's the truth, isn't it? Abby, I'm fifty-eight years old; I don't have time to be beating around the bush like that."

"Speaking of the truth, Mama, you were fifty-eight years old during the first Clinton presidency. " I smiled coyly at Kitty. "So how much is this cutie?"

"Two hundred and fifty—if I remember correctly. It was so many years ago. And of course that's after converting it into dollars."

I was immensely relieved; she'd paid a fair price, even way back then. It was, after all, a replica of excellent quality and unusual size.

"Even in today's somewhat repressed market," I burbled, "I bet I could still get you ten grand for that—should you ever wish to sell. You did good, Kitty."

"I hope so, Abby, because what I meant to say was two hundred and fifty *thousand* dollars."

8

"Earth to Abby, come in, Abby."

It was three weeks later and I was still stewing over the events that transpired the night of Kitty Bohring's party and their many repercussions. In the time-honored spirit of "kill the messenger," Kitty was no longer speaking to me. On the other hand, just a few minutes of posing as a fake blue blood had turned my life upside down.

Disclaimers did absolutely no good. I would like to think that most folks knew I wasn't royalty—at least in their heads. But if they did, that didn't stop them from thinking of me as a celebrity. Everywhere I went, even in the produce aisles of my Harris Teeter, people pointed and whispered. Some even asked for autographs, and they were sorely disappointed if I signed their grocery lists as Abigail Washburn. In their minds I was a *somebody* just for pretending to be one—like Paris Hilton, I suppose.

But then there were those folks who thought my disclaimer was just for show and that I really was royalty. For them I was the princess of the peninsula. The fact that I owned and ran an antiques store was part of my disguise. Who, or what, I was hiding from was fodder for a dozen different tales, none of which seemed to have anything to do with the principality of Weisbladderbadden. My favorite story was that I was the granddaughter of Anastasia, and was waiting for the day when I would be crowned empress of all of Russia. That day, by the way, was imminent, now that communism was a thing of the past (one version had it that I was already quietly assembling my court).

At any rate, as a result of that one evening, I was suddenly the belle of Charleston. The invitations poured in and business boomed. I was in need of both a social secretary—other than Mama—and another hand in the shop. Greg, who is happier on a shrimp boat than any place on earth other than our bed, was distinctly not overjoyed by the prospect of becoming Charleston's "first man." As for me, there is only so much smiling the human body can endure before even the perkiest of us begins to feel mandibular pain. Is it any wonder then that the genuine blue bloods are sometimes photographed looking as if they've been caught preparing for their colonoscopies?

I was scurrying from my car to my shop's back entrance when Bob assaulted me with his annoying "earth to Abby" cliché. "Oops," he said, "on second thought, maybe I better let you orbit in peace."

I breathed deeply, of what I hoped was cleansing salt air. Unfortunately it was early Monday morning and the garbage trucks were late. All of King Street, even my fairly sedate part of it, smelled like the College of Charleston had partied hard over the weekend.

"I'm sorry, Bob. I probably look like a bitch on heels."

"But a very good-looking one. Hey, can I buy you a cup of coffee?"

"I'd love that, but I'm interviewing someone to help out in the shop. In fact, I was supposed to meet her ten minutes ago."

"Through help wanted ads?"

"Yeah, afraid so. I don't know how long this position will last, so I didn't think it was worth it to go through an agency. You want to come sit in on the interview? Give me your thoughts afterward?"

Bob and Rob—the Rob-Bobs, as they are affectionately known—are very successful antiques dealers themselves. Their shop, The Finer Things, is one of those places that appeals to folks who'd been vying for my attention as of late. To enter, one must ring the bell and be scrutinized via a sideways glance (although the Rob-Bobs vehemently deny this), but once inside, a customer feels like a member of an exclusive club. A handsome young stud, or a gorgeous young nymph, from the College of Charleston drama department is always on duty to charm the pants off the men and women customers alike. While they're being charmed, the customers—referred to as "guests"—are treated to champagne, coffee, and a variety of finger foods. In the background the soothing sounds of soft classical musical have begun to hypnotize those lucky enough to be buzzed through. When they've consumed enough to feel somewhat beholden, one of the Rob-Bobs will step in and offer a guided tour of the shop, as if it was a museum.

Each piece in The Finer Things has a story, and often, by the time the tale has been spun, the guests will be bidding against each other for the right to own this piece of history. It is an interesting way to do business, but far too labor intensive for me. Besides, it smacks of some of the churches my friends dragged me to as I was growing up in the very buckle of the Bible Belt. The right music, a little snack, a spirited lecture—by the end of the experience you actually *want* to part with your money. But once you're home, then what? At least shoppers can return most items. Still, I think manipulation should be reserved for stiff muscles and potter's clay, not two-legged pigeons with too little willpower to resist college kids and cheap champagne (I've seen them switch the labels).

"I'd love to come sit in on your interview," Bob said.

"You sure Rob won't mind?"

"Hey, I own half the business. I can be late if I want. Besides, the high tide floats all boats. We've hired another shark—it's a she. She started yesterday. That's what I came to tell you."

"You've hired a docent?"

"Ha ha, very funny. Her name is Sandy. She's in her early seventies, very well turned out, has beautifully coiffed hair—although that shade of red looks totally unnatural at her age. But who cares, everyone colors their hair now, right?"

"Not Mama."

"That's because Betty Anderson and June Cleaver would never have colored theirs."

"You're so right. Anyway, this woman really knows her antiques. What's more, she knows how to handle

Rob. All she has to do is give him the *look*, and he jumps three feet."

I tried in vain to stifle a giggle. "You know, that really *is* funny, because your new saleslady sounds exactly like his mother. How Freudian is that?"

Bob grimaced. "Abby, what is Rob's mother's name?"

"Sandra Gold . . . Why slap me up the side of the head and call me Marvin three days from Sunday! You poor, poor dear."

"What did you just say? About Marvin?"

"Oh nothing; it was just an expression my daddy used whenever he was shocked by something—which was rarely, I assure you. Tell me, how did this happen?"

"It was my fault. She made a comment about sitting around our town house all day being bored. So Rob suggested she look into volunteer work. She said she'd already done enough mitzvoth to last her three life-times. Then I—schlemiel that I am—told her that she could always come and help us organize the stock-room. I thought that might scare her off. Instead she said she thought it was a wonderful idea, but you know how anal our Rob is—no pun intended—he couldn't bear anyone reorganizing his precious stock, so bingo, she was instantly promoted to sales associate. And do you know what the worst thing about it is?"

"She's good?"

"She's awesome! Hurricane Sandy. She racked up a hundred thousand dollars worth of sales in just one afternoon. Then she went home and insisted on making us a celebratory supper—in *my* kitchen. Abby, what kind of supper is scrambled eggs with smoked salmon?"

"High in protein?" I glanced at my watch. "Jeepers creepers, I gotta run. You coming?"

"I might as well; it's not like they'll miss me over at Casa de la Goldburg."

Wynnell flew at me like a bat from a cavern at dusk. "Abby, where have you been? You're late."

"I know. Bob and I got to talking and—"

"She's here." My buddy was suddenly speaking like a ventriloquist, through her teeth, but her voice wasn't being thrown anywhere.

"I'd hope so. Did you put her back there in the corner where I've got that Eastlake living room ensemble set up?"

"That's what you told me to do, but—"

"Then we're all set. Bob's going to sit in, by the way. He wants to get some hiring pointers—in case they decide to hire over at The Finer Things." I winked at him. "All right then, Wynnell, I'll just let you get back to minding the shop. I know it's in good hands. Oh, if you get a chance, bring us some coffee, will you?"

"Yes, boss," she said, with a dollop of sarcasm and two scoops of acerbity.

I tiptoed back to the corner in question. Walking quietly is part of my interviewing process. I make allowances for human behaviors like pit-sniffing, head-scratching, or nose-picking, because we all do them when we think we're alone, but making nasty, leering faces into the small mirror that hangs above the East-lake love seat, or performing the Nazi salute (I've seen it done), tend to raise red flags with me. Once I observed a woman get on her knees and pretend she was me. When I promptly showed her to the door, she had the nerve to be miffed.

Despite a dearth of caffeine that morning, I breezed into the homey nook, my perk factor cranked to the max. "Good morning, Miss Cheng."

My interviewee stood and turned. I did a double take.

"C.J.! As I live and breathe!"

"Hey, Abby. Aren't you going to give your sister-in-law a kiss and a peck, and a hug around the neck? Of course in your case you'll have to jump to do it." She laughed good-naturedly.

I made her bend down for the kiss and the peck, but instead of the hug, I gave her a playful smack on the bottom. "You *aren't* Miss Cheng. I skipped my Starbucks routine on account of you." I lowered my voice to a whisper. "Now I have to drink Wynnell's coffee."

"I *heard* that," Wynnell growled from somewhere unseen, which just confirmed my belief that my shop was far too small.

"Well everybody, since there is no interview, and we don't open for another twenty minutes, why don't we all sit down."

Bob and I sat, but C.J., bless her oversized heart, seemed too nervous to sit. "Actually, Abby, I am Miss Cheng."

"Isn't that a Chinese name?" Bob asked.

"Yes, and I am Chinese."

I smiled at my friend, who is five feet ten and has mouse brown hair. "I thought you were a Ledbetter from Shelby, North Carolina."

"That's true too, but Abby, don't you remember that Granny Ledbetter said she found me on the front porch in a basket?"

"Yes. She claimed that giant stork dropped you off."

"The fact that you believe that story," Bob said dryly, "is one of the reasons we love you so much."

C.J.'s large gray eyes filled with tears. "Then maybe you should start loving me less, because I no longer believe it. You see, my Great-uncle Billy died three weeks ago—"

"Oh C.J., I'm so sorry," Bob and I said as one.

She thoughtfully nodded at each of us. "That's all right; you didn't know him. Anyway, when Great-aunt Nanny was going through his things she found some letters and some newspaper clippings. I didn't bring them today because they're all in either Russian or Chinese, and I know how parochial y'all's educations have been. Anyway, Great-uncle Billy was a Russian major in college, although he became a vet, and when a group of Russian farmers came to Shelby to study goat husbandry, the government asked if they could stay with him."

She took a deep breath. "One of the farmers was a young woman—Svetlana Neerkovich—who'd fallen in love with a Chinese exchange student. His name was Cheng Shin Jou—in Chinese, the family name comes first. Anyway, she was eight and a half months pregnant but no one in her group knew it, on account of my birth mama was a very big-boned lady. And she was scared to death too that anyone would find out, because they might kick her out of the collective. Then one dark and stormy night she gave birth, and not only did Great-uncle Billy help out, but he put the baby in a basket and set it on Granny Ledbetter's front porch, because he knew she had a soft spot for young'uns."

"You had me right up until 'dark and stormy night,'" I said, and flashed my friend a warm smile to welcome her home.

"I'm afraid she had me until 'young'uns,'" Bob said. "Does anyone *really* say that?"

C.J. sprang to life like a tyrannosaurus that had been napping only to discover a herd of herbivores trampling across its tail. "Dang it, I'm telling the truth, Abby! Stick an acorn up my nose, blast it out with a garden hose!"

"Ouch! You're serious, aren't you?"

"More serious than a meeting house full of preachers on Judgment Day. And you know what? It turns out I'm really three years *older* than I thought. How cool is that?"

"Bummer," Bob said.

"You really are half Chinese?" I said.

"Yes, ma'am, my birth daddy was from Beijing. Somehow Granny managed to get me a copy of a birth certificate with his name on it, but she never told me about it. Why do you think that is, Abby? Do you think she did something illegal?"

"You mean like stole two eyes of newt from a government supply house and held them ransom? That kind of thing?"

"Abby!"

"I don't know, C.J. Maybe she was trying to protect

you; even as recently as twenty-five years ago, Shelby wasn't exactly a bastion of diversity."

"Oh yeah, Abby—Bob—I know you guys like to call me C.J., which stands for Calamity Jane, but my name isn't even Jane, so now you'll have to think of a new name I guess."

"Will I be able to pronounce it?"

C.J.—I mean, whoever she is—snorts when she's happy, and she let out a horse-pleasing one now. "I hope so. My mama named me Cheng."

67

9

*E*xcuse me?"

"She was mad at her lover, and pretty much just wanted to get rid of me, so she decided that whatever was good enough for him as a last name was going to be good enough for his baby's first name as well. Granny never did invest anything along those lines because she never anticipated the day when the secret would come out."

"I see. Now it is all just as obvious as the pimple on Bob's nose."

I was only joking, but Bob, the poor man, yanked a silver compact out of his pocket and desperately scanned his proboscis for a grease-clogged follicle. "Abby," he boomed in his basso profundo, "one more prank like that and you're off our Halloween guest list."

Believe me, that's all the warning I would need for the next five months. No one, but no one, gives Halloween parties like the Rob-Bobs. Folks have been known to put off dying in order to attend, and more than a few have returned from the dead in time to enjoy these fabulous events. There are even stories of people who have been *long* dead—Marie Antoinette, comes to mind—who somehow managed to put in an appearance. In her case, fellow partygoers were more impressed with the fact that she carried her head tucked under her arm than that she'd somehow managed to hop over an ocean and skip ahead two centuries.

Along about then Wynnell trotted back bearing a mahogany and ivory tray bearing four mismatched mugs of undrinkable coffee. "What did I miss?"

I faked a yawn. "Nothing much—except that C.J.'s parents were both communists. Her mama's a Russian and her daddy's Chinese and her real name is Cheng Cheng and she's been asked to open a panda preserve in the mountains of western North Carolina. Now tell me, Wynnell, which part of this little tale isn't true?"

Wynnell didn't even blink. "It's all true, except for the panda part."

"*What*? How did you know?"

My friend has eyebrows like a pair of black shoe brushes, except they usually form an unbroken straight line. Now, however, she'd managed to jam them together into a steep-sided vee.

"Abby, didn't you talk to C.J.'s Aunt Nanny at all at the wedding?"

"Of course—well, a little."

It looked as if the lower half of C.J.'s long broad face was going to break off and fall on my good hardwood floor. "Are you saying that my Aunt Nanny knew all this and didn't tell me? I thought sure Uncle Billy would have been considerate enough to take that secret to his grave."

"Maybe he thought that the considerate thing to do was give her a chance to talk to him about it," Wynnell said. "Anyway, Abby, C.J., I wasn't trying to keep it a secret from either of you. I simply didn't know it was a secret. But while we're at it, C.J., *Ni how ma?*"

"*Wo how shi shi ne,*" C.J. said, happy as a 160-pound lark again. She turned to me. "So Abby, how about it? Do I have the job? You know that I'm a good sales-woman, and I understand your style—such as it is."

"But you love living in Sewanee, Tennessee, with my brother. Or have you forgotten that you're well on your way to becoming an Episcopal priest's wife?"

"Ooh, Abby, but you see, I'm not. Toy and I are sepa-rated."

Wynnell, Bob, and I all stared silently at the big galoot from Shelby.

Wynnell spoke first. "I get it; you're joking, right?"

C.J. shook her head. "You know I don't have a sense of humor."

"But C.J.," I cried, "how can you do that? Don't you love Toy? He adores you!"

"No he doesn't, Abby. He adores the *idea* of having a wife so that someday he can be a parish priest in a small town where he knows everyone and can solve all their problems. But it isn't *me* he's in love with."

"He *told* you this?"

"I'm out of here," Bob said, rising. "This is family business."

"Me too," Wynnell said wisely.

"No," C.J. said. "You're both my family too. Besides, sooner or later, what I tell Abby will get back to you. Right, Abby?"

I felt like a worm on a hot sidewalk. "Well—maybe later. Certainly not sooner. Okay, so I can't keep a secret; what would you like to know about each other?"

"*She* said it," Bob blared, not me.

"Abby," Wynnell said, "you know that I think you're the salt of the earth, the veritable pillar of indiscretion."

"So anyway, Abby," C.J. said, "here I am, back in Charleston, on account of Shelby's just too small for me these days. So I was thinking about what to do, and then I saw your ad; it was like a match made in Hell."

"You mean *Heaven*, right?"

"Ooh, don't be silly, Abby. You keep your shop three degrees hotter than The Finer Things, and you pay your employees a lot less."

Watching Wynnell scowl is like watching a conga line of tarantulas. "Is that true, Abby? About the pay?"

"From what I hear, both things are true," Bob boomed.

"Thanks," I hissed softly.

"Abby," C.J. said, adopting a motherly tone, although she was twenty years my junior, "when your store is too warm for comfort on hot days you lose customers. You want them to walk in and say, 'My that feels good. I could stay in here forever.' Then you make sure that they do—just not like Cousin Penelope Ledbetter who lived in the Pine Hollow IGA for twenty-four years and raised herself three young'uns in there from start to finish, and had already started in on a granddaughter."

"C.J., you read that in a book."

"No siree, ma'am. You ask anyone in Shelby. Poor old Frank and Ida Cornmeister, the couple who owned the store, never could figure out how come they couldn't seem to keep Twinkies and Charmin in stock. It wasn't until Cousin Ludmilla Ledbetter—Cousin Penelope's granddaughter—got caught stealing a box of Krispy Kremes, and the police insisted on driving her home, that they discovered three generations of people had been living in that store all along."

"C.J.'s right about one thing," Bob said. "People will hang around a lot longer if they feel comfortable."

"You're hired," I said. "Does Mama know that you and the son who hung the moon just for her are separated?"

"No, but I was planning to tell Mozella tonight, irrespective of whether or not you gave me the job. Honest, Abby."

"Where are you staying? In a motel?"

"No, I'm staying at CHAS."

"Come again?"

"It's an acronym for Charleston House for Absentee Shelbyites. The rooms are very small, but the rates are low—kinda like the ceilings." She chuckled good-naturedly.

"I don't care if the rooms are free. You're staying with Greg and me. You're family, C.J. You always will be; even if the day comes when you really are shed of my self-absorbed brother."

"Abby, I can't put you out like that. I don't mind bumping my head on the ceiling. I really don't."

"Tough titty said the kitty. You're staying with me, and that's that."

C.J. glowed with gratitude. "Thanks, Abby, you're a Carolina peach. You know, most people associate peaches with Georgia, but that's only thanks to better marketing. South Carolina actually produces more peaches than does Georgia."

"Gotta love this one," Bob said.

"Hey, that's not fair," Wynnell cried.

I turned to my second best friend in the entire world. "You know, I'd love to have you and Ed move in as well, but I only have the two bedrooms, dear. As it is, she'll be bunking with Mama. Besides, Wynnell, you have a perfectly good house of your own, don't you? Nothing's happened since yesterday, has it?"

"My house is fine! What I meant is, *I* want company for a change. Ed and I never have guests. Everyone said, 'Move to Charleston and you'll have a constant stream of visitors.' Well, pooh on that. Our two beautiful guest rooms just sit empty gathering dust."

I felt a wave of relief sweep over me. In fact, it would have swept me off my feet had I not already been sitting down. To put it mildly, C.J., by any name, is high maintenance.

It's quite possible that my sister-in-law felt similarly; she accepted Wynnell's offer immediately. One would think she might have expressed some level of indecision out of consideration for me, but oh no.

Bob, bless his heart, decided to distract me. "Abby, have you given any thought to our previous conversation?"

"Not really—"

"What conversation was that?" C.J. said. The big galoot was also without guile.

"Bob's mother has come to stay with them," I said. "*Indefinitely*, it seems. He wants me to help him find a way to send her packing back up to Charlotte."

"Ladies, this is strictly confidential," Bob said. "If Rob ever found out, he'd send me packing off to Toledo."

"Sure thing," Wynnell said. She pretended to put on a thinking cap.

C.J. might be as silly as a canister full of putty, but she generally doesn't need time to think. "Bob, how about if your Aunt Nanny came down to stay for a while?"

"That would be great, C.J., except for the fact that I don't have an Aunt Nanny."

"Sure, you do." She winked broadly. "She's your father's widowed sister-in-law, remember?" She was, in fact, referring to one of her own aunts.

A smile spread slowly across Bob's recently exfoliated cheeks. "He did have an older brother who no one kept in touch with much after he decided to seek his fortune in California."

"Did he find it?" Wynnell asked.

"No, yes—I guess that depends. He became moderately successful producing soft porn movies; that's why the family disowned him. My coming out was made easier than it could have been, thanks to Uncle Harold."

"Perfect," C.J. said. "Aunt Nanny will have a field day with this."

"Wait just one cotton-picking minute," I said. "Is this Aunt Nanny a goat?"

"Abby, don't be insulting. Her daughter was a bridesmaid at my wedding; you know that she finally passed the DNA test."

"But does she have a beard?"

"I'll remind her to shave, and on a daily basis too, if that will make you feel better."

I sighed. Never had life been fuller, or strangely happier. With C.J. back working for me, my children doing well in their various pursuits, and my husband, Greg, happy as a hickey with his cousin Booger Boy on a shrimp boat, what could possibly go wrong?

Being the toast of the town can go to one's head after several toasts. After a while I could barely lift my noggin off the bed. Thank goodness Wynnell and C.J. were both friends, as well as competent. They kept the Den of Antiquity running smoothly. Just as long as my ego could survive knowing that they didn't need my input in order to keep the shop afloat, there was no reason for me *not* to stay away.

Although frankly—and I don't mean this as a put-down of the good folks of greater Charleston—there is only so much socializing one can do in a city this size without getting bored. I was wined and dined by the South of Broad set, then the Old Village of Mount Pleasant set, followed by the James Island set, until I'd gotten in all the islands, and as far inland as Summerville. But over and over again the same topics of conversation raised their genteel heads, and the same bloodlines were compared, albeit from somewhat different perspectives.

The one thing upon which everyone could agree was that there was no place quite as special as Charleston, and Charlestonians were to be given special credit for having chosen to be born in the Holy City. When I expressed my discomfort with this attitude one evening at a dinner party for twenty, at the residence of Lloyd and Florence Knudsen, eighteen pairs of eyes looked my way disapprovingly. One pair of eyes remained placid, while the remaining pair belonged to me.

"I never go anywhere else on vacation," said Mable Stoutsman. "Why should I? I'm already there."

Everyone laughed and nodded their agreement.

"But don't you have any desire to see Paris in springtime," I asked, "or walk along the Great Wall of China, or maybe take a boat up the Amazon to visit tribal villages?"

"None whatsoever," said Deidre Matthews.

"There's a Great Wall of China restaurant on King Street," Albert Winslow said, much to everyone's amusement.

"I really can't help that I'm from off," I said.

There were sighs of pity all around.

"Your guest is eating the centerpiece," Jill Manners said.

Neither Greg nor Mama could accompany me that evening, so I'd brought C.J.'s Aunt Nanny. Sure enough the sweet old lady was nibbling on the greenery surrounding an impressive spray of apricot-colored azaleas. She looked as happy as a hog in a mud wallow.

"Aunt Nanny," I whispered, "that's just a decoration."

"Then they should have labeled it as such," she said. She turned to Jill. "Tattletale."

"Why I never!"

"Then maybe you should try it, dear. Most people find it quite disagreeable, but my dear Billy and I always thought it aided our digestion. Who knows, you might be one of the lucky few to feel its benefits."

Jill leaned over Aunt Nanny as if she weren't even there. "Abby, who *is* this eccentric woman anyway? She's not a Pinckney, is she?"

By then I'd had it with the likes of Jill Manners, and was about to launch into a lecture on *good* manners, when a liveried wait person showed up on Aunt Nanny's right with a tray of tomato aspic. I'm not saying Aunt Nanny was raised in a barn, but she most probably had rather humble beginnings. The sudden materialization of a waiter in a black tuxedo was too much for her. She bleated in misery as she threw up her arms as a sign of surrender. Unfortunately, one of those long spindly arms—a forearm, I believe—knocked a bowl of aspic, top side down, onto the Knudsens' authentic Persian carpet.

Florence Knudsen emitted a howl of despair and then appeared to slip into catatonic shock. Her husband Lloyd betrayed his low-born, perhaps even "off," origins with a string of invectives, some of which even I had never before heard. Meanwhile the waiter's face turned a macaw scarlet and he attempted to flee back into the kitchen. Following him, just as close as bird lice, was our irate and belittling host. As for most of the other guests, years of rubbernecking along the I-26 corridor to Columbia (sometimes referred to as Death Row) had given them the ability to see everything that was going on without leaving their seats.

"You see what you've done," Jill hissed to poor Aunt Nanny.

I told myself to remain professional. Blot, blot, blot— that's what a professional would do. But with what? My napkin? It looked pretty, and had been folded beautifully, as a matter of fact, but it was pure polyester, and barely soaked up the condensation left on my hand from my water glass.

But wait! There was indeed something within reach. Jill Manners was wearing a blue satin sheath that was strapless. In order to guard against the chill of the evening, or perhaps an overcooled room, her ensemble included a matching pashmina shawl that she'd draped (with a great deal of dramatic flair) over the back of her chair. Six feet of wool and silk was just what I needed to undo Aunt Nanny's boo-boo.

"Nooooo!" Jill threw herself at her pashmina as it slithered off the back of her chair, but it was too late.

Just as I thought, the shawl was exceptionally absorbent; from now on I highly recommend pashminas for blotting up tomato aspic from Persian carpets. Since Aunt Nanny, who only drinks clover wine, was sipping club soda that night, I had everything I needed to do a bang-up job on cleaning the Knudsens' carpet. I did have a little extra help that night: first, the carpet in question had been well protected with Scotchgard or a similar substance; and second, Aunt Nanny couldn't help herself and licked the bulk of the aspic right off the carpet before I even had a chance to blot.

Aside from Jill's now red and purple pashmina, my efforts at restoring the Knudsens' carpet to its former glory would be over—except for one very important thing.

10

"You're got to be mistaken, Mrs. Washburn," Lloyd said, and bashed his left fist into the palm of his right hand. Ah, so he was a lefty.

"Abby knows her carpets," Florence managed to say between sobs. "I trust her, Lloyd. What are we going to do?"

"Where did you purchase this carpet?" I asked gently.

"Where else?" he demanded. "The best place in town, of course."

"But Mr. Knudsen, I assure you, I would never pass off a machine-made copy as a hand-made original. In fact, I have only ever sold three—no, make that four—mass-produced carpets, and each one had a fascinating provenance. Elvis was said to have—"

"I don't give a dog's ear what Elvis did on your carpet, Mrs. Washburn. It wasn't your shop I was referring to, but the one with them two gay boys."

"That would be The Finer Things, and as they are both well over eighteen, I believe the proper word would be 'men.'"

"Yeah, whatever. Sit right here, ma'am, while I go get the bill of sale. That dang thing cost too much to be a reproduction."

He left me with Florence in what, I suppose these days, one is supposed to call the formal living room (their massive home was a new house in a gated community, one that Lloyd Knudsen himself developed by destroying a pine forest). The family room could have housed a small third world village, or two Buckeyes and one of their children; the dining room was large enough to seat ten Charlestonians, even the transplants among us; but the living room was barely large enough to accommodate two nearly life-size Raggedy Anne and Andy Dolls, after which the small space was decorated.

"Florence, dear, do you mind awfully if I put Andy on the floor so I can sit? It's been a long day."

"I'd rather you held him on your lap, Abby. He could get a complex down there."

"In that case, I'll just stand. If he can develop a complex sitting on the floor, no telling what would happen if he sat on my lap."

"Are you making fun of me, Abby?"

"No, ma'am. Absolutely not."

It was actually a relief to see Lloyd return, triumphantly waving a sheet of paper. "*Authenticity guaranteed.* It says so right here. So, Mrs. Washburn, this leads me to believe that one of y'all is lying."

"Or perhaps there is another explanation."

He folded his hands, resting them carefully on what was the beginning of a paunch. "Yeah? Like what? Maybe a spaceship zapped it up and made a switch?"

"Anything's possible, although some things—like that—don't seem probable. Tell me, do you have a maid?"

"We use a cleaning service," Florence said, for which she received a glare from her husband.

"We could afford a maid," he said. "You know, a real one, with a uniform and all—just like on a TV show—but heck, Florence and I ain't all that messy. Are we, hon?"

"I believe you," I said. "I was just wondering aloud. Do you think the cleaning service might have switched rugs on you?"

"Yeah, and next week they're gonna switch wives, and I ain't gonna notice until it's my birthday. Look, Mrs. Wiggins, this ain't just any old rug. This here is an authentic Persian carpet from—from—" He glared at his wife for not having finished his sentence. "Florence, where the hell was that again?"

"Uh—I don't remember, Lloyd."

"You playing stupid, again, Florence, or this time did you really hide your brain under a rock? It didn't take a very big rock, did it, Florence? No siree, it was more like a pebble, wasn't it?"

"I think it had something to do with a breeze," she said.

"Yeah, that's it: Taliban Breeze, although it ain't got nothing to do with them bad guys, I assure you."

"That would be Tabriz, sir."

"Nah, that ain't right."

His dismissal of what I knew to be the truth really hiked my hackles. "Look, sir, I know what I'm talking about. I may not know much about chopping down virgin forests, or cluttering marsh views with ten thousand square foot homes, but I know something about Middle Eastern carpets."

"Make up your mind, little lady. A minute ago you were calling it something else altogether."

"Tabriz *is* in the Middle East," I said. Then, as painful as it was, I adhered to Mama's admonishments to always be a lady, so I refrained from adding what I was really thinking. But had I, it might have gone something like this: *Didn't you study geography in Chester, or Gaffney—or wherever it is you're really from?* I might even have turned to his wife and said: *Florence, why on earth are you living with this Neanderthal?*

"Mrs. Washburn," the caveman said, "you're wrong about this one, and you flapping your gums like this is just a waste of my time. I'm calling the police and reporting a stolen rug."

He pronounced it POH-leece. In less than five minutes Lloyd Knudsen had gone from being a pillar of the Charleston community to being a hot-tempered social climber from the Upcountry region of South Carolina. His speech habits alone were enough to get him ejected from the dinner tables of even the lowest rungs of the Lowcountry social ladder. It was clear that he had married far above his station in life, and were it not for the big bucks his business as an environmental rapist brought in, I wouldn't have even been there listening to his abusive tirades.

I looked at his bill of sale again. "Mr. Knudsen, this receipt is three years old."

"That's right. *I* hang on to my receipts. I'm a businessman, Mrs. Washburn. I take it you don't do the same?"

"This house wasn't even finished then," Florence said. "The carpet was our first purchase for it."

"Florence, just hush up, will ya? That ain't got anything to do with nothing. What was your point, little lady?"

"My point, big—I mean, sir, my point is that you don't have a legal leg to stand on. In three years time you could have done anything with the original, and gotten a machine-made one that sort of looks like it. How are the police to know that you didn't make the switch? No offense intended, sir."

I was with Greg and Booger Boy once when they netted a puffer fish. That's almost exactly how Lloyd Knudsen looked just now, only less compelling.

"How dare a little tart like you insinuate that I stole my own carpet? What would be the point? Insurance fraud?"

Tart? If only I could tell him to shut his pie hole. Oh why did having good manners have to come with a price? My daughter Susan would have verbally tied him into knots by now—not that she wasn't properly raised; she was. But times have changed, and what was shocking just ten years ago doesn't even turn a head these days.

"Florence," I said with a quick bob of my head, "that was a lovely dinner. Thank you so much for including me and Aunt Nanny. I would like to return the favor sometime. Good night."

Being such a tiny tart, I can turn on a dime, which is what I did. I like to think that I walked regally away. At any rate, I didn't look back once at my fuming host.

* * *

I waited until the next morning before contacting Rob, and even then it was at his place of business. In retrospect the delay was due to the fact that I was hoping to catch him on one of the many days that his mother took off to work on her tan. Rob didn't mind it when his mom was a "no show"——I think he much preferred it, in fact—but he couldn't very well come right out and flatly refuse her help. And believe me, he'd already tried all the more subtle approaches.

The beefcake who saw me ring the bell mouthed the words *We're closed* and waved a hand that appeared to be a mite loosely attached. I pointed to the OPEN sign. He shrugged and mouthed something again, and soon we were engaged in a battle of gestures—not all of them as polite as they should have been. Suddenly, out of nowhere, Rob's mother appeared and buzzed me in.

"I'm sorry about that, Abby. Stanley is new, and of course another drama student from the College of Charleston. He also just got the lead role in *that play*, as they call it, although everyone knows it's *Macbeth*, so he's a bit full of himself today. Would you like me to call him over to apologize?"

"Hmm, that is really tempting, but I need to speak to Rob."

"He's closing with a customer right now. Perhaps I can help you." Her diction was Old Charlotte, as rare these days as a four-sided triangle.

If I didn't already know that Mrs. Goldburg was impossible to live with, just looking at her would have been enough to prejudice me against the woman. Whereas Mama carried eccentricity to the max by wearing fifties outfits, with Rob's mother the pendulum swung in the other direction; she was Junior League on steroids. For her, linen—the more wrinkled, the better—was the holy grail of fabrics, followed closely by cashmere. Silk ran a poor third. Cotton was for summer only, and polyester was merely a curse word you flung at Democrats come election time.

Every stripped and colored hair on her head was somehow held into place without looking lacquered, and the miracles wrought by Charlotte's finest plastic surgeon were maintained by Botox tune-ups and a plethora of minor nips and tucks. In short, the woman was about as natural as a veggie burger.

"No, I'll just wait over here by the noshes, thank you."

"Noshes! That's a good one. You're such a quick study, Abby. Too bad you and my Robby didn't meet years ago."

"I don't think that would have done either of us any good."

"Come again?"

"Rob would still be gay; I can't turn men straight, Mrs. Goldburg—nobody can. And besides, until about five years ago I wasn't someone you'd want to bring home to introduce to Mama. Not with that second head. I'm telling you, it wasn't a pretty sight, especially not on bad hair days. And those weeks when I'd forget to wax our lips—"

"Abby, are you making fun of me?"

"Not really, Mrs. G. But Bob is my friend too, and I just hate that you don't think he's good enough for Rob."

She glanced around before cupping one hand to her mouth as a shield. "But his aunt really is—well, peculiar would be an understatement. Yesterday, when she thought no one was looking, I saw her open a door by butting it with her head."

"You didn't!"

"But I did."

When we both realized that she'd inadvertently punned, we burst into peals of unladylike laughter. That's when Rob, of course, materialized out of nowhere.

"How are my two favorite ladies doing? Why so mirthful this fine-feathered morning?"

"Mornings can't be feathered," I said. "Although mourning doves can."

"Good one, Abby."

"I don't get it, Robby."

"It's just a little wordplay Abby and I like to engage in."

Mrs. Goldburg shot me a triumphant look that seemed to say, *Wordplay, foreplay, they're practically the same thing in my book. You should have held out for my Robby instead of marrying that detective cum shrimper.*

I shot back one that said, *Just remember, sister, that you and I have both been divorced and that in this town you can't be anyone with the D word in your past.*

"Rob, darling," I actually said, "I need a moment of your time."

"Can it possibly wait? I have an eighteenth century commode at stake. I'm just on my way back to the office to get an appraisal that I had done on it by Sotheby's."

"I'm sure your mother can bring home the sale. We both know she's an extremely talented people person, or she wouldn't even be working for you. Right?"

"Right, but—"

"There, you see, Mrs. Goldburg? There was absolutely no need to worry; I told you he'd say yes. Your son has total confidence in you. Now go out there and make him proud."

"Yes, but—"

At this point Rob had his hands on his hips and was about to huff and puff and blow down my house of bravado. I snagged one of his arms and dragged him off behind a Philadelphia hutch circa 1830.

"So help me, Abby, this better be good."

"Hang on to your socks, Mr. Wolf, because this little pig has some information that just might knock you flat on your big ol' lupine bottom."

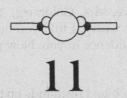

11

Y ou're serious?" Rob said for the bazillionth time.
"I can't really blame Mr. Knudsen for being
angry; I would have been too. But that didn't
stop me from leaving in a snit. I swear, Rob, when am I
ever going to grow up?"

He didn't even hear my confession of bad behavior. "I
remember selling him that rug, feeling at the time that
it was like taking blood money. Believe it or not, Abby, it
wasn't just your charm and your wit that lured us down
to the Lowcountry, nor was it the lucre to be made off all
the filthy rich retiring to the peninsula. A lot of it had to
do with the vistas that Pat Conroy brought to life in his
novels, and which we got to see for ourselves every
time we crossed one of the bridges. Now it's all high
rise condos and business complexes. Look how Mount
Pleasant has grown from a sleepy fishing village bor-
dered by marshes to a real city with bumper-to-bumper
traffic on Highway 17. The *it* factor that brought outsid-
ers down here in the first place is getting damn hard to
find. And do you know who I blame? Developers!
They're the very sons of Satan himself."

"Believe me, Rob, you're preaching to the choir."

Rob had to pause and catch his breath, just like some real preachers. "Sorry, Abby. I probably wouldn't be so emotional on the subject if I wasn't feeling so guilty. I'm every bit as greedy as Lloyd Knudsen. The only difference is that I don't chop down trees and pollute marshes. When he and that mousy little wife of his came and practically wanted to buy out my place, I was as pleased as punch. I'd like to think that I'd draw the line somewhere—Hitler surely—but heck, I'd probably even sell to George W, and you know how I feel about him."

"What's done is done, so quit beating yourself up. Can you think of any explanation for how the copy showed up in place of the original rug? And trust me, Rob, it *isn't* an original Persian Tabriz. I'll sign a paper right now turning everything in my shop over to you if it turns out I'm wrong. That's how sure I am."

"Hey chill, Abby. I believe you—although there are a few things in your Den of Iniquity I've had my eye on."

I laughed. "You don't need double entendre to enter my den; cold hard cash will do fine. And, of course, as a fellow dealer you get a twenty percent discount."

"Fair enough. Quite seriously, you do have that Meissen candelabra tucked away in a corner on an ugly pine table, and which, I'm happy to say, is already vastly underpriced."

"That candelabra is Meissen porcelain?"

"Yes, but in all fairness, it is a very early mark and not well stamped." He paused and lightly bit his lower lip. "I was just thinking," he continued, "what if it was the wife who switched out the rugs?"

"Florence?"

"I'd forgotten her name. Anyway, I had this distinct impression that he treated her like a piece of Shih Tzu—minus the dog."

"He still does."

"Do you think he beats her?"

"I don't know. You think she's selling off the family jewels—so to speak?"

"Could be. I'd have to think of an excuse, but I could swing by to see if some of the other major pieces I sold them are still there."

"Would you? I mean, don't you think it's strange to have two very large expensive carpets turn out to be fake in such a short period of time?"

"No. Strange things happen all the time, Abby. Why not here? It's called coincidence."

"Yes, but that I should be the one to discover this coincidence?"

"Abby, look, I said I'd swing by there. Now sweetie, I've really got to get back to these customers. Ma means well, but you know how she can be."

"Was the Shih Tzu a female dog?"

"Abby, that's my mother," he said, but walked off smiling.

There is Charleston, and then there is *North* Charleston. They are separate cities and not meant to be compared. To do so would be needlessly unkind. For example, one does not compare a piece of gravel with a gem-grade diamond, although both are pebbles and both have merit in their own way. That some Charlestonians playfully refer to North Charleston as Upchuck is merely an indication that these folks lack maturity, and has nothing to do with the reality of things. So what, if Charleston is undeniably the fairer of the two cities? That is surely no reason to boast.

At any rate, Rivers Avenue, home to car dealerships and strip malls, is exactly where one would expect to find Pasha's Palace, and frankly, the vaguely Taj Mahal appearance of the blindingly white building rather dresses up this otherwise mundane stretch of highway. Knowing that parking spaces would be at a premium, I focused on positive thoughts, and sure enough, after circling the lot five times I found a space only six rows back, and less than half of it was in a rain puddle.

As I attempted to do the "Charleston walk" (one saunters on the shady side of the street, thereby minimizing perspiration) I noticed that most of the license plates were from out of state. How odd. Then it occurred to me that our tourists were watching television as well as dining out in the evenings, and were taking advantage of the ridiculously low prices at Pasha's Palace before heading back home. But what were they getting? Surely not handmade rugs.

So intent was I on examining the first large carpet I came across that I didn't see the lanky young man who practically hurled himself at me until he was inches from my face. I stifled my cry of alarm by clamping a hand firmly over my mouth. Unfortunately, in doing so I accidentally whacked him in the groin with my latest Moo Moo bag. The poor lad staggered backward, hopped up and down several times, then with a pinched look on his face gamely went back to work.

"Looking to buy a carpet?" he asked through clenched teeth.

"Perhaps. Can you tell me something about them?"

The boy had long blond hair tied neatly back with a stretchy band, but he would have looked so much nicer had it been shorter. I gave myself a gentle mental slap. I was there on an unofficial investigation, not to do a make-over. Still, it was nice to see that when he picked up a carpet, it was with fingers that sported clean, well-trimmed nails.

"You've got good taste, ma'am. These here are the top of the line. They are one hundred percent wool, with more stitches per inch than any of the others. Feel how thick the pile is."

"It does feel very good, but with such thick pile, how can the weaver cram in more stitches? They are handmade, aren't they?"

"Oh, no ma'am. Like I said, these are all top of the line. You *don't* want them handmade rugs. The stitches in those things tend to be crooked and the colors are uneven." He lowered his voice. "Besides, those carpets are made by pheasants in bare feet and some of them smell."

"What smells? The barefoot *pheasants*, their feet, or the carpets?"

"The carpets—although maybe some of them pheasants smell too; they don't have a lot of water in the desert." He chuckled, no doubt proud of his worldly knowledge. "I reckon that's why they call it that."

"I bet you're right. I hadn't really thought of that. Anyway, doesn't Pasha's Palace sell any handmade carpets?"

"No, ma'am. Not as long as I've been here."

"And how long is that?"

"Two weeks, ma'am."

"Do you sell any silk carpets?"

"We had one; somebody bought it yesterday. Most of what we have are the synthetics. They're cheaper than the wool, and most folks think they wear better, but that's because they've listened to the wrong salesman's hype. Now me, I actually took a course on Oriental carpets. I'm not saying I'm an expert or anything, but I do know me a thing or two."

"A course? At the College of Charleston?"

Paul—at least according to his name badge—reddened slightly. "I watched a DVD in the break room. But it's like three hours long. If you make it all the way through, they start you on the fast track to management."

"Well, good for you. That's what we need in this country: more motivated young people like you." I shut my mouth quickly before any of the sarcasm could drip out and possibly ruin a decent wool rug.

Although poor Paul, bless his heart, did his darnedest to sell me a mass produced rug, and even excused himself twice to speak to the manager (whereupon the prices plummeted to an embarrassingly low level), I just wasn't in the market. But he showed me a broad selection, and what I learned from the experience was that Pasha's Palace was not only seriously undercutting the home improvement stores, but making a killing while they were at it. It's not every customer who will ask for a discount, or for that matter who will stick around long enough to be offered one.

* * *

When I finally arrived at the Den of Antiquity, I found Wynnell and Cheng at each other's throats. Literally.

"What on earth are you doing?" I demanded. I was not in a mood to play arbitress to two alpha women, both half again as large as me.

"C.J. was trying on this Victorian garnet necklace from the jewelry case, but it got caught in her hair."

"My name is *Cheng*."

"That explains why Wynnell's hands are around your throat, Cheng. Why do you appear to be strangling her?"

"Because Wynnell was trying on this gold locket and the chain got caught in her unibrow. When I finally got that loose and tried to undo the clasp, my ring got caught in her hair."

"It's not a unibrow," Wynnell growled.

"Ladies, this is not a jewelry emporium. And where are the customers?"

"We don't have any, Abby. C.J.—I mean, Cheng—hung the CLOSED sign on the door so she could talk to your brother."

"You *what*?" I had half a mind to toss both women out into the street, tangled together or not.

"Abby," Cheng whined, "do you want us to get back together, or what?"

"Frankly, Cheng, knowing Toy a whole lot better than you do—and let's not even go there—I might be tempted to say 'what.'"

"Go where, Abby?"

"She means that you've slept with him and she hasn't," Wynnell said. "At least I hope she hasn't."

"But I haven't slept with Toy either; that's the problem."

That's all it took to get the pair apart—that, a couple of shrieks, and some huge hunks of hair. They staggered away from each other like prize fighters when a round has been called.

"Why do you mean you haven't?" I said.

"Exactly what I said, Abby."

"Is my brother . . . well, is he impotent?"

"No."

"I don't understand."

"It's not important. Can we change the subject? I think I see some women about to try the door."

"Pretend they tried five minutes ago—or whenever. Toy's my brother, Cheng, so you have to tell me."

"And Abby's my best friend, Wang," Wynnell said, "so I get to listen in."

"You see how she treats me?" Cheng said.

"Wynnell, this *isn't* funny," I hissed. "What if I called you Wynnell Crawdad, instead of Wynnell Crawford? How would you like that?"

"Okay, I'll behave."

"Now spill it, Cheng," I said.

"Abby, I just can't bring myself to—uh, *do it* with a white man."

"Run that by me again, please."

"No offense, Abby, but I find Caucasians kind of yucky."

"I'm still not quite comprehending this. Yucky how? In what way"

"Y'all's skin, for one thing: it's too hairy. And while I'm being frank, you smell a bit like wet dogs, even when you're dry."

"Cheng, that's racist! I've never heard such blatant

racism in all my born days. If you were my employer, instead of the other way around, I could probably sue you."

"You tell her, Abby," Wynnell said. She glared at Cheng beneath her unibrow.

"Wynnell," I growled, "I'll thank you to butt out of this."

"But she offended me too." My friend did a quick sniff test. "Stale lavender soap? Maybe. Yesterday's Secret? Maybe. But definitely not wet dog."

"Besides," I said, "what about Granny Ledbetter and Aunt Nanny, and that entire clan? And if you think Toy is too hairy and smells a bit too much like Fido—"

"Funny thing," Cheng said, a nostalgic smile spreading across her massive face, "Granny Ledbetter always smelled like feta cheese. Aunt Nanny smells that way too, don't you think?"

"Hmm, I think you're right. But Cheng, look here, your mother was a white Russian, so you are half Caucasian, and for all the years we've known each other, I've smelled just fine to you. So here's the deal: I'm going to keep on smelling fine to you, and you're going to keep on being the loving, goofy C.J.—I mean Cheng—you've always been, or you no longer work here. *Comprende?*"

"Yes, Abby. I'm sorry."

She sounded sorry too, so I was about to wrap my short doggy arms (perhaps I'd been a Chihuahua in a former life) around her when one of the customers not only knocked on the door, she practically broke it down.

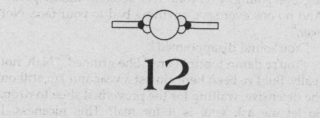

12

It always pays to be courteous—well, most of the time it does. I brushed some hair out of my eyes and put on my perky saleslady face. Then, despite the continued banging, I took ladylike steps to the door. I even managed to turn the dead bolt with deliberate slowness.

"Good morning, ladies," I said as I stood aside to usher them out of the May humidity.

Three ladies sailed through, but a fourth stopped just inside. It was immediately clear by the frown lines on her face that she was not a believer in Botox, and that she'd been the one responsible for the annoying racket.

"How may I help you?" I said.

"You can stop being so perky, for one thing."

"Excuse me?"

"When I moved here from Michigan, I anticipated there'd be times when I'd have to fight that damn Civil War all over again. That's what friends who'd moved here from Kalamazoo warned us about. But aside from letters to the editor complaining about Yankees ruining everything, everyone has been so damn polite. And no one ever says anything bad to your face. Not ever."

"You sound disappointed."

"You're damn tootin' I am." She grinned. "Nah, not really. But I've been here almost a year and I'm still on the defensive, waiting for the proverbial shoe to drop. So let me ask you, is it for real? This niceness, I mean?"

She was a large woman and sweating profusely (Southern women don't sweat, we dew), so I steered her toward the office, where I keep a box of tissues. There, she accepted the guest chair, which is nearest the air-conditioning vent.

"My name is Abby, by the way."

"Yes, I know. I'm Andrea Wheating."

"Well, Andrea, I have heard stories of northern transplants who've been accosted by ill-mannered locals and told to go home. Happily, these stories are few and far in between."

She flashed me a smile. "Good. Abby, you don't remember me, do you?"

I shrugged. "Should I?"

"Oh say it isn't so!"

"You're not a long lost relative of Daddy's, are you?"

She brightened considerably. "Your father has relatives in Michigan?"

"Sadly, my father has passed, but his granddaddy, Great Grandpa Wiggins, liked sowing seeds as much as Johnny Appleseed."

"Cool. To my knowledge, we don't have any Wiginses in our family tree, so that's not why I'm here.

You sold me—oh shoot; I knew I should have written it down. It has something to do with bees and a jar."

"Ah, a Bijar! That's the name of a city in Iran. Describe the carpet please."

She did better than that; she extracted a photo from her purse. And yes, I remembered her carpet. In fact, I remembered it as well as my first date with my husband, Greg. Then again, Greg took me to the Red Lobster and I had a giant margarita and got so tipsy that I ended up in the men's room by mistake, and it was only on my way *out* that I noticed the urinals.

At any rate, the carpet I sold Andrea Wheating was mid-nineteenth century, and although it had been in constant use, it was in excellent condition. It had a triple floral border—the background was orange, the flowers blue—a large cream insert, with an orange medallion inside that, and a bazillion flowers woven everywhere, but in a symmetrical, formal design. It was a real showstopper and, quite honestly, the price tag was a heart stopper.

"Are you asking me to buy it back?" I asked. "Because I will, assuming we can agree upon a price."

"*Agree* upon a price? What kind of crap is that? I want a complete refund, of course."

I could feel the blood drain from my cheeks. "But you see, dear, that's not the way most antiques stores operate; that's why we post signs that say all sales are final. It's too easy for someone—not you, of course—to take a one-of-a-kind item home, then bring back something that resembles that item and demand a refund. How can I—the dealer—prove that what you've returned *isn't* what I sold you?"

"Listen, Abby, I'm not trying to pull a fast one on you; I'm just trying to get my money back on a piece of junk I bought from you on good faith."

"And now it's time for you to listen up, Andrea: I *don't* sell junk. Case closed."

She was silent for a moment. To her credit, I could tell that she was trying her level best to control her temper.

"Look, I bought what you told me was a genuine Persian carpet for my formal living room, and it turns out that I have a cheap knockoff made in Beijing—or wherever it is in China that they mass produce the fake Orientals. I thought this might happen, so I already have an appointment set up with my lawyer."

"Wait just one cotton-pickin' minute, missy," I said, hopping mad myself. "You're besmirching my reputation at my place of business. I stand behind that carpet. It was the genuine article."

She fished a second item out of her purse. "You see this? I had B. S. Heuchera out to the house at the crack of dawn this morning. It cost me an arm and a leg to do it, but here's his report. Surely you know Mr. Heuchera, Abby."

Every antique dealer in the Southeast knew and feared Barry Sullivan Heuchera, if only because his syndicated column, "The Finer Things" (and yes, the title was stolen directly from the Rob-Bobs' shop), could make or break a dealer's reputation. Barry Sullivan—privately we called him B.S. for short—had a way with words, rather than a depth of knowledge upon which to draw. I was skeptical that he could even tell a genuine antique wool carpet from a recently made synthetic one.

I scanned the report. "Hmm. Well, this is certainly interesting. Tell me, Andrea, what made you choose him? And why now?"

"Lloyd Knudsen called me last night—you mean now you're not denying that what's in this report is true?"

"What did you say? Did you say 'Knudsen'?"

"We—the upper middle class—have friends too, Abby."

"What am I, a *knaidlach*?" As long as I had to be something, I'd rather be a matzo ball than chopped liver.

"What? Are you making jokes at my expense?"

"No, I gave up humor for Lent. But back to this report: I'm sure B. S. Heuchera meant well, but— Andrea, may I possibly go back with you to your house and look at it myself?"

"Well, I don't know—"

"I'll make you a baroness."

"Really? You have that power? I mean, I heard you were a princess of some kind, but I thought that Americans can't have titles. Which brings up an interesting point that the ladies in my bridge club were discussing—"

"Their titles aren't recognized by the government here," I said. "But the next time you're in Europe and want a good table at a restaurant, just say you're Baroness Wheating from Charleston and see what happens." I cleared my throat softly. "Or not."

Andrea chortled. "Abby, I know you're pulling my Yankee leg, but I love it. Do you want to ride with me, or do you prefer to follow in your own car?"

"I'll ride with you," I said.

* * *

Andrea Wheating lived in a seaside mansion on the Isle of Palms, just down from Charleston's premier public beach. To get there from downtown meant crossing the Cooper River on North America's longest cable-stayed bridge. As one climbs up and over the harbor one can see all of Mount Pleasant and as far north as Dewees Island. To the west is Daniel Island, of course, and on a clear day the chimneys and vents of Nucor Steel are visible floating on the horizon, while to the east is Pinckney Island, and beyond that the container ships diminish in size until they become indistinguishable from distant seabirds.

As a little girl we used to take the old Grace Memorial Bridge across on family vacations to the beach. At its best the GMB seemed to be built out of a boy's erector set, and was pitched at a nose-bleed angle, so that cars appeared to be launching themselves into the sky, rather than crossing a broad estuary. Everyone I knew, including Daddy, had grown nervous at the thought of crossing this bridge, and with good reason: lots of folks died in the attempt, and lots of folks had attempted to die from these dizzying heights. It didn't help either that there were tales of the bridge being haunted, of unrecovered bodies entombed forever in the massive concrete pilings.

Today, riding with Andrea, I was happier than ever that, after five years of aggravating construction, the new bridge had finally been completed. Andrea, however, was the world's second worst driver (behind only Mama). I discovered after riding only one block with her that she had a lead foot and took the speed limits merely as suggestions. What's more, she zagged when she should have zigged, and vice versa; she never once used her turn signals, although she did use a lot of rude hand signals; she jerked to stops in one-third the recommended space; and once she jumped out and left the car running at a red light while examining a window display. Of course she failed to make it back to the car before the light turned green again, providing me with yet another excuse to color my hair.

That said, I wouldn't have missed going out to her house with her for the world. It's one thing to have rich friends, but this was taking it to a whole new level. I'd actually driven past Andrea's house on many occasions—we go by there every time we have out-of-town guests we want to impress—but never without a drool bag in my lap.

Although mere words can't do it justice, I am willing to give it my old Winthrop College try. The house has three floors and was designed as the vacation home of a wealthy builder. Since the builder eventually hoped to retire there, he used the finest materials and took no shortcuts. As a result, what sleeps twenty-four and could have eventually ended up as rental property is now a showplace. U.S. presidents, both sitting and former, have used the residence on both official and nonofficial trips.

Because the exterior was built to resemble Tara from *Gone with the Wind*, it has been the location of a number of films, including that short-lived television do-gooder show, *Miami Nice*. With all this publicity, one would think that Andrea Wheating would be paranoid about security, but there is no front gate, and the only privacy fence is a row of Sabal palms under-planted with variegated Japanese pittosporum.

The oval drive wraps around a bronze fountain featuring a pair of dolphins (presumably mother and off-spring). The front doors are appropriately massive, and daunting, until one notices that there is a normal size door embedded into one of the monstrosities. Andrea didn't bother to use a key, metal or otherwise. Instead, she just pushed a button.

"Thackeray, it's me. Open up."

Immediately, the normal door was opened by a butler in tails, straight out of a P.G. Wodehouse novel—except that this one was very young, and to-die-for handsome. "Good day, madam."

"Thackeray, I'll have my usual, and Mrs. Wiggins will have—"

I jumped right on it. "Sweet tea."

Thackeray rolled his eyes. "Will y'all be having any corn pone with that, ma'am?" he asked in the most exaggerated Southern accent this side of Hollywood.

"Now Thackeray, be a dear and just get the drinks please, and maybe some light finger food." She waited until the butler, who walked like he had boards in his pants, had turned a corner before addressing me.

"Sorry about that, Abby. He's English, you know. He thinks we Americans are terribly uncivilized, especially Southerners. It's the movies, you know, that are responsible for giving the English that stereotype. Anyway, Thackeray used to work for Buckingham Palace—gosh darn it, I should have told him that you're some kind of royalty. He would have globbed onto you like nobody's business."

Now there was an image I just might file away for future use. As obnoxious as he was, Thackeray cut a handsome figure in his morning suit. Still, the line between condescension and hostility seemed too fine to distinguish under pressure, so I was determined to swallow as little of my sweet tea—assuming it ever arrived—as possible.

"Andrea," I said, turning up my perkometer a little higher than usual, "please show me that carpet."

She led me straightaway into a living room fit for a king, a room even Thackeray might approve of. Although most of the furniture was twentieth century, they were quality pieces made in North Carolina, the capital of furniture making in the United States. The floral sofas and lightly stuffed armchairs were remarkably traditional, not at all "beachy," as one might expect to find in a house so close to the ocean that the breaking waves were all that could be seen through the expanse of glass at the far end.

I will admit to being mesmerized by the view, and that Andrea had to remind me to look down. But then instantly I was on my knees, choking back a cry of despair.

13

"It's a forgery," I sobbed in a hoarse whisper into my cell phone.

"*A forgery?*" Bob bellowed into my ear. "Abby, how can a carpet be a forgery?"

"I don't know!" I realized with a start just how loud I must have been speaking. Andrea was staring at me from across the room, but at least Thackeray had the training to ignore the wild machinations of— No he hadn't; he was grinning from ear to ear. I'd have bet dollars to doughnuts that Thackeray was yet another drama student at the College of Charleston. With nothing to lose, I decided to heed a lesson from the book of "The Wise Words of Abigail Washburn, Chapter Eight, Verse Two": When caught staring at the headlights and with no time to jump, you might as well wave.

"Are you there?" Bob demanded.

"Drawn and quartered, and about to be hung on the village gates for all to see."

"Then at least the worst part is over."

"Ha ha. Bob, what do I do? How do I stall Andrea? She seems like a nice enough person—a good sport

106

even—but she wants to go to the police. Funny, but she didn't mention the police when she came to the shop this morning."

"What did you say her name is again?"

"Andrea Wheating."

"It couldn't be—could it?"

"How should I know? You haven't told me what 'it' is."

"Where's she from?"

"Michigan."

"Getting closer, feeling warmer. Do you know where in Michigan?"

"Kazoo . . . Kalamazoo, that's it."

"Hot, hot, hot!"

"Weird, weird, weird, but you're still a dear friend."

"Where are you now, Abby?"

"Isle of Palms, just down from the public beach."

"Go with her to Coconut Joe's and snag an outside table. I'll be there in twenty."

"What if she doesn't like seafood?"

"Then she can eat chicken. Or a salad."

"Shall I tell her you're coming?"

"No!"

His *no* was so loud that I fumbled with the phone, thereby making a total fool of myself.

"Is anything else wrong, Abby?" Bob has a basso profundo voice, but Andrea booms pretty well herself.

I shook my head. "Shoot, a monkey, Bob," I hissed. "Can you keep it down? She already thinks I'm a total incompetent, if not an out and out thief. What if she refuses to come to lunch altogether?"

"Nobody from Kalamazoo, Michigan, ever turned down a free lunch," he said, and hung up.

Coconut Joe's restaurant is upstairs facing the sea. In the afternoon, when the breezes shift and come off the Atlantic Ocean, lunch there can be a truly delightful experience. The food and service are great too, a fact of which Andrea was well aware, because she offered to drive.

Thackeray wanted to come as well, but Andrea ordered him to clear away our drinks and make sure he had all the ingredients to prepare a proper beef Wellington for some guests she was having over that night.

Then she nudged me. Dunce that I was, she had to nudge me twice.

"Anyone special?" I asked.

"Why yes, as a matter of fact. The head of the household at Buckingham Palace, Mr. Michael Grimswater. He says he knows you quite well, Thackeray, and he's looking for a chance to catch up. Tut tut, cheerio, and all that sort of rot."

Once outside, Andrea couldn't stop laughing, if indeed one could call the loud trumpets and snorts coming from her proper laughs. Without meaning to be rude, I can only describe it as if someone had spliced together two *National Geographic* nature tapes, one on elephants, the other on wart hogs. At any rate, long after we were seated at our table, Andrea was still emitting the occasional honk. Because school year was still in session, I was indeed able to snag an outdoor table facing the ocean. Mercifully, her back was turned to the other diners and she missed out on their expressions and, I believe, most of their comments.

I saw Bob Steuben coming toward us from the bar area, but I didn't expect him to sneak up behind Andrea and put his hands over her eyes.

"Quick," he said, "what is the main ingredient in kangaroo tail soup, Miss Kalamazoo?"

Andrea not only managed to jump straight off her seat several inches, but to somehow swivel in the air before plastering herself on Bob like a barnacle on a piling. There was no kissing, to be sure, just the pressing of leathery tanned flesh against pale freckled flesh. The entire time, Andrea was shrieking like a banshee on steroids. Customers and waiters who'd formerly been snickering at wild hog and pachyderm sounds now found themselves in the primate house just before feeding time.

Trying to think fast on my little feet, I dashed to the specials board and erased it with the back of my blouse. Then I wrote: *Long lost lovers. She was just rescued from a desert island. Been there fifteen years, bless her heart.*

Tobias, the highest ranking waiter, is a real sweetheart. When he saw what I'd written, he held up the board, whereupon there was enthusiastic applause and an empty bread basket was passed around to collect money so the poor leathery woman could buy a bottle of sunscreen and some new clothes.

At last the effusive and prolonged greeting was over—at least to the point where I could convince them to sit down. Tobias brought the bread basket over and gave each of the startled "lovers" a peck on the cheek.

"What was that all about?" Bob asked. "Is he single? Not that I'm in the market, but it doesn't hurt to know what's out there."

"Tobias is straight," I said. "He's also French; they kiss everyone."

Andrea was more pragmatic. "What's the money for?"

"Your fellow diners took up a collection for you. Wasn't that thoughtful of them?"

"A collection? Whatever for?"

"I told them that you'd been stranded on a desert island for fifteen years, à la Tom Hanks in *Castaway*. They thought you might need some new things."

Andrea jumped up and took a series of deep bows, which inspired a standing ovation, the donation of more cash, and the demand for a speech.

"Keep it short," I begged. "We have a crime to discuss."

"It was a dark and stormy night," Andrea began, her face deadly serious. "My lover, Reginald"—she gestured at Bob—"and I were standing on the poop deck, utterly pooped from an evening of tepid sex, when a giant origami type wave washed me overboard. Reginald heard me cry out, but couldn't see, and neither could the captain, who has astigmatism and needs new glasses in the worst possible way. Thankfully, I was washed ashore on a desert island, where I subsisted for fifteen years on a diet of coconuts, fish, and radicchio. Then one day the captain got a better medical plan, some new specs, and here I am. By the way, meeting Reginald here today was totally unplanned. I only wish he had waited for me. Even if the Church came through and gave him an annulment, how would he explain his thirteen kids?"

She took another bow, but instead of more applause, the air rang with boos as poor Bob was pelted with dinner rolls and virtually anything that could be flung *except* for money and heavy water glasses. While Tobias tried to gain control of his dining room, I crawled under the table with my newly arrived order of blackened chicken, red beans and rice, and fried plantains. As a mother I am quite aware of the five second rule, and have at times extended it to thirty seconds, so I was well supplied with bread.

Nothing can restore order quite like a sincere threat to call the cops, especially where local businessmen might be caught lunching with secretaries or receptionists—at least of some description or another. When order was returned and it was safe to resume eating above lap level, my calm gaze met the flashing eyes of a rather angry Bob, who turned them on Andrea.

"Yes, Andy, I am glad to see you, but *thirteen* children? Did you have to throw that in?" he said.

"Well you know that's what she wanted," Andrea said.

"What who wanted?" I said.

"How long have you been down here, for Pete's sake?" Bob asked.

"A year this July," Andrea said.

"So how do you two know each other?" I asked.

"And you never thought to look me up?"

"I didn't think you'd want to hear from me," Andrea said. "Not after the way things ended between you and Melissa."

"Who the heck is Melissa?" I asked.

"Andrea, that was sixteen years ago. Besides, I could have helped you to settle in down here."

"Bob, are y'all talking about your ex-wife?" I said.

"Abby, shut up," they said in unison.

"Damn, Yankees," I muttered.

That got their attention. They both apologized, then I apologized, after which Bob explained that Andrea was his former sister-in-law. The last bombshell was Andrea's.

"Speaking of children," she said, "at least in theory, it might not be too late to produce one. That is to say, I'm divorcing what's his name."

"Edward?" Bob said.

"Heavens no! He was three husbands ago. This mistake is Chalmers Wheating III. This one is actually leaving *me*, can you believe that?"

"I can't believe that," Bob said, sounding as serious as a Baptist preacher come Judgment Day.

"How interesting," I said. It's a Southern euphemism for, *Yes, I can surely believe it, based on your thoroughly unpredictable whacky behavior.* In that regard it's very much like exclaiming, *What a tiny little baby!* when forced to admire a newborn that looks just like Mr. Magoo.

"Yeah, he said it was too hot for him. He said that since he was going to Hell anyway, he didn't want to sit through a bunch of previews during his time spent on earth."

"Can we finally get down to business?" I whined.

"By all means," Andrea said, having the nerve to suddenly sound impatient. "You'll never guess what happened, Bob— Hey, do you two know each other?"

Bob winked at me—at least I hope he did. Given that he wears glasses and doesn't have discernible eyelashes, it was hard to tell.

"If this was the 1970s, Abby would be our fag hag."

"Now I'm just a hag," I said, strangely flattered.

She ignored my self-deprecating humor. "*Our?*" she asked archly.

"Yes, I've been in a committed relationship for eleven years. But no divorces. My people still aren't allowed to engage in legalized monogamy. Somehow, it seems, it will have a deleterious effect on the institution of marriage."

"You were always so droll, Bob; I can't wait to hear the details."

"Maybe tonight? Over cream of lichen soup and musk-oxen steaks. The musk oxen are farm raised, of course. I found this place up in Vermont that even packs a few homegrown tundra berries in with your order for garnish. It's all very good; in fact, I think I'll order some more."

Andrea laughed delightedly. "I see that you're still into weird cooking. Well, I'm still into eating it."

I drummed on the table, which, given the size of my digits, went unnoticed. "We're here to discuss a carport that's a fogy," I bellowed. "I mean a carpet that's a forgery!"

Fortunately, when I bellow, the decibels rise just above the level of the average conversation, so nobody other than my luncheon companions heard me.

"Abby, you're certainly right about that," Bob said, "so please explain. We're all ears."

The bellowing had me hoarse, so I cleared my throat.

"Bob, Andrea, although I have no doubt that Lloyd Knudsen's carpet is not a handmade Tabriz, I can't vouch for the fact that it isn't the one Rob sold him."

"Rob and I don't sell schlock!" Bob is as Waspy as a nest full of yellow jackets, but over the years he's picked up a smattering of Yiddish phrases from his partner.

"Don't get your tighty whites in a bunch, sweetie," Andrea said. "Abby knows that you don't sell junk."

"Anyway," I said, "the Bijar I sold to Andrea is a different story. I was in love with that carpet; I almost didn't put it up for sale. In fact—and I shouldn't be saying this—I had it in my living room for three years before putting it in my shop."

Andrea feigned shock. "*What?* You sold me a used carpet?"

"That's the beauty of owning an antiques store," Bob boomed. "You get to try out the merchandise at home and it doesn't lower the value."

"What fun," Andrea said.

"My point," I said, "is that I am intimately acquainted with your Bijar. When we had boring guests, I studied its pattern. Likewise, on those occasions when a loved one might get it into his, or her, head to lecture me—not that it happened often—I studied its pattern. If I could draw, I could recreate it on this napkin. Had I sent it out for a cleaning and gotten back a rug that looked similar, I would have immediately spotted the substitution.

"Now the really weird thing is, when Andrea sent this rug out, she got back an *exact* copy, the only difference being that they were woven from different materials. That means one of two things: either the cleaners had access to a machine-made rug that was copied from the original *before* I bought it at auction, or, through some technogadget wizardry of some sort, they were able to make a replica. Obviously they then kept the original, and most probably for resale."

Bob raised his glass of chardonnay. "Well thought out, Abby. Brava!"

"Except for one thing," Andrea said.

14

"Pray tell, what might that be?" I asked. You can bet that I was slightly annoyed.

"I never sent it out to be cleaned."

Oops. "You didn't? Not even once?"

"No, Abby. It's too big. Did *you* send it out when it graced your living room floor?"

"Uh . . . no. I had somebody come in. It's just that sending carpets out seems to have caught on lately here."

"Yeah, well so have a lot of things that make no sense to me. Like wearing lined linen clothes in the summertime. Linen is great for summer because it's an open material that breathes. The moment you line it with polyester, you may as well be wearing a plastic bag."

"A wrinkled plastic bag," Bob said. "Abby calls the women who wear lined linen the 'Linen Ladies.'"

"I knew I liked you," Andrea said, her voice building to a crescendo.

"Okay," I said, "let's review. At Kitty Bohring's huge—"

"Fiasco," Andrea said.

"Were you there?" I asked.

"Of course; all the filthy rich were. I was just three people behind you in the receiving line. I heard every word."

"Then you know I'm not royalty."

"I should hope not. From the books I've read—so this is all *allegedly*, mind you—particularly about the English royal family, you'd have had to spend far more time committing adultery than even I—and I hate competitors of any sort. So if I thought that you were really a royal—even just the Continental kind—we wouldn't be sitting at the same table." She grinned, and I noticed for the first time that she had exceptionally large teeth. One tooth in particular was quite enormous.

"Anyway," I said, feeling a bit like a harried tour director, "Kitty had a gigantic seventh century Aubusson carpet that she bought in Paris decades ago. Today, the real McCoy would be easily worth at least one hundred and fifty grand. At some point, someone switched carpets on her—or not. I have no way of knowing for sure. But she did send it out to be cleaned a couple of months prior to the fiasco."

Andrea laid her stubby but well-manicured fingers on my arm. "And next we have the hot-tempered, wife-beating—again *allegedly*—Lloyd Knudsen. Lloyd sent his carpet out to be cleaned, whereas someone should have cleaned his clock."

"I take it you don't like him," Bob said.

"Loathe, would be an understatement. But the icky little man doesn't get it; he thinks just because he built my house and that we're both rich, we're somehow friends. Abby, I would much rather have a mature butler than that muscle-building Thackeray, but I'm afraid Lloyd is going to show up some night and try to climb into my bed. Do you know that I have a restraining order on him?"

When Bob and I gasp together it sounds a bit like Aunt Nanny settling into an afternoon nap. "No," I said. "Has he assaulted you?"

"He harasses me. He shows up at all hours of the night, rings the bell, pounds on the door, and when I won't answer it he stands out in the street with a megaphone and yells 'Slut.'"

"Icky is the perfect word to describe him then," I said. "Just like a fungus."

We were all distracted then by a seven tier chain of kites that floated by just out of reach. The breeze had shifted so it was coming from the ocean, a sure sign that it was now the afternoon. I looked past the kite out to sea. The Atlantic at this latitude is an uninspiring greenish color that becomes leaden gray on cloudy days, but like any sea, its horizon beckons and promises. Were I able to swim, or even sail, straight across the ocean, I would end up in Casablanca, Morocco, which is in North Africa. They have some beautiful rugs there, but without the cachet of the ones to be found in the eastern Mediterranean area. Still, someday I was going to visit Morocco and—

"Earth to Abby," Bob said. "Come in, Abby, wherever you are."

"I'm in the Casbah," I said, "doing a little personal shopping."

"Well, we need you here to help us figure out what to do."

"And just so to be clear," Andrea said, "after hearing all this, I'm not expecting a refund or anything like that. For all you know, I *do* have a brother who's a master forger."

I laughed, mostly out of relief. While I do respect the "buyer's remorse" rule on high ticket items, my merchandise is generally not returnable. Sure, I often let customers take a piece home to see how "it fits," but they invariably bring it back the next day, sometimes within hours.

"It's not the forgery so much as the production," Bob said. "I mean, with computers these days you can copy just about any image. But to translate it from the image to the actual product—well, that would take a factory, wouldn't it? What do you think? China?"

"Yes," Andrea said, "but so far that's only three carpets that we know of so far, and we have no proof that two of these were even genuine antiques to begin with."

"And let's not forget," I added, "the splendid original I bought at Pasha's Palace for Cheng and Toy's wedding, but now, since she finds him repulsive and they're separating, I no longer have to give to them—" I paused to catch my breath. "—and the fact that Gwendolyn Spears, former manager of said establishment, was pulled from the bay wrapped in a gorgeous Tabriz original. I'd say there's something definitely fishy in Mudville—to mix a metaphor."

"Unless it's a mudfish,"

Andrea appeared hopelessly lost. *"What?"*

"There are various varieties of mudfish," Bob said. "The African mudfish can actually live for months without water—"

"Robert Steuben, I don't give a rat's patootie about a mudfish! Abby, when was this that you saw an original Oriental carpet for sale at Pasha's Palace?"

"Just a day or two before the nice young manager, Gwendolyn Spears, was pulled from the harbor."

"Yes, of course. I was in there about that time too. No offense, guys, but I was looking for an inexpensive carpet to put down on the floor of Thackeray's new room. He might look well-trained in that monkey suit, but he prefers to eat in his room, and there are mornings when I have to get the gardener to come in and hose him down. Anyway, I nearly dropped my dentures when I came across a whole pile of fabulous antique rugs at unbelievable prices." She grabbed my hand and squeezed so hard that I nearly dropped some viable teeth. "You do understand, don't you, dear, if I bought a few?"

"You wear dentures?" Bob asked. "I have a partial that I find really irritating. I can't imagine a complete set of false chompers."

Andrea and I focused identical withering glares on our male companion. After the three second glare requirement, I turned to her with a smile—well, at the very least it was a pleasant expression.

"Forgive me, Andrea, but I'd have to ask this of anyone I spoke to: on what exactly did you base your conclusion that they were antique?"

She didn't recoil, but her eyes flashed, warning me to tread carefully. "Forgive *me*, Abby, but if someone were to ask how old you were, I would guess that you were somewhere in your forties. Am I correct?" She didn't wait for an answer. "I can see that you color your hair, but other than that I'm guessing you haven't had any major work done. Still, there's no stopping Old Man Time from leaving his mark; even the best preserved of us look just that—preserved."

"Ouch," Bob said. I wanted to punch him.

"Point made," I said. "However, antique carpets get their patina from the wear of feet, sunlight, and the occasional spillage. But ever since wealthy foreign tourists discovered the joys of collecting antique Persian carpets, their vendors have discovered ways of turning new carpets into old."

Some of the fire left Andrea's eyes. "I guess I shouldn't be surprised. But tell me how."

"The dyes in new carpets are too bright to emulate the antique, so they're bleached with chemicals— sometimes harsh chemicals like calcium chloride—or maybe something as everyday as lemon juice. Of course then the acid has to be neutralized, or it will eat the carpet."

"It's like getting a perm," Bob said, who happens to be very nearly bald. "Abby, may I add a few things?"

"Go for it, big guy."

He grinned; a big guy he's not. "New carpets are also buried in the ground for a while, or sometimes rubbed with coffee grounds to give them that certain patina. One of the most interesting ways of giving them that 'lived with' look is to apply a flammable substance to both sides of the carpet, light it, and then instantly douse the flames. Then the scorched fibers are scraped off, but what is left is very convincingly old."

"As would be I," said Andrea. She shook her head. "Abby, I owe you a huge apology."

I almost told her that no apology was needed, but that would have been rude. "Apology accepted. Still, whatever their age, the carpets you saw were certainly a departure for Pasha's Palace. I was there just this morning, and every one of them was brand spanking new."

Bob cleared his throat, an action that was loud enough and apparently with enough promise to tempt several sea gulls to land on the railing not ten feet away. They cocked their heads expectantly.

"Stupid little buggers," he growled. "Now where was I?"

"I don't know," I said. "You were still getting ready to launch."

He grinned again. "Stop it, Abby. *Anyway*, it seems pretty clear to me that Gwendolyn Spears was trying to send Abby a message by selling her that Tabriz at a ridiculously low price—well, giving it to her, actually—and that she later paid with her life. Do Tweedledee and Tweedledum know about this?"

"Who are *they*?" Andrea asked, dropping her fork, scaring the sea gulls away.

"Two of Charleston's not-so-finest," I said, glancing around. "If I was paranoid I'd think they were following me. But to answer your question, Bob, they later came to my house for a deposition and I told them everything I know, but I don't think they believed a word. I am, after all, just a lowly antiques dealer."

"Who has a penchant for solving crimes." He turned proudly to Andrea. "Abby is the Sherlock Holmes of Charleston—but without the drug habit."

"Are you her Watson?" Andrea sounded distinctly envious to me.

"I'm only one of her many admirers," Bob said. "But I'm sure she has room in her coterie of disciples for one more—don't you, Abby?"

"The more the merrier," I said. "And the first item on our agenda should be coming up with a way to find out just how many carpets in Charleston have been switched. Any bright ideas on how to do that?"

"We could put an ad in the paper," Andrea said. "In it we'd ask people to contact us—I mean, you—if they think they've been swindled."

I shook my head vehemently. "The weight of all those lawyers camped out on my beautiful antebellum piazza will cause it to cave in, resulting in bodily injury to some, thereby precipitating a multitude of lawsuits against yours truly. I couldn't possibly win all the lawsuits, and would be forced to flee the Holy City in the dark of the night disguised as George Stephanopoulos to spend the rest of my life on the island of Mykonos, which will be very pleasant until the real George shows up on vacation with his wife, at which point I'll be exposed as a fraud and shipped off to a nunnery, and then who will care for my cat?"

"*What?*"

"I think Abby would prefer another idea," Bob said. "Hey, I know, what about a carpet clinic?"

"Expound, Bob," I said. "Briefly—sort of."

"Well, we could start with Andrea's idea . . . " He

paused long enough to let Andrea beam. " . . . of placing an ad in the Charleston *Post and Courier.* The ad says that for fifty dollars we will come to your home, assuming it is within a ten mile radius of the Battery, and we'll give you a short, written appraisal of your carpet that will be suitable for insurance purposes. We will also give you tips on what you should or should not be doing to extend its wear."

"I like it," I said. "But make that *two hundred* dollars a visit."

Bob whistled, attracting the attention of the last table of diners other than ourselves. "But Abby, isn't that a little steep? With the economy the way it is, a lot of people won't be able to afford that."

"Exactly. Bob, I don't mean to be snobbish, but we want to weed out the people who bought their rugs at Pasha's Palace or Home Depot for under a thousand dollars. Besides, people who pay a lot for a particular item are often likely to think more of an appraisal that is also pretty, uh—"

"Overpriced?" Andrea said.

"I think I get it," Bob said. "And hey, we do have mileage to consider, and our time is worth something, right?"

"Look at it this way," I said, "if we were plumbers or electricians making house calls, would we think twice about charging that much?"

"Touché."

Since Andrea had driven me out to the Isle of Palms, it was agreed that Bob would drive me back to the Den of Antiquity. After all, The Finer Things is situated just across the street. As it was such a beautiful afternoon, we detoured back through Sullivan's Island, hugging the coast so I could see two of my favorite houses. These aren't the monstrosities of the über rich, or built as summer rentals for parties of twenty or more, but eccentric, single-family dwellings.

The first is a so-called "hurricane proof" house that resembles a flying saucer, or a residence on the old TV show the *Jetsons*. As all the surfaces are rounded, the wind supposedly keeps right on going. The second home was created out of an underground bunker, which used to belong to the United States Navy. The entry is fronted by an expanse of glass, through which one can view a stately chandelier, but the roof is a thick blanket of grass and shrubs, and even small trees. It looks like something straight out of a fairy tale.

"I'd love to live there," Bob said. "I've heard there are dozens of underground rooms. The potential for a good wine cellar is, well—through the roof!" He demonstrated his appreciation for his own joke with a hearty belly laugh.

"You've obviously never been inside; it presents some real decorating challenges. Not only that, but I'd find all those rooms kind of spooky at night."

"Abby, you know I'm not afraid of ghosts."

"That's because you've never met one. You'd change your tune really fast if you had."

"Do you have a tail?"

"Hmm, not last time I checked. Do you?"

"Not a wagging type tail. I mean, is Greg having you followed again?"

"What?"

As it doesn't do me much good to just turn my head, because then all I see is the back of my seat, I undid my belt and climbed into a kneeling position. There was indeed a car idling about a hundred feet behind us, and I was able to catch a glimpse of the driver before he put it into reverse. Despite clipping a large chunk from a yucca plant, he did some fancy driving and was soon out of sight.

"Abby," Bob said, "you look as if you just saw one of those ghosts right now."

15

"For your information, Bob, they no longer like being referred to as ghosts. The preferred term now is Apparition Americans."

"Isn't that a bit racist?"

"How so? It applies equally to deceased Americans of all races."

"Isn't saying Apparition American making fun of hyphenated Americans, even if most copy editors leave out the hyphens these days?"

"That's exactly the point that Apparition Americans are trying to make. They think that unless one gives the continent of racial origin in each case, then one is assuming that there exists a norm—a regular American, so to speak. You don't speak of *European* Americans, do you?"

"Abby, you're hopeless."

"So is Mama."

"Why, pray tell, are you dragging *her* into this conversation?"

"Because the guy driving that car was one of her paramours."

"Did you say *one* of her paramours? How many does she have?"

"She'll tell me she isn't seeing anyone, but just about every night of the week she has a different gentleman caller. And lately some of them have even gotten halfway to first base. Heck, I caught one of them kissing the top of her head the other night."

"Mozella gets a peck on the noggin. How sweet! Now how about this guy we just saw?"

"He's not a guy; his name is Big Larry McNamara."

"What do you mean he's not a guy?"

"Well, he is, but he's also as big as Texas and Rhode Island combined. And he's really weird. He talks in a down-home, good old boy drawl when he thinks you're listening, but then he switches to California mystery English when he thinks you're not."

"California mystery English?"

"You know, what you hear on television—for the most part."

"Ah, when they're not mocking the South, Minnesota, etcetera."

"Anyway, Big Larry was there when Detective Tweedledee pulled Gwendolyn from the harbor. He actually assisted me in not getting trampled by the crowd. Then he somehow positioned himself into being Mama's date at the fiasco of the twenty-first century. But there's more to it than that. He's got his eye on me. I felt it immediately. This just confirms it."

Bob shook his head slowly from side to side and exhaled dramatically. "Abby, we're getting a little full of ourselves, aren't we?"

"You haven't met this creep. If you knew him, you wouldn't be saying that."

"Oh no, don't get me wrong. I'm sure Lecherous Larry is a creep; I'll take your word for that. What I meant is, it's a little premature to declare your royal debut at the Bohring mansion as the fiasco of the century—isn't it?"

We laughed all the way back to King Street as we tried to imagine worse scenarios. Unfortunately, we were rather successful.

I might not spend much time there, but I actually have a home. It's a beautiful Georgian Revival at 7 Squiggle Lane, in the much coveted lower part of the peninsula south of Broad Street. That, of course, is what makes me an S.O.B. In addition to my very handsome husband, Greg, our house is inhabited by a fifteen pound marmalade tabby cat named Dmitri. And, of course, Mama.

Dmitri was named after one of Erica Kane's innumerable husbands. She, by the way, is the star of one of television's longest running soap operas, and no, I am not ashamed to admit that I've been watching it for thirty-odd years. I got hooked in college but am slowly getting unhooked, as yesteryear's beefcakes and power brokers grow portly or long in the tooth, and most of the players are now the ages of my own children.

The day before Bob and I were to start our house-to-house carpet appraisal clinic (Rob was none too thrilled with the idea and begged off), I took off early from work, and when I opened the front door I got the surprise of my life. Standing in my foyer, with only a white Turkish towel slung low around his narrow hips, was a six-foot-tall, deeply tanned man with a glass of sweet tea in his hand. He held the drink out to me, his azure eyes twinkling mischievously.

"Hey babe, I thought you'd never get here."

Standing just as expectantly beside my lover was a much shorter male, one with a good deal more body hair.

"If it isn't my two favorite guys in all of Charleston," I said happily.

Greg, still smelling slightly fishy, gave me a quick kiss on the lips. "Surprised?"

The shorter male settled for wrapping himself around my legs and purring loudly.

"Yes, I'm surprised. You're never home this early. How long have you been standing there like that?"

"Really? Not more than a minute."

"Then how did you know when to expect me?"

"I had Wynnell call me when you left work."

"What happened, Greg? Was the shrimping bad today?"

"Rotten is more like it. Fishing altogether wasn't worth our time. In fact, I'm thinking of staying home tomorrow. If you can spare a couple of hours, I thought we might hang out together. You know, play tourists in our own town. It might be really fun. We could start tonight even, by going out to eat. I vote for Slightly North of Broad. What about you? Remember, your vote always trumps mine."

"Uh . . . yeah, sure. SNOB sounds great." Frankly, I would have preferred Magnolias, which is right across the street.

"Wait a minute. I saw those wheels turning in your head. You're holding back, Abby. Out with it."

"Wheels? What are you talking about?"

"I only work with Booger Boy on a shrimp boat, hon; I don't have boogers for brains. I used to be a detective, remember?"

When you're caught and there is no way out, you can either confess immediately or stall a bit and hope that some *spin*formation comes to you in the interim. I chose the latter course, one that I learned from our government. For them, at least, it seems to work very well.

"Let's eat first, and I'll tell you everything while we're waiting for dessert to arrive," I said.

"And since we don't have reservations, and it's a weekday night, we don't need to eat right away," Greg said.

Dmitri, always a jealous cat, stopped purring.

After strengthening our bonds of marriage, we'd dined sumptuously. I started with a cup of red bean soup, which was slow cooked with peppers, onions, celery, and garlic, and topped with jalapeno salsa and sour cream. Despite the fact that he had spent the day at sea, Greg chose mussels as his appetizer. They were poached in white wine, garlic, parsley, and a touch of butter.

For my main course I picked the jumbo lump crab cakes, which were served over a sauté of corn, okra, roasted yellow squash, and grape tomatoes. To keep things interesting, my darling ordered the skinless sautéed duck breast, leg confit with plum glaze, braised greens, mashed sweet potatoes, and honey thyme reduction. Of course we both had multiple helpings of warm, freshly baked bread,

Greg hasn't met a crème brûlée he didn't like, and I'm pretty sure I can say the same thing about triple chocolate cake. After we placed our orders he turned to me. "Did you enjoy your dinner?"

"It was fantastic. And you?"

"I've never had a bad meal here yet."

"Good. Uh . . . then maybe you won't mind so much calling up a couple of guy friends and going golfing?"

"Abby, was that a statement or a question? I swear, sometimes I think you should have been a Canadian."

"It was a declarative sentence, unless you object strongly, in which case it was a very weakly posed question—one not at all worth getting upset about."

"And why the heck should I get upset having a day to spend on the golf course with my friends? What aren't you telling me?"

At that very second the waitperson, whose name was Jance, but who was of yet undetermined gender, sidled up between the two of us. "Excuse me, but did yinz say decafe, or regular coffee with dessert?"

"Regular," Greg growled. "Who knows how late I'm going to be up tonight?"

"Decaffeinated," I said. "I intend to fall into bed the second I walk in the door. Who knows, I might be asleep before I even get there."

Jance laughed, without divulging any clues. "Coming right up."

"Are you from Pittsburgh?" I asked, forcing a bit of cheer.

"Yes. How did you know?"

"You said 'yinz.' That seems to be a Pittsburghism."

"Well, shoot. I've lived here two years; I was hoping I sounded like yinz—I mean *y'all*, by now."

"Did you move here with your family?" Greg asked.

"Yes, sir." Jance started to turn away.

"How do your parents like it?" I asked.

"Oh no, ma'am, it wasn't my parents. I moved down here with my spouse."

"Evil word, spouse," Greg said after Jance was out of earshot. "It gives no clues. Okay, Abby, no more excuses. Out with it."

"I have to work tomorrow."

"That's *it*? You made ants and a gorilla just for that?"

"You mean *gantzeh megillah*," I said. It's a Yiddish expression we learned from Rob, which essentially means a big deal. Foreign languages have never been my sweetie's strong point.

"Whatever," Greg said, his azure eyes now twin stormy seas. "You know how I hate lies."

"I'm *not* lying; Bob and I are conducting a carpet appraisal clinic. We'll be busy all day."

"Where is this clinic? Your shop, or his?"

"Actually, we're visiting our clients in their homes."

"You *what*?"

"Honey, didn't I show you our ad in the paper?"

"If you did, I sure the heck don't remember it. Abby, do you know how dangerous that could be?"

"Yes, but like I said, Bob will be with me."

"No offense, because he's your—I mean, *our*—friend and all, but Bob is a tad on the skinny side."

"That may be, but he has a black belt."

"He *does*?"

"Yes." What self-respecting gay man in this country doesn't own a nice black leather belt? Perhaps even a brown leather belt as well?

"How come it's never come up in conversation before?"

"He's modest, that's why—especially in that area. You know that if it had to do with cooking, we'd never stop hearing the last of it."

"You've got a point. So how many days is this clinic anyway?"

"Just two—tomorrow and Saturday. After that, my weekends will be free until—oh, crapolla and a pocketful of posies. It's *him* again."

"*Him* who? Abby, are you trying to change the subject?"

"Two tables behind you, one table over toward the door, there's this guy built like a professional wrestler gone to seed. Mama's been dating him, which is neither here nor there, but what is important is that he's been following me. And no, I'm not trying to change the subject."

Fortunately, Greg has seen me survive enough scrapes with truly dangerous characters to trust my judgment. Also, as a former detective, he was savvy enough not to turn immediately. Instead he started coughing. He told me later that his intent was to cough just hard enough to have an excuse to turn his head. The last thing either of us expected was for Godzilla to leap to his feet, cover the distance between our tables in what appeared to be a single bound, and then attempt to do the Heimlich on my dearly beloved husband.

"*Stauuugh*," Greg managed to say, the veins at his temples bulging in frustration.

"He said stop!" I shouted. "He's not choking!"

"Just remain calm, little lady," the giant said. "I've done this a million times."

"Leave him alone!" this mouse roared.

Big Larry, however, was bent on saving Greg's life. I'd read that in many cases the Heimlich maneuver can result in broken ribs. That might seem like a small price to pay for one's life, but was far to steep a fee for just a quick look-see of the man who'd been tailing me. But what was I to do? Grab the wine bottle off our table, jump up on a chair, and whack the wacko over the head? What if Greg got cut by the glass?

"Stop him!" I climbed on the table and again implored the other diners to come to Greg's aid. No one moved a muscle. It was if we'd been eating in Madame Tousaud's Wax Museum. What made the scene especially weird was that a local television station, which had been filming an author interview in the corner, now had its camera trained on us. Yet neither the crew nor the interviewer was making a move to help us. As for the stuck-up author, she couldn't even be bothered to look our way. Needless to say, I made a mental note to never buy a copy of Ramat Sreym's books again.

Think, Abby, think. But there wasn't time to think. Suddenly the answer came to me! I'd do what any red-blooded American would do if he, or she, were in my situation.

16

I cupped my hands and shouted directly into Big Larry's left ear. "We're going to sue you. Do you hear me? S-U-E, *sue*. Let go of him this second. If my husband has as much as a hairline facture on just one rib, we'll take everything you own, even the bloomers off your mama."

Arms the size of wharf pilings immediately released poor Greg, who slumped forward across our table whilst emitting an eerie groan. For what may have only been a few seconds, but seemed like an eternity, I entertained the possibility that the love of my life might have expired right there in front of me.

They say that in some near-death experiences one's life flashes before one's eyes, but I've never heard it said that when watching a spouse die, the future flashes in front of the survivor's eyes. I'd selfishly put off retiring, and now we would never know what it would be like to wake up each morning with a fresh day to spend together. Unless I remarried (and I was not about to train a new husband), I would have to do without the comfort of growing old alongside a best friend, someone who would always look out for me. In the future, when I had only enough energy to sit on the front porch and watch the world go by, the other rocker would always be empty.

I can't remember which came first: my loud anguished cry of utter emotional pain, or the violent movement of Greg's shoulders. Whichever, my vocalization was cut short as Greg leaped to his feet, turned, and, as he explained to me later, throwing all his weight into the swing, connected his right fist with Big Larry's jaw. It might not have been the crack heard around the nation, but virtually everyone in Slightly North of Broad heard skin-covered knuckles connect with jowl-covered bone.

Big Larry stood stock still for a second, teetered back and forth several inches like a skyscraper in a strong wind, and then crumpled in his tracks. It was like watching a building being demolished by dynamite on TV. Much to my surprise, there was scattered applause.

"Timber!" some wag yelled. Just so you know, it wasn't me.

Three hundred pounds hitting the floor created enough of a tremor so that folks on the sidewalk peered through the windows. When they saw the television crew, which had now moved into close range, the pedestrians flooded into the SNOB, no doubt looking for their fifteen seconds of fame. The diners, all of whom had been as useless to me as last year's stock tips, suddenly sprang to life. They jumped to their feet and milled about, comparing notes with their table mates, a few even thinking to ask the arrogant author for her autograph. But do you think anyone thought to ask Greg if he was all right? Or even to inquire after the welfare of Reclining Larry, for that matter?

Thank heavens the manager saw fit to call the paramedics, who called the police. Greg was taken to the University of South Carolina Medical Center, which mercifully is only a few minutes away by ambulance. At the E.R., he was immediately taken to be X-rayed, but as I was sitting in the waiting room, biting my nails, I glanced up at wall-mounted television and saw a replay of some of the worst minutes of my life.

I couldn't believe how awful I looked. I'd taken great pains to restore my hair and makeup to their preafternoon delight state before going out to dinner at SNOB. But the videotape taken by the local TV station made me look like a two-bit streetwalker who'd been on a four week binge after first throwing away her comb and soap.

"Ugh. I can't believe they let someone like that into Slightly North of Broad."

"*Mama?*" It was a somewhat rhetorical question, because if there were other women dressed liked Beaver's mother, Charleston would be the place to find them.

"Abby, what are you doing here?"

"Mama, that was *me* you just saw on television. That's Greg they're showing being carried out on the stretcher. Although he's actually in X ray now."

"Are you sure?"

"Of course I'm sure. We just came from SNOB. Isn't that why you're here? I thought maybe the paramedics called you."

"No, darling, you know I visit the sick list from Grace Episcopal. Greg? You thought the paramedics called *me*? Abby, are you all right?"

"Yes, Mama. I've been trying to tell you that it's Greg who's injured, maybe even seriously so. Anyway, I thought you were watching that stupid newscast."

"Abby, you know I haven't watched news shows of any kind since Howard Cronkite signed off. What happened? It wasn't terrorists, was it?"

"Sort of—not really. Look Mama, it was that monster boyfriend of yours. We were minding our own business, having a romantic dinner, when Greg started coughing. Suddenly your idiot boyfriend leaps across the room, grabs poor Greg, and nearly squeezes him to death."

Mama looked horrified. "I'm so sorry, Abby. Sometimes Guillermo doesn't know his own strength. It's all those years working out in the Georgia State Penitentiary, you see. But inside he's really as gentle as a mouse."

"Big Larry is Guillermo?"

"Gracious me, no! Big Larry is Big Larry; he's just a friend. Guillermo is my man friend—if you get my drift, dear. Not that we've engaged in any acts that are inappropriate for a couple who have yet to unite in the bonds of holy matrimony. But just as soon as Guillermo can save up enough money to get back down to Chile to see if his wife is still alive, we'll know how to proceed. He has no compunctions against joining the Episcopal Church, so that might be the easiest route to follow."

I stared at the woman who endured unspeakable

agony for thirty-six hours just to bring me into this cruel world. I loved her unconditionally, but didn't that mean—in addition to feeling warm and fuzzy toward her upon occasion—an obligation to protect her from harm? Lately it seemed as if the harm was likely to be her own doing.

"Mama, let me get this straight—and please correct me in case I'm having a flashback to the seventies and I heard everything wrong: you're dating an ex-con from Chile?"

"Isn't that exciting, dear? Guillermo Estevez. His ancestors were conquistadors."

"Oh goody; they raped and pillaged the Incas."

"Is that sarcasm, Abby?"

"Bingo. Why was he in the big house?"

"The what? Oh, you mean the slammer. He was innocent, Abby. And he was only the getaway driver. It's not like he was the one who went in and shot the security guard in both feet—before shooting himself in both feet. That, by the way, was a total accident. The safety wouldn't stay on. At any rate, Guillermo was paroled after thirteen years for good behavior."

"Your boyfriend was involved in *that* robbery? I read about that in *People* magazine, for heaven's sake! 'The world's most incompetent bank robber,' the caption read."

Mama patted her pearls proudly. "Do you remember reading that he had an accomplice? That was Guillermo!"

Screaming in hospitals is discouraged. Pulling one's hair out is not such a good idea for a woman whose hormones are beginning to wane, and especially not on the day before one is scheduled to see clients. I might have settled for lying on the floor and kicking my arms and legs (without the scream) but it was a *hospital* E.R., and who knows what, besides feet, had last touched that linoleum.

I closed my eyes so I could go to my secret spot; this is something my therapist taught me to do on those occasions when I found myself under unbearable stress. Unfortunately, Mama and Guillermo had beaten me to the spot and were locked in a not so chaste embrace. I tried to exile them in my imagination but they wouldn't budge. I even went so far as to dump a load of garden compost on them, but they merely shrugged and resumed their necking.

Upon opening my eyes, just as I was emitting the first syllable of a high-pitched shriek (it began with the letters M.A.), I noticed a wheelchair being pushed my way. In it was the very familiar head and shoulders of my darling husband.

I ran to greet him, but stopped short of throwing myself in his lap when I noticed that his right arm was in a sling. "Greg!"

"Easy, Abby, easy."

"What's the verdict? What did that man do to you?"

"You should be asking what I did to him. Sweetheart, I broke three bones in my hand, and one bone in my wrist, and cracked two others, when I punched him in the jaw. Lord only knows what he looks like."

"Isn't he back there somewhere?"

"No. I heard he was taken to Roper Hospital."

"That's odd. I wonder why. Greg, what about your ribs?"

"Ah, more bad news, I'm afraid. One is cracked and three are bruised. Fortunately, they're all on the same side."

"How long will you be in the hospital?"

"As long as it takes for you to check me out."

"*What?* You're kidding, right?"

"Abby, you know they don't keep you in hospitals anymore unless you're dying, or darn close to it. Besides, hospitals are where all the germs are at. You do know what my chances of catching a disease here are, don't you?"

He had a point. Greg really was better off taking his aching body home; he'd certainly get more rest there. At least I wouldn't be shining a light in his eyes every half hour, or taking his temperature every whip stitch in a weird attempt to get back at my tenth grade biology teacher—not that a real nurse would ever do such a thing; I'm just saying that I wouldn't.

"But who's going to take care of you at home?" I asked. "You know, until you get the hang of things? At least here they have orderlies that can assist you with certain functions." I gestured with my chin at the tall young man who'd pushed his wheelchair.

"What Abby's really saying," Mama said, "is who will help you use 'the little boys' room?'"

"Mama Wiggins!" Greg said, turning the color of fresh salmon.

"It's all right, Greg," Mama said. "I was married once, you know. And I've had lovers. I am familiar with the male anatomy—all those hoses and things they possess. It's nothing to be embarrassed about." She turned to me. "Besides, Abby, I'll take care of Greg.

I already live with you; why not let me earn my keep? You don't even have to worry about staying home tomorrow. All I ask in return is that during his recuperation I get to be the one to plan and prepare all the food, as well as be responsible for the housework."

I didn't know which bothered me more: her use of the word lovers, her reference to hoses, in the *plural*, or her blatant bid to insinuate herself into our good graces. Surely Greg would find a diplomatic way to turn down her kind but totally inappropriate offer. On the other hand, having just emerged from the bowels of a bandaging room, my beloved had no way to know that my mother was dating an ex-bandit.

"Mozella," he said with a smile, "your generosity is exceeded only by your good looks. I would be delighted to take you up on your generous proposition."

"That's ridiculous, Mama," I cried. "You can't even look at a turkey neck without blushing."

Greg winked at me. "Shh, don't dissuade her, darling. I'm having too much fun. Besides, what she can't do, you can."

"In a pig's ear," I growled. But of course I was going to agree to the arrangement. I'd taken my wedding vows seriously—both times. And if I ever took them again, I'd be just as sincere the third time around.

The doctor had given Greg some choice chemicals to help him sleep through the night, and sure enough, he slept like a teenager. When Bob came to pick me up, my husband was still zonked, but not for long, because Mama, wearing a pinafore apron over her full skirt dress, was frying bacon in the kitchen.

When bacon molecules hit Greg's nostrils he goes from deep sleep to wide-awake starvation mode in three seconds flat. Throw in blueberry pancakes and fresh ground coffee, and he's capable of breaking through walls to get at it.

"So how was your evening?" Bob said when we were in the car.

Oops. There had been so much going on that I'd forgotten to call my best friends. What would have been the point anyway? To make them worry?

"Did you see the local news last night, Bob?"

"Just caught a snatch of it: something about a crazy tourist couple at SNOB accosting an older man. Hate to say it, Abby, but for a second I thought the woman was you, but then they showed a close-up of her face. That's when I thought, 'Bob, you really need to get your vision checked again, and soon, because there is no way that woman looks like our Abby.' I mean, seriously, that woman hadn't exfoliated in a month of Sundays and her roots were showing like a mangrove swamp at low tide."

I cleared my throat so loud that somewhere, someone in Homeland Security was no doubt rubbing a sore ear. "I'll have you know that I just had my hair done, and—not that it's any of your business—I do exfoliate with a prescription cream. And how do you know anything about mangrove swamps, since we don't have them this far north?"

"Yuth a minuth, Abby, while I take my footh out of my mouth."

"Then I forgive you."

"In that case I'm sorry."

Having made peace with each other, we took the quaint Ashley River Bridge with its stone pillars over to James Island, hung a left on Wesley Drive, then a right on Maybank Highway. Just before the highway crosses the Stono River, it cuts through the middle of Green Acres, a municipal golf course. This bizarre bit of suburban planning leaves motorists and golfers alike cringing. I always steel myself for the thud of a golf ball against my windshield. But the fact is that too many golf carts have been turned into scrap metal upon encountering the steel frame of an automobile, so of course it's the fate of the golfers that is the main concern. There has been talk of building a golf cart bridge over the road, but such a project would cost millions of dollars, and why should the municipality have to shell out for something that only a few people in the community get to enjoy?

I asked Bob the same question.

"I'm not Solomon," he said. "Abby, we were so poor growing up—"

"How poor were you?"

"Abby, it's not a joke."

"Sorry. Continue."

"My parents moved up from Kentucky the year I was born. My father had contracted black lung working in the coal mines and was essentially unemployable; he died when I was nine. My mother took in ironing, in addition to raising us eight kids.

"At any rate, she had an arrangement with our neighbors. Mr. Teitlebaum down the block was an early riser; he saved his coffee grounds for us. It was my job to collect them. My father always pretended he

145

liked his coffee light, but even when I was little, I knew he was aware of what was going on. Mrs. McGregor was in the habit of making too much soup—like every other day in the winter. You'd think that after a while she'd figure out how to adjust her recipe. Anyway, that's pretty much the way we lived."

"Wow, you weren't kidding. And I thought I had it tough because I had to choose between a secondhand gown for the junior prom or not going. For the senior prom, of course, I got a new one. Hey, how did you and your ex meet? At a ball game?"

"This is going to sound corny, Abby, but her family and mine were from the same hollow back in Kentucky. Folks often kept in touch as they moved out—if they could. Her family first moved to Toledo, then after a while her daddy got a job as an assistant manager of an IGA in Kalamazoo. The next thing we heard is that he owned it. From then on it was nothing but up for the Crabtrees."

"Forgive me for asking this, Bob, but were y'all kin?"

"Abby! How can you even *ask* that?"

"Sorry, again."

He laughed. "Of course we were. Not close enough so that I have two heads, but in those hollows—we called them 'hollers'—we were all related somehow, on account of we didn't let strangers get that close."

Maybank Highway had morphed into Bohicket Road, and we were fast approaching our turnoff into Runaway Slave Plantation. Named after a tiny little freshwater spring that doesn't even show up on most maps, the plantation produced primarily rice, tea, and badly scarred people. During the War of Northern Aggression all the buildings were burned to the ground.

"Was Andrea brought up poor, or wealthy?" I asked quickly.

"When I married Melissa, the family was upwardly mobile—solid middle class."

"Do you trust her?"

"Yes, I do. Why all the questions, Abby?"

"No reason—just idle curiosity."

"Yeah, *right.*"

We turned between two imposing brick columns. Ahead of us a single lane dirt road, straight as a needle, disappeared into the artificial dusk created by an allée of ancient oak trees. Their overhanging boughs were draped with Spanish moss, and in places the moss grew so heavy its own weight had torn it from the trees and it lay in the road in great gray clumps, like sleeping armadillos.

The dusk was always ahead of us, the road seeming endless, but at last the landscape brightened and out of the gloam a shape arose that was, at first, incomprehensible. Bob stopped the car.

"Holy Toledo ," he said.

"Holy *merde,*" I said.

17

"Abby, do you see what I see?"

"It's not a little drummer boy, is it?"

"*That* would be easier to believe. Tell me, do you think we made a mistake? That this is a hotel of some kind?"

I shook my head. "Her directions were clear." I tapped a paper in my lap. "And it says right here that it's a very large house."

"Look at that garage, Abby. *Six* doors. Who, besides Jay Leno, owns six cars?"

We had, of course, brought cameras, and what better place to start? I've been to the White House before (only as a tourist!), and this house reminded me of it. It certainly wasn't any smaller. Or any less white. I've often wondered what it is that the owners of these megamansions do to support their lifestyles. Well, today, by golly, I was going to find out.

Both Bob and I were somewhat taken back when a woman in tennis attire answered the door. Oh well, tennis pro, instead of a liveried butler; at least it was something.

"We're here to evaluate a Persian carpet," Bob said.

The woman smiled. "Are you sure you have the right house?"

"This is Runaway Slave Plantation, isn't it?"

"Yes, that *was* the name of the plantation; of course now it's just a house. But there are actually several built on the old plantation site. What's the name of the family you want? Maybe I know them."

Bob turned to me. "Abby, it's all yours."

I'd spent half an hour that morning over breakfast trying to get a handle on that one name. It had come in an e-mail from someone named Marianne, who'd warned me that her last name was French Huguenot and perhaps a bit tricky. What she meant was that there are a lot of these names in the Lowcountry, and they do present a challenge to newcomers, sometimes even to linguists. Over the centuries pronunciations can change so that a family name, or a place name, bears little resemblance to its origin across the Great Pond.

"Uh . . . " I stared at the slip of paper in my hand where the name was written: *Beauxoiseux*. If I remembered my high school French correctly, it was the combination of two words: beautiful and birds.

Her eyes twinkled. "If it's the family I think you want, you pronounce just four letters in their name."

"Are you sure?" I handed her the paper.

"Yes, that's us. The thing is, nobody hereabouts could pronounce our name, and after a generation or two of hearing it mispronounced so much, we just kind of went along with the flow. Don't ask me exactly when it happened, but by the time I was growing up folks were already pronouncing it 'Bexis.' That's what our friends call us, so I know if someone calls on the phone and asks for anyone else, a red flag goes up.

"But hey, I knew who y'all were all along, and I was just flapping my gums to see what you'd do. Sorry about that. As you can imagine, it can get mighty lonely way out here. I can't imagine how my ancestors survived in the days when they had to hitch a horse up to a buggy and drive that long way back into town."

"Didn't a slave do the hitching and the driving?" Bob said.

"Touché. At least until the mid-nineteenth century. My point is that the loneliness must have been so much more acute back then. Gracious me, where are my manners? Please, do come in." She stepped aside and with vigorous arm motions shooed us up the steps like we were errant chickens in need of corralling.

At the great set of bronze doors, which soared about twenty feet, she stopped and put her thumb in front of a little glass plate. Instantly a smaller door, one I hadn't even noticed set inside one of the large doors, swung wide open. It was reminiscent of Andrea's front door, but way cooler.

"One can never be too safe—especially out here. And just so we're clear on things, you've been under surveillance since the moment you turned onto our dirt road."

"You're kidding," Bob said.

"Holy Toledo," she said.

"You could *hear* inside our car?"

Until then she'd seemed like an affable native, one who liked to tease newer arrivals, but in a good-natured sort of way. Now she would have come across as downright ominous, if not for the fact that she also thought she'd gone a mite too far.

"I shouldn't have said that. But really, y'all, it's nothing the government hasn't been doing ever since . . . " She pressed a hand over her mouth and with the other beckoned us to enter first.

I was torn: on one hand, I wanted to dash into the megamansion, camera flashing; and on the other, I wanted Bob to wrestle her to the ground and force her, if necessary, to finish her sentence about the government eavesdropping on its private citizens. *And* not just through our phone system either. I swear that two or three weeks ago, or thereabouts, when I was sitting on the john, I heard the faint voice of Vice President Dick Cheney.

Bob did come to my aid by giving me a gentle push. The next thing I knew I found myself in a foyer with a ceiling that must have soared straight up for thirty feet or more. Bob later said that looking straight up that high put a crick in his neck that hung around for several days.

"Well, well, would you look at that," he and I said simultaneously.

Marianne snorted, apparently in agreement. "That means you don't approve."

"I didn't say that," I said.

"You've been well-brought-up, Mrs. Washburn, so you didn't have to come right out and say it; I read between the lines. As it happens, I share your sentiments. Think what a creative person, such as you, could do with all this wasted space. Unfortunately, this is my brother's house. They removed his tonsils when he was five, and along with them they removed his imagination."

"I didn't realize we shared the same brother," Bob said.

Marianne's laugh was rather pleasant. "I knew I liked you two. You might be wondering what it is that I'm doing here. Well, Clayton and his family are in China for three years selling coffin nails to people who can't afford them, and I offered to act as live-in caretaker. It's not that I'm such a generous big sister; *au contraire*, I'm rather niggardly with my limited resources, and I can't stand Clayton, his wife, or two out of their five children. Did I mention that I was dirt poor?"

"You did mention limited resources," I said, feeling curiously elated by the revelation.

"Ah yes. As y'all may know—especially you, Mrs. Washburn, given that you have a Deep South accent— many fine, old Southern families are as poor as a mule skinner on a camel train. Our fortunes were lost during the Late Unpleasantness, and we"—she sighed dramatically—"never learned how to roll up our own sleeves to get them back. My brother, however, is a notable exception; he could sell solar heating in Hell, if you'll pardon the vulgarity. At any rate, I live by my lonesome in the thirteen rooms of the northeast wing, but I'm fixing to move out in late August when Clayton returns from Asia. As big as this monstrosity is, it can't contain the two of us."

"Do the Chinese really buy *that* many coffin nails?" Bob asked. As I don't want his question to be misinterpreted as a regional slur, I must point out that it is only folks from a particular neighborhood in Toledo who can be a little slow on the uptake from time to time.

"She means," I said, "the business of selling cigarettes. And I'm guessing her brother is a high-ranking marketing exec, and not someone selling cartons on some street corner. But even then, he must be doing exceptionally well to get all this."

"Oh, didn't I mention that Clayton owns Smokes and Croaks? And that he already has forty factories over there? I heard somewhere that in thirty years a hundred Chinese a minute will die, thanks to my dear, sweet brother."

"What a scumbag," I said.

Bob didn't comment. Instead he was glancing around at the enormous space, still in apparent disbelief. "Surely, living here can't be all that bad," he said.

Marianne put her hands on her hips; this was either an indication of extreme spunk or at least one Yankee ancestor. "Before my brother left for China he donated a million and a half to the pet project of a certain senator—he's not from South Carolina, by the way—on the condition that he vote to make gay marriage unconstitutional, should he ever get the chance. There was another stipulation as well: this senator is to introduce a bill that will require all gays and lesbians to register nationally as sexual deviants, whose agenda it was to destroy the family. Of course the bill doesn't stand a chance of passing, but it will stir up a lot of ugly discussion.

"Anyway, the Sunday after Clayton made this donation, his pastor's wife confessed to the congregation that she'd been carrying on a five year affair with Clayton, and that at least two of her children were probably his. Clayton, who was already in Beijing by then with his family, denied the allegations, and of course Gloria, his wife, believed him. They always do—if the husband has enough money. But wait, the story doesn't stop there, because after the wife confessed in front of the entire congregation that she'd been sleeping with Clayton, then her husband—the *pastor*—said he'd slept with Clayton too. Don't you just love it?"

Bob was blushing. I knew him well enough to know that he was more embarrassed at being outed than angry at hypocrites like Clayton Beauxoiseux.

"Why did you look at me when you told us that story? Do you think I'm gay?"

"Give me a break, Mr. Steuben. You're practically a walking stereotype."

"I am *not* effeminate."

"I quite agree; I never said you were. But you're around forty, aren't you?"

"So?"

"Sorry, but in Charleston that makes you too old to be a metrosexual. And you, sir, have clean fingernails, your eyebrows are trimmed, and there aren't any bushes growing out of your ears."

Bob appeared immensely relieved. "That's *it*?"

"That, and the fact that I've been throwing pheromones your way by the billions, but you haven't reciprocated with a single one of your own. This is quite all right, mind you. I don't have to sleep with *every* man who walks in the door—not that many do walk in way out here." She turned to me and whispered behind the back of her hand, "You wouldn't believe how many times I've had to call the cable repairman."

I flashed her a reluctant smile. "If you don't mind, could we please see the carpet now? We have quite a busy schedule."

"Certainly."

Then, much to my immense disappointment, instead of leading us into the main portion of the house, we exited through a side door of the foyer, walked down a long bare hallway, and stepped into an industrial-size elevator. Marianne pushed the third floor button.

"I only get to use the top floor of the northeast wing, but I get the entire floor. Does that make it a penthouse?" She laughed.

I looked around, simultaneously trying to take everything in and keep the green-eyed monster at bay. "Who did your decorating?"

"Sheila Cohen. Isn't she fabulous?"

"Only the best. We *are* talking about the Sheila Cohen from London, right?"

"Right. Of course Clayton paid for it all. That's another reason I have to get out of here; I feel like this is all blood money." She ushered me into a large room that was being used for storage. When I say storage, don't think a for minute of boxes, plastic bags, and cardboard wardrobes. Think herds of tables, chairs, and sofas, huddling together by style and wood type. Lining the perimeter of the room, like a stockade, were dozens of paintings, some of which I recognized from Christie's catalogue. The furniture pile on the right side of the room did not extend as far as it did on the left, due to a mound of rugs approximately a yard high. As if that wasn't enough opulence in one spot, over everything hung a twinkling sky made of crystal chandeliers.

"Holy Toledo, Cleveland, and Cincinnati," I said.

"What about Charleston? After all, it is known as the Holy City."

"Whatever," I said. "Where did all this stuff come from?"

Marianne kicked at a painting that had the nerve to try and sneak an inch past the doorjamb. "Don't let this stuff fool you. If you look closely you'll see that the paintings are student copies made in Chinese art schools, and the furniture is Indonesian. They're intended for the home decorating trade. Gloria, my sister-in-law, is shipping it back because she wants to open a decorating studio when they return to stay." She picked up the errant painting; it depicted two leopards, one lying on its back. "You see, it doesn't even have a signature." She put it down again, exactly where she'd found it.

Duh. I'd seen copies of paintings just like it dozens of times before. The same thing was true for most of the other artwork. As for the furniture, it was indeed Indonesian. While there are master craftsmen on that island nation capable of producing outstanding pieces, what was assembled in this room was, by and large, a clear waste of rain forest. It was also very marketable to people who desired a lot of visual bang for their bucks, although the odds were that in twenty years most of the things in that room would end up on the secondhand market.

"Why it is that Gloria couldn't use one of her own bazillion rooms to store this junk in is beyond me," Marianne said, and gave the leopard painting a second kick for good measure. Fortunately, at least so far, she'd been kicking only the frame.

"Are the rugs all cheap knockoffs as well?" I asked.

Marianne grinned. "Nope, and that's why we're here. In her last, rather terse, communiqué, Gloria said she was shipping some rugs she'd picked up in Shanghai. She said she'd bought them from a shop off a back street near the Bundt, and some of them were undoubtedly junk but there were bound to be a few good pieces in there. At any rate, I'm supposed to have my pick. You see, everytime a load of this crap shows up in port, I'm the one who has to see it through customs. This carpet is supposed to be my payment—ha ha."

Bob and I exchanged worried glances; we were standing next to a veritable mountain of carpets and already running a half hour behind schedule. Even just flipping through the entire pile would take another thirty minutes, and it was hardly the kind of service we'd advertised in the paper.

"I know what you're thinking," Marianne said, "which is why I'm prepared to make you an offer you can't refuse."

18

I'm afraid there isn't such an offer," Bob said. "We have obligations." His tone made it clear that if, indeed, he'd been initially charmed by Marianne, he no longer felt that way.

"Suit yourself," she said, and whispered into my ear.

"Get out of town!" I said in response.

"I kid you not."

"Robert, you may wish to reconsider."

"Abby, we're not children; these are the same as contractual obligations."

"But you know as well as I do that these people may not be there when we show up."

"They will if we show on time—and if we call first."

"He does have a point," I said. "That is why cell phones were invented."

"What if you split your time? Mr. Steuben could meet the appointments, and you, Mrs. Washburn, could take me up on this exceptional offer."

"I don't think that's practical," Bob said. "We've arranged our day in a semicircle; our last appointment is in Mount Pleasant, which, as you know, is in the opposite direction. How would Mrs. Washburn get home? But besides being impractical, there is the ethical issue to consider. These people were given a verbal agreement—and a written one as well, if you count the newspaper ad—that two experts would come to their homes to evaluate their carpets. Having just one show up is like—well, it's like being promised Barbra Streisand and Ricky Martin at same concert and then just getting Ricky. Okay, so maybe Abby and I don't quite equate Babs to Ricky, but the principle is the same."

I must admit that if I were on the receiving end of Marianne's mirth, I would find it a bit irritating myself. "Mr. Steuben," she said, after laughing far too long, "you don't think I'd live out here by myself for three plus years without at least one car at my disposal, do you? I'll have Sedgwick drive her home in my brother's Aston Martin."

"Sedgwick?" I said.

"The chauffeur. Nice old man; knows not to ramble—on, and on, and on."

Bob's thinning pate glistened in the light of a hundred chandeliers. "You said you lived alone!"

"Well yes, of course I did. One never includes the staff—does one?"

I will never get stinking rich whilst being married to a shrimper and owning a secondhand shop (isn't that what an antiques store *really* is?). To date, Marianne's skeevy brother appeared to be the wealthiest person with whom I'd ever rubbed shoulders—okay, it was only by proxy—so I might as well enjoy it.

"How large a staff does it take to run a house this size?" I asked.

"When the family's in residence . . . " She moved her lips, as she counted on her fingers. " . . . twenty-three. When it's just me, then there's only five: the chauffeur, the cook, the housekeeper, the maid, and the grounds-keeper. As you saw, I had to open the door myself, because the housekeeper is in town now, grocery shopping."

I pretended to play a miniature violin. Bob looked horrified, but Marianne laughed hysterically.

"Yes, I know, I have it easy. I went to college with girls who didn't even have a maid. Not a single one! Their mothers actually scrubbed the family toilet and expected the girls to do so when they got married. Can you imagine a well-bred gentleman wanting to marry a young lady whose hand had been inside a toilet bowl?"

"I think they use brushes," Bob said. "But then what do I know about that? Abby, what do you use?"

Pretending to be horrified myself, I gave Bob a play-ful smack and shoved him toward the door. "Run along, dear, and keep our appointments. But be care-ful not to get lost."

The poor man actually looked afraid to step back into the hallway, and I didn't blame him. Even with a St. Bernard with a keg to lead the way, I'm not sure I'd have been brave enough to try and find my way back to the front door.

Marianne came to the rescue by speaking softly into an intercom that I had missed on my way in. Within seconds (or so it seemed to me) a young woman in a gray and white maid's uniform appeared from around the corner.

"Yes, ma'am?"

"Please escort this gentleman to the front door."

"Yes, ma'am."

"Nice enough guy," Marianne said when Bob was out of earshot, "but he seems a bit uptight."

"William Tell's crossbow wasn't wound that tight."

"I went to finishing school in Switzerland; William was just a legend."

"Yes, but don't tell the Swiss that."

She chortled with delight. "Okay, Abby, as I promised, you get to keep any single *one* of these carpets that your little heart desires—uh, no offense intended."

"None taken—at your *large*-esse."

She whooped with glee. "Stop it! Now really, Abby, I mean it. I've taken quite a shine to you, and you know what they say about girls who've spent too much time in boarding school."

"They're spoiled rotten?" I stepped adroitly aside, lest she desire to frolic with me among the fringes, so to speak. "Let's get to work, shall we?"

Although one could hardly call it work. The mountain of wool and silk included some of the finest designs and most meticulous work I'd ever laid eyes on. Some of the Persian carpets had been executed by the hands of women, and some were executed by the hands of men who had executed women. And, of course, there were some by men who were innocent of such things. Each and every rug was exquisite: there wasn't a clunker among them.

I counted only twenty Chinese rugs, the rest having found their way to the Shanghai shop via the living rooms of foreigners or wealthy Chinese. There was one other possibility.

"Did the shop your sister-in-law bought these from import some from the West?"

Marianne shrugged. "I don't think so—but I guess there's always the possibility. I just know that they arrived in one big shipment, and that I had to go down to the dock and pick them up. Then I had to convince the customs official that they were for personal use. He was like, yeah right. It wasn't until he called over another official who recognized the family name that he believed me."

"That you might actually have enough room in all your houses for that many rugs?"

"Yeah. So which one do you want?"

That was easy. About a third of the way through the pile my eye was drawn to a mid-nineteenth-century Bokhara carpet. It wasn't the most valuable one in the pile—I would have felt too guilty about taking *that* one—but to me it had the most appeal.

We had recently redecorated our guest room, following the old dictum: neutral tones make pleasant zones, for visiting bones—or something like that. Then again, it's possible I made up that saying. At any rate, I needed a nice warm color to add a little spice, and this brick red Bokhara, with its black and pale cream designs, was just the ticket.

I'd pulled several candidates aside, and when Marianne asked which one I wanted, I began to roll up the winner.

"Oh, no need to do that, Abby." She strode over to the nearest wall where, also unnoticed by me, there was another intercom. Immediately a hidden panel in the side of the room opened and a middle-aged man in a business suit stepped in. The most memorable thing about this character was that the breast pocket of his jacket sported sunglasses instead of a handkerchief.

Marianne looked at me looking at him, and convulsed into giggles. She tried hiding her mouth behind her hand, which just made things worse.

"What's so damn funny?" I said.

"You."

"Well, you have to admit, not everyone has people popping out of walls like it's normal."

"He didn't exactly pop out of a wall. That's a legitimate door. This is Delbert, by the way. He's Daddy's idea. Daddy's afraid I'll be kidnapped, so when I said I'd be driving you into town, I forgot to mention that Delbert will be riding with us." She turned to her bodyguard. "The red carpet there on your left is for her. Please roll it and put it in the trunk of my black Mercedes limo."

"Yes, ma'am."

She gestured to me with her head to follow her out the door through which we'd entered; apparently it was *not* all right to watch the staff carry out their duties. Appearing aloof and indifferent is actually a sign of respect, as it shows that the master trusts his servants—except they are not called by those names anymore. I wondered what someone like Marianne Beauxoiseux thought of someone like Kitty Bohring from Chicago.

"I suppose," I said, "that you were there for the social fiasco of the year—hee hee."

"*You* were there?"

"Don't tell me that you weren't!" I grinned slyly. "There was even a princess."

"Hmm. I don't suppose you're referring to Jenny Breakwater's baby shower, are you?"

"You bet I am."

"I mean how ironic is that! I'm telling you, I wouldn't have guessed she was pregnant in a million years. That just shows how good couture can hide a multitude of sins—no pun intended."

"For shizzle," I mumbled.

"I beg your pardon?"

"Nothing—it was just some short-lived slang that deserved an early death." Whew! Even a small wit, if quick enough, can get one out of most tight situations.

"But come to think of it, Charles and Camilla left the day *before* Jenny's baby shower, and she hasn't been given the title of princess yet. So which party were you thinking of, Abby?"

"Kitty Bohring's?" I felt it safer to pose it as a question.

Marianne shuddered as she folded her arms across her chest. "Gracious no, Abby. Our sort doesn't go to those, uh, *things*."

"*Things*? You make them sound like diseases."

"I'm sorry; I've offended you now, haven't I? What I mean to say is that—well, surely you must know what it's like where you come from on *off*. Where is that in your case?"

"Rock Hill."

"North Carolina is such a beautiful state."

"Rock Hill is in *South* Carolina—just like Charleston."

"It *is*? Oh well, geography was never my strong point. And anyway, before I went to that finishing school in Switzerland, I was at Miss Amy's Preparatory School on Long Island. The only thing they were

preparing us for was the perpetuation of the species—
ours of course. If you get what I mean."

"The stinking rich."

"I love it when you say that; it sounds so naughty."

"Trust me, Marianne, it sounds positively evil to us
cake-eaters, so you might want to watch out."

"Huh?"

"Never mind. Thanks again for the rug."

"Thank *you*, Abby. You've really made my day. Ever
since moving back home I've felt terribly alone. I
thought getting an apartment of my own might help—
I could make friends on my own, invite them over. You
know, live like a regular person. But now, after meeting you, I'm not so sure that I want to do that."

Oh crap, I thought. What if I'd done something to
make this woman-child want to run off and join a con-
vent? The poor nuns hadn't done anything to deserve
the likes of her.

I made a hasty decision to bite the bullet. "What is it
you might want to do instead?"

"Keep picking out some stuff I like from the store-
room, and then go over the list of men that Mama and
Daddy have already preapproved. The list is a season
old and will need some updating, but I can still get
started, can't I?"

"I suppose," I said, feeling perhaps a wee bit let
down.

"Come on," she said with a laugh. "Delbert will already be waiting for us downstairs."

Because the rug was for my guest room, I directed
Delbert to drop me off at Squiggle Lane, instead of my

shop. Having already made up her fickle mind to tie the knot with someone *suitable*, rather than expend any energy to acquire a new friend, Marianne barely acknowledged my good-bye. Well that was just peachy keen with me; after all, I was old enough to be her mother.

The carpet was both heavy and unwieldy, so I was much relieved when Greg answered the bell immediately.

"Whoa," he said, "what have you got there? You didn't fly home on your work, did you?"

"I gave up flying on carpets for Lent, remember? It's awfully dangerous; there's nothing to hang on to."

Greg stooped down and planted a kiss on me before relieving me of my precious acquisition. "I'll never ride on one in the nude again, that's for sure. I had pretty good control of mine, but the rug burn was not something I'd anticipated."

I asked my one-armed darling to carry the Bokhara to the guest room, which he cheerfully did. Since Greg has an inborn sense of composition, he placed the rug exactly where I wanted it, without me having to ask. He whistled as he worked, and not just some mindless notes either, but "Here Comes the Sun," from the Beatles album *Abbey Road*. In order to make the carpet lie absolutely flat, he rolled the ends under the opposite way and then held them there for a minute.

"Isn't it gorgeous?" I said.

He whistled ominously to a slow stop. "How much did you pay for it?"

"Nothing, if that's what you're worried about. It was a gift from Marianne Beauxoiseux. Don't ask me how to spell that name right now, but take my word for it, they are truly among the crème de la crème of Charleston high society. They wouldn't be caught dead at the home of someone like Kitty Bohring. Okay, now tell me what you think of the carpet."

"The colors are beautiful, and the pattern is unusual. But Abby, it's just not you."

"What do you mean by that? Greg, you *know* I love Oriental carpets. We have them in the living room, the bedroom, the dining room, and I sell them in my shop, for heaven's sake. You're talking nonsense, dear."

Greg hopped to his feet and made a move as if to hug me. I deftly dodged him. "Abby, since when have you settled for a machine-made replica when you could afford the real thing?"

"*What?* Look who's talking nonsense now! For your information, Gregory Thomas Washburn, I examined that carpet and it's the real McCoy."

"It's not." He had the audacity to look me right in the eye.

"Oh yeah? You want to bet? What do you want bet?"

"What would any red-blooded American husband in the South want to bet?"

"Fine. That's how sure I am. If I lose, when you recover you get to play eighteen rounds of golf every Saturday for six weeks in a row. And of course makeup days for rain. But if I win—and I will—I get six deluxe treatments at Lazy Susan's, that new spa that's opening up in Summerville. The deluxe package, by the way, includes the twenty-four-carat gold leaf facial peel."

Greg smiled. "So they're going to gild the lily, just to peel it off again?"

"Compliments aren't going to get you anywhere, darling, because you're losing this bet. Do we have a deal?"

"Deal."

"Okay. Now, I know you're not going to take just my word for it, but I want you to look with me anyway. Think of it as a way of humoring the old ball and chain."

"Sure."

"Please, Greg, pretty—*what* did you say?"

"You said it, hon, I didn't; I was just agreeing—to look, I mean. I certainly wasn't calling you an old ball and chain."

"Who stole my husband and inhabits his body even as I speak?"

"Come on, Abby, just prove your point. It's almost lunchtime, and I plan to watch a movie on TMC while I eat."

I dropped to my knees and, all the while willing my face to remain a mask of indifference, flipped back a corner of the carpet. "You see this row of stitches, dear? And the rows on either side of it? You see how they—oh my fathers!" I shrieked. "This can't be right. Someone's playing a joke on me."

"Hon, could the carpet have been switched at this Marianne woman's house?"

"It had to have been switched! That's the only explanation. But *why*? Is this how the über rich get their kicks?"

The love of my life shrugged. "Beats me. I don't know any über rich. The Rob-Bobs are as wealthy as it gets for me. Look hon, given that someone pulled the rug out from under you—pun intended, I'm afraid—you don't have to honor this bet. I can't take time off work most Saturdays anyway."

"No! A bet's a bet; I insist on honoring your win. Greg, can we TiVo this movie, pick up some fast food, and head right back out there?"

"And do what? Have it out with her at the front door? You know she won't answer the bell. Does she have security cameras?"

"Does she ever! She has it rigged so she can see inside your car once you pass through the pillars and head up their dirt lane."

"Ah, one of *those* kind of rich. We had some of those up in Charlotte too. I just didn't know any of them personally. At any rate, they're almost a different species altogether. Funny thing is, the nouveau riche *think* they've made it to the top until they meet one of these blue-blood über rich; that's when they realize they've barely even started up the ladder. Abby, I say write this one off to experience. You didn't pay anything for this rug—except for some pride—so enjoy it for what it is: beautiful in its own right.

"I guess," I said.

But if I ever saw Marianne Über-Rich-Beauxoiseux again, I was going to wring her neck—well, metaphorically speaking. I'm capable of wringing out a dish rag, but not much more. Still, the girl was going to rue the day she'd made a fool out of Abigail Merely-Well-to-Do Washburn.

19

I was ashamed to get on the phone when Bob called late that afternoon. "So Abby," he boomed into my ear, "what happened after I left? What was the offer you couldn't refuse?"

Although the truth is often stranger than fiction, in the end it makes things simpler for everyone. I told Bob what a boob I'd been and apologized for having left him in the lurch.

"No apology needed, Abby. Love means never having to say you're sorry, right?"

"Bull skins," I growled.

"You can say that again. That was one of the stupidest lines of dialogue I've ever read—or heard. Well, I was able to keep nine out of the twelve appointments on our schedule; two called and canceled, and the third slammed the door in my face when she saw that I wasn't Rob."

"That poor baby. If only she knew."

"Yeah, right. Anyway, I got nipped by three dogs, scratched by a cat, shat on by a free-flying parakeet, and had gum pressed into my hair by a pair of two-year-old twins. Abby, you didn't warn me about the perils of house calls."

"It's like the pain of childbirth, Bob. Mercifully, you forget it after a while. So, did you uncover anything of interest?"

"I'll say, or I wouldn't have lasted that long."

"Do tell!"

"Well, George and Myrna Saunders at 1137 Fish Grove Mar—"

"Save the details for later, sweetie. Just give me an overview now."

"All right." I heard him shuffle papers. "Seven of the nine people had been led to believe they'd purchased handmade, antique carpets. In fact, five of these carpets came with rather extensive paperwork detailing origins, composition, etcetera. But all seven of these carpets were machine-woven from new wool, and probably in the twenty-first century."

I was dismayed but not surprised. "Can you think of anything these carpets might have in common?"

"Oh yes. At one time or another every single one of them was sent out to Magic Genie Cleaners."

"Aha! Now we're getting somewhere." Suddenly my mood went from despair to one where I felt like doing the happy dance.

"Maybe—if we had a genie of our own. I did some checking and discovered that Magic Genie Cleaners folded about six months ago. The businesses on either side say they have no idea where the owner or his employees went, and the Better Business Bureau seems reluctant to hand out information willy-nilly to just any old Tom, Dick, and Harry."

"Or Bobby."

If glares could have been transmitted over wires as electric signals, I'm sure I would have dropped the phone.

"Oops, that just slipped out. Sorry. So how many visits do we have scheduled for tomorrow?"

"Just ten. Abby, I've been thinking. Given that I've already been bitten, scratched, and shat upon—i.e., initiated—why don't I continue doing this tomorrow, and you try and dig up some info on Magic Genie Cleaners? Maybe Greg can use his detective skills to help you. At the very least you have your feminine wiles, your perky personality, and, of course, that bodacious bod of yours to use as weapons of mass distraction."

"Sucking up to me will get you nowhere, Robert. But sure, okay. I'll play Colombo."

"With Greg?"

"Without. Greg's a stickler for following the letter of the law. What fun is there in that? I'll do it with Mama."

"Oy vey," Bob moaned, and hung up.

Believe it or not, Mama enjoys my company. It's not that she doesn't have a life; she plays bridge, mahjongg, and Scrabble, belongs to a book club, is on the Altar Guild at Grace Episcopal Church, is an active member of their sisterhood, needlepoints kneelers for the church as well, and is enrolled in a beginners' class to learn the jitterbug. Nonetheless, she finds our escapades "refreshing," despite the fact that she often complains mightily at the time.

When I picked her up the next morning, she was

wearing a blue full circle skirt, a crisp white blouse, and a red and white polka-dot kerchief that covered her hair. Those who know Mama well would not have been surprised to see that she was carrying a wicker hamper. If it wasn't for the character lines on her face, I might have thought Mama was Doris Day all set for a picnic.

"I left Cary Grant at home," I said. "I was tired of his wisecracking."

"Did you bring Rock Hudson?"

"As promised; he's in the trunk. What's in the basket, Mama?"

"Guess."

"Fried chicken, biscuits, celery and carrot sticks, brownies—and a thermos of sweet tea."

"And potato salad, dear. Didn't I raise you right? And made with Duke's mayonnaise, of course."

"Mama, we're not leaving the city limits. I bet there's a Kentucky Fried Chicken within biscuit-heaving distance."

My petite progenitress smiled sadly. "I *didn't* raise you right; I can see that. Fast food is just not the same. Oh it might taste a sight better than my cooking, and it might be better for you as well, but it's not the same."

"I can't argue with that."

My acquiescence made Mama happy, so she was content to sing ponderous Episcopal hymns all the way to Upchuck. We took Interstate 26 west as far as the Mark Clark Expressway, and then backtracked south a couple of blocks on Rivers Avenue. By the time we got to the abandoned building that had once been Magic Genie Cleaners, Mama had switched over to show tunes.

Allow me to state right here that there is nothing wrong with the way Mama sings, just as long as no one, or no thing, is compelled to listen to her. If Mama could be convinced to sing at prisons across the country, and threatened the prison populations with repeat performances, there would be no recidivism. At any rate, I cringed as I opened my car door, because at that very moment Mama was raising my car roof with a rousing rendition of the theme from *Oklahoma!*

"Mama, please," I hissed in vain.

Although I know from experience that my mother's caterwauling can set cats wailing and dogs to howling, it is impossible for her to sing both soprano and baritone simultaneously; her three previous attempts failed miserably. Thus, when I heard a very stirring male baritone join Mama's operatic soprano, I began to look around for a second singer. Sure enough, in the doorway of a neighboring business called Finnaster's Finnery, stood a tall handsome man with silver curls.

Mama spotted him about the same time, turned azalea pink and clammed up in the middle of a word. The gentleman finished the verse by himself, and then bowed in Mama's direction as he clapped.

"Brava, madam, brava."

"I think you have an exceptionally fine voice," I said.

"Nonsense, dear," Mama said. "Do you really think so?"

"Not only that, but I think he looks like an Irish Omar Sharif."

"Get out of town," Mama said as she fluffed up her crinolines and patted her hair.

"Don't look now, folks, but Mozella Wiggins seems to be smitten with a perfect stranger."

"I most certainly am not!"

If actions speak louder than words, Mama decided it was time to drag out the bullhorn. From her white patent leather purse (it was summer, after all) she extracted the one item ladies of her generation never leave home without: their spackling kits. I believe they are also known as compacts. At some point in history a few women got to together and decreed that worn lipstick was uncool, that it took away from their feminine mystique, but that reapplying it at the table did not destroy the illusion. So it was that while the handsome stranger watched, Mama repainted the door to her stomach, secure in her belief that she was somehow invisible as long as she could see her reflection in her magic compact. (Applying powder is quite another thing, and must be done in the privacy of the ladies' room.)

When she was satisfied with the image she wished to project, she snapped the gold tone case shut with a flourish and returned it safely to her purse. The next step in her seduction was to reach into the depths of her prodigious bosom and whisk out a beautifully embroidered and heavily scented handkerchief. This she waved about her at arm's length as if to charm the native into a state of cooperative somnolence.

"Yoo-hoo, young man," she called, without first consulting me, "may we speak with you?"

Irish Omar nodded and smiled, but stood his ground, waiting for us to come to him. Perhaps he'd been hypnotized by Mama's hankie and was incapable of locomotion. Or perhaps I was hallucinating, and had been for the past twenty-four hours, due to stress. Whatever the reason, Mama stopped dead still about six yards away, and the three of us traded stares for so long I had to borrow a pair of retinas from a passerby just to see anything from there on out.

Omar from the Emerald Island spoke first. "Mozella Wiggins, as I live and breathe, is that really you?"

"Why Fagin Finnaster, if this doesn't beat all, nothing does! What on earth are you doing down here on the coast?"

"Me? I've been living down here since 1952, that's what. Ever since my Lula Mae passed on. And yourself?"

"I came down just three years ago to be near my daughter. This is Abby right here. Abby, say hello to Mr. Finnaster. His wife, Lula Mae, and I were roomies at Winthrop College for Women, *and* we were bridesmaids in each other's wedding parties. I know you've seen her picture a million times."

Fagin Finnaster stepped forward with an outstretched hand. Despite having silver hair, he was well-preserved for a man of his years.

"Pleased to meet you, ma'am. And call me Fig, like my friends do—seeing as how we're both adults."

Mama turned to me. "Lula Mae died of breast cancer two years after they were married; mammograms weren't available back then."

"I'm sorry to hear that," I said.

"Fig, did you ever remarry?" Mama asked.

He smiled sadly. "Nah, not officially anyway. Just couldn't see punching the forever card with anyone else. How about you, Mozella? From time to time word of Rock Hill filters down here, so I know about your husband getting called Up Yonder, thanks to that sea gull, and him leaving you with two little ones, but nothing about you since then."

"Well, I never remarried," Mama said, and giggled shamelessly.

"Although she does have a boyfriend," I said.

"I most certainly do not!"

"His name is Big Larry," I said.

"We're just friends," Mama said.

"The post office gave him his own zip code last year, but Bell South has been slow to follow up with the area code. You might want to check before you call." To be sure, the Devil made me do it.

Fig laughed at my joke, even though he undoubtedly saw Mama kick my ankle with the point of her white patent leather pump. "What brings you two ladies to North Charleston—I mean, I'm assuming you live downtown someplace. Mozella, you always seemed like an S.O.B. to me. No offense intended, of course."

Mama's face glowed with pride. "We most certainly do live downtown." The truth is my mother couldn't afford to live downtown on her own, but what the heck, if she didn't feel compelled to mention it, then neither did I.

"We were looking for the Magic Genie Cleaners," I said. "Did they move?"

Fig pursed his lips as if to spit, but then remembered there were ladies present. He swallowed instead.

"They cleared out, lock, stock, and barrel, about a month ago. It was the strangest thing. It was like this movie I saw when I was a kid, in which an Indian camp disappeared overnight, and the next morning the white men who came to attack it found only warm coals where the campfires had been. The movie was sad and kind of romantic, but this Magic Genie Cleaners business was just downright irritating. For the next week or two I had their customers demanding to know what happened to their things." He chuckled unexpectedly. "On the plus side I sold two complete saltwater setups to those folks, and believe me, those things aren't cheap."

"Fig, whatever got you into selling fish?" Mama asked.

Forgetting my manners, I slipped in front of her. "Do you know where the Magic Genie Cleaners people might have gone?"

He shrugged. "Why don't you ladies come inside where it's a mite cooler." We took him up on the offer, but I had a feeling—just pure woman's intuition—that he wanted to get us out of sight of busy Rivers Avenue.

Inside it was a warren of gurgling tanks. Dozens of the aquariums served as temporary homes to the usual tropical fish to be found in most pet stores, but there was an entire room devoted exclusively to saltwater tanks. These were my favorite. The intricate shapes of the corals, the gently waving anemones, jewel-toned fish—all proved that magic *could* be had for a price.

Fig excused himself to say something to an assistant, then steered us to a back room. Like storage rooms anywhere, it contained stock, a toilet reserved just for employees, and a messy lunch table surrounded by folding chairs. He asked us to sit.

"I didn't get along with the owners from the beginning. You see, their drivers didn't respect my reserved parking sign out back. When I called the owners to ask them to move their trucks, they claimed the lot out back was community property. It wasn't, of course, but they were nasty as hell—pardon my French, ladies—so I let it slide. What I mean is, they were tire-cutting nasty and I didn't want any trouble. Neither did Andy Garcia, the feller on the other side of them. Anyways, 'bout all I can tell you, young lady, is that their trucks had Chester County license plates."

Mama patted her pearls, which is sign of many things, but in this case was the preamble to a flirtation. I'd have staked a Louis XIV chair (completely original) on that.

"Fig," she said, "why don't you—"

"Tell us," I said, "have you, yourself, ever used Magic Genie Cleaners?"

"Why Abigail Louise, how rude of you!"

I totally ignored Mama's comment, which, while not necessarily rude, was certainly the most aggravating thing I could have done.

Fig, having neither a daughter nor a wife, was oblivious to our mother-daughter power struggle. "Well now, ma'am," he said to me, "the answer to that may surprise you. You might think that I wouldn't, on account of their nastiness, but you see, I was born and raised a God-fearing Presbyterian, and I learned in Sunday school that one should always turn the other cheek. Besides, I figured that by throwing a little business their way, I might get them to cooperate some."

"And did they?"

"Not in the least. They stayed as ornery as mean dogs—although some of the counter people were right nice. But they never stayed around long."

"Did they at least do a good job?"

"Funny you should ask. On shirts and the like they did, but they always came back in bags that had another dry cleaner's name on them. But the kicker—"

"What was the name?"

"I can't rightly remember. Something about a little Dutch girl—I think. But what I started to tell you was that I had them pick up this carpet that Lula Mae had inherited from her Grandmother Tibbins—well, not *inherited*, exactly, but got as a wedding present. It was supposed to be an early inheritance, which was a good thing, on account of Granny Tibbins died seven years after Lula Mae passed."

Mama waved her arm excitedly like a schoolgirl who finally knew a correct answer. "I remember that rug! It was blue, wasn't it? With orange whatchamacallits. Lula Mae said that when she was a little girl she used to call it her Granny's Purring Rug. She said that she thought the rug was really called that because her granny's rocking chair was in that room, and the old woman, bless her heart, was always snoring. Of course the adults were saying *Persian*, not purring."

We all laughed, until Fig, bless *his* heart, wiped away what I hoped was a tear that had been induced by a happy memory. "Mozella, you're still a hoot, but I'm not yet done with my story."

"Press on," I urged.

"So anyway, they pick up the carpet, and it takes them six doggone weeks to clean the bloody thing, and then when they do bring it back, well—"

"It isn't the same one." I clamped a petite paw over an equally petite maw.

"Abby!" Mama said sharply. "Don't interrupt with such nonsense."

"But she's right on the mark," Fig said.

"Go *figure*," Mama said, but nobody laughed.

"How different was it?" I asked.

20

At first the rug I got back looked identical to me—minus the dirt, of course. Granny Tibbins had gotten it for her wedding, and it was already *supposedly* an antique then. And to my knowledge Granny had never had it professionally cleaned. So anyway, the colors were much brighter, especially the blue background, which made the orange whatchamacallits really stand out.

"But what I didn't check to see at first was that Granny had hand-stitched Lula Mae's and my initials on one of the whatchamacallits—designs, I would call them—in a slightly darker shade. It was the kind of thing that would pop out to Lula Mae and me every time we walked into the room and looked down, but nobody else would notice until we pointed it out. In fact, it was always fun asking first-time visitors to look for our initials."

"Kind of like *Where's Waldo*," Mama said.

"What?"

"Never mind," I said. "So the rug you got in return didn't have the initials. Is there any chance they might have come off during the cleaning process?"

"I thought about that. But it's not like they were painted on, or written on with a pen or a marker. They were stitched on really well. Fat letters too, that looped all the way through the rug and back again. They were just hard to see at first because the color difference was so subtle."

"Was there anything else different about the rug you got back from the cleaners?"

He nodded, slowly at first, but faster when he saw that I was a respectful and receptive audience. "I took to studying the rug after that, and other rugs too. Heck"—he grinned shyly—"I even started visiting those high-end antique shops down on King Street."

"My Abby owns one!" Mama squealed. "The Den of Antiquity. Did you go in there?"

Fig winked at me. "I might have. At any rate, Abby—may I call you that?"

"Her name is *Mrs*. Gregory Washburn," Mama said.

I beamed with pleasure. "Yes, please call me Abby."

"Anyway, Abby, a lot of the older rugs, and the more expensive ones, don't seem as well made."

"Hear, hear," Mama said.

"Why is that, Abby?"

"Ah, you must be referring to uneven stitches and such. Was Grandmother Tibbins original rug one of those?"

"Yeah, I'm afraid so. The thing is, even though I'm pissed—pardon my French again—"

"That wasn't French," Mama snapped. "Really Fig, how would you like it if the French said, 'Pardon my English'?"

"Actually, Mama, they do."

Mama bathed me with a loving glare.

"Please, Fig, continue," I said.

"What I'm trying to say is that even though I'm really ticked that it's not the same rug, I'm kind of relieved at the same time. The rug they substituted looks so much nicer."

"That's because you're not snooty and pretentious," Mama said. Apparently she couldn't make up her mind whether she was still making a play for the handsome widower.

"Fig," I said, "can you tell me anything about this Andy Garcia, the guy who owned the restaurant on the other side of Magic Genie Cleaners?"

"Andy was a first-class guy. His parents were from Mexico, but Andy was born and raised right here in Charleston. Spoke English like the native he was. Andy's dream was to own an authentic Mexican restaurant, not one that catered to the night-out crowd, but to Hispanic workers."

"The illegal immigrants," Mama said, before her lips all but disappeared.

"It was a brave venture, but doomed from the start. He kept his prices low by serving mainly peasant dishes family style, so the place was always packed, but the city health department and the Federal Department of Immigration were always riding on his buttocks—pardon my English. They kept him jumping through hoops, filling out forms, and paying fines for minor infractions. Then one day someone from the Magic Genie Cleaners hierarchy shows up and asks Andy if maybe he needs a little help dealing with the bureaucracy.

"Well, Andy had seen enough movies to know that this sounded an awful lot like protection money, so he wasn't about to start something that was just going to escalate and he said no. Shortly after that some of Andy's customers got assaulted coming and going from Casa de Mama Mia. The first couple of times it happened, Andy called the police, but a fat lot of good it did because everyone ran away; the customers ran away as well. It was a crazy scene."

"Why did they run if they were innocent?" Mama asked.

"This is your chance to say illegal immigrants, Mama."

"Why Abigail Washburn, are you implying that I'm prejudiced? Because I most certainly am *not*. I am quite aware that our own ancestors landed on this continent without the local inhabitants' permission. But just so you know, it's a fact that most of the Indians were killed off by the diseases that we brought with us, not by our guns."

"Please excuse her," I said. "She doesn't like to say Native Americans because she was born in America, which, strictly speaking, makes her a native of America, and ergo a native American with a small N. But at any rate, I can guess what happened to the restaurant: the customers stopped coming and poor Andy Garcia had to give up on his dream."

"Exactly."

"Fig," I said, "are you sure the shakedown men were from Magic Genie Cleaners?"

"I'm darn sure that at least one of them was. You see, the first time they beat up on the customers, I was

185

locking up my store and I heard the fight. I went over to see what was going on, and that's when I recognized this one guy; you can't mistake him for anyone else. He has shoulder-length bright red hair—curly, mind you—and a mean old scar that starts above his right eyebrow and continues across the bridge of his nose, makes a sharp downward turn, and ends up just beside the left corner of his mouth. Really nasty-looking scar. Maybe put there with a box cutter."

"Ick," said Mama. "I'm not sure Lula Mae would approve of this."

"Of what, Mama?"

"Well, it isn't my place to say it, but—"

"We really must be going," I said.

"That's not what I was going to say, dear."

I kicked Mama under the messy lunch table. Unfortunately I forgot that I was wearing open-toed sandals.

"Loach, gouramis, and neon tetra," I exclaimed with a great deal of emotion.

"Why Abigail Louise, I taught you not to swear."

Fig roared with laughter.

"I fail to see what's so funny," Mama said. Her eyes had narrowed to mere slits, which in Mama-speak means you're on pretty shaky ground, no matter who you are.

I looked helplessly at Fig. "You better tell her, because she won't believe me."

He got right to it. "Mozella, your baby girl didn't swear; those are names of fish species. Where did you learn that, Abby?"

"In the distant past my son Charlie had an aquarium. He tried just every kind of fish there was, and then settled on fried."

"Shhh, better not say that too loud." He pointed a thumb to the showroom.

We both laughed.

"I don't get that," Mama said. "Fish can't hear."

I struggled to my functioning foot. "You've been very generous with your time, Fig. We really appreciate that, don't we, Mama?"

"You tell *me*, Abby, since you're doing the talking on my behalf."

"Mama!"

"What?" She tried to sound like an innocent little girl. What mattered is that she gathered her voluminous skirts and stood.

"Ladies," Fig said, before gallantly ushering us into the showroom, "I'd bet you dollars to doughnuts that these words are going to fall on deaf ears. Nonetheless, I feel obligated to say them. Stay clear of anyone, or anything, that has to do with Magic Genie Cleaners. They're bad news."

Outside in the brilliant sunshine the empty building next door didn't seem quite so ominous. Plenty of businesses close in the first few years, and as for the boarded-up restaurant adjacent to it, wasn't it in the highest risk category? I'd been overreacting as usual. Doing the "Abby thing," as Greg sometimes says. Well, it was time to step back and get some perspective.

"Abby," Mama said, as if handed a cue card, "I have an idea."

"I bet I know! Let's bop on over to Northwoods

Mall, since we're so close, and get pedicures *and* manicures. My treat. Are you willing to have flowers painted on your big toes this time?"

"Shoot a monkey," Mama said, shaking her well-lacquered head, "if that doesn't take the cake, nothing does."

"What?"

"I just never thought I'd see the day when the flesh of my flesh would put pleasure over duty."

"Mama, that's not fair. What am I supposed to do? Track down a gang of thugs and punch their lights out?"

"Gracious no, dear. A proper lady never engages in fisticuffs. That's why we have husbands and gentlemen friends."

"Like Big Larry?"

She looked away momentarily as the corners of her mouth tugged upward. "I'm just saying that we still have work to do, and that there is always a way to get it done."

There were several men named Andrew Garcia in the Charleston area telephone book, so I asked Mama to pick which one to start with. I'm not saying she's telepathic—okay, I *am* saying that she does have an uncanny ability to know who's calling, even without looking at caller ID. She can also guess exactly how many pennies (jelly beans, etc.) there are in a jar, but she never enters those contests, because she thinks they'll lead to gambling. Perhaps in her case they would. At any rate, I use Mama's gifts only when they're offered: I don't want to be the one responsible for leading her down that path of destruction.

He answered on the first ring. "Andy here."

"Mr. Garcia, you don't know me, but—"

"Excuse me, but I don't take calls from strange—"

"I'm not a stranger! Not really."

"Yeah? Not really how?"

"Fig's my uncle," I said, lying between the smallest of gaps between two of my top left molars. But it was *sort* of the truth. Had Lula Mae and Daddy lived, and our parents kept in touch, I'm sure that Toy and I would have thought of them as family. Heck, the way Mama was carrying on, if Daddy hadn't come along just in time, Fig might well have been my daddy, which is a sight closer than an uncle.

"Well, in that case, what's this about, ma'am? If you don't mind me asking."

"I hate to say this over the phone, Andy, because it involves *you know who*. You might say that I'm a private detective and that I'm doing my best to expose them for the crooks they are. I wouldn't use your name, of course: I swear on a pile of dead kittens, and I love cats more than anything in the world."

Mama poked me in the ribs. "Abby, that was horrible! How could you even say that?"

"Who was that? And what did you say your name was again?"

I was losing him. "Abigail Washburn. Look, is there a McDonald's, or someplace like that, near you where we could meet? We're just outside Uncle Fig's place."

"Let me speak to him."

There was a chance that my cell phone reception might be spotty inside the store and ruin my everything, so I palmed my cell phone and held it as far from my mouth as possible. "Mama, go get *Uncle* Fig and bring him here. Andy wants to speak to him."

"But he's not your—"

"*Favorite* uncle," I said, just in case Andy could still hear me. "Mama, please do as I say and go get Uncle Fig."

Fortunately Mama gathered her petticoats and was back in a flash with Fig. He winked as he took the phone. I was too nervous to listen in so I walked over to the empty building that had once been used as a dry cleaning store. The doors were locked and there was nothing to see through the windows except for sills lined with dead flies, lying belly up, and a bare counter. There weren't even any chairs in the lobby. As for the vast area behind the counter, it could have been previously occupied by any business. Gone were the rotating racks one associates with the dry cleaning business. Absent was the glorious scent of formaldehyde.

"Abby." This time Mama poked me in the back with her index finger.

I shrieked. "Mama! I'm practically middle-aged. I could have a heart attack."

"You *are* middle-aged, dear. Although it is a mystery, seeing as how I just barely reached that milestone myself." She pointed toward Fig. "Andy wants to talk to you."

My heart still thumping like that of a witless teenager in a horror movie, I scurried over to my newly created uncle and grabbed the phone.

"Hello?"

"This is your last chance, Mrs. Washburn: is Fig really your uncle?"

I bit my lip before answering. "No."

"Meet me in fifteen minutes, just outside the mall entrance to Dillard's. What do you look like?"

"I'm four feet nine. Look down."

"Very funny."

"I'm serious. What do you look like?"

"I'm six feet two and have sandy hair."

"Ha ha."

"I'm serious as well. See you."

He hung up.

21

Northwoods Mall began life as a flat, one-story affair that might have given tall people claustrophobia. A few years ago it underwent some renovations that brought both light and life into it. Folks tell me that it feels much airier now, and judging by the crowds that day, they were right.

One would think that with so many stores at her disposal—and a hundred dollars cash pressed into her hand—Mama would be happy to wander off and amuse herself for a half hour or so. Of course one would be wrong. It wasn't until I'd upped the ante to three hundred—which meant finding an ATM—that I got rid of her, and even then I didn't trust her.

Perhaps Andy Garcia wasn't to be trusted either, because by the time I finally got to the Dillard's mall entrance, there wasn't anyone standing there, short or tall—except for me. I was only five minutes late. In a city like Charleston (and by extension, North Charleston) where the living is easy, that was almost like being early.

No sooner had I decided to give Andy Garcia ten

more minutes than a man matching his description popped out of nowhere.

"*Mr. Garcia?* Where did you come from all at once?"

"Actually, I've been watching you for the last five minutes from the other side of the perfume counter. I used to date the woman who works there. Still, she almost made me buy some. Man, that stuff's expensive."

"You find that amusing, do you? Watching me grow panicked?"

He touched my elbow lightly. "We need to start walking. You're being stalked by a real nutcase."

"Me?"

"A wack job, if I've ever seen one."

"Where? Who?"

"She ducked in that formal store a minute or two after you arrived, when your back was turned. She's hiding behind that mannequin in the long red dress."

My stomach sank, while the hair on the back of my neck rose. "Uh-oh. What does she look like?"

"She's an old woman in a costume of some kind— like in *I Love Lucy.*"

Although I already knew the wacko's identity, there was an infinitesimal chance I was wrong. After all, just that morning I'd heard on the news that a flock of pigs was spotted flying over Cincinnati. I always swore that would never happen.

Andy put his hand even with my head and then raised it several inches. "She's about this tall, I guess."

"Okay, I confess. That nutcase is my mama. She's afraid you're going to make a pair of gloves out of me."

He laughed, showing lovely white teeth. "Mrs. Washburn, I hope you don't mind me saying so, but I couldn't make much more than one glove out of you."

"Just for that, bear with me, and follow me into the store."

"Sure, I'm game."

I led him straight to the mannequin in red, where we stopped and I pretended to look around. "Mr. Sanford," I said, "I'm telling you, I did see a chimpanzee come in here; I'm not making it up."

"I'm not accusing you of lying, Mrs. Washburn, but the three other reports we had were of an escapee from a mental institution, not an ape. Two of those reports were official, by the way. They describe her as being wild-eyed, with stringy gray hair, and dressed in a 1950s costume."

"Yes, that's it! A chimpanzee in a dress. Did the reports mention how it smelled? I mean it smelled like—well, like woof!"

"Like *woof*?" Mama tumbled out from within the folds of the red gown. "What is that supposed to mean? That I smell like a dog? Abigail Louise Wiggins Timberlake Washburn, how could you? And after all I've done for you too? Who else would have endured fifty-six hours of unbearably painful labor just to bring you into this world?"

"Mama, it was thirty-six, not fifty-six. And we were only yanking your chain because you were spying on us."

"As well I should. You'd consented to meet a total stranger—a marked man yet—on the spur of the moment. Someone needed to keep tabs on you. Then I

194

spotted this oddball hanging out in the perfume section, and he was making the goo-goo eyes at you, which would have made it impossible for the Mexican gentlemen and you to rendezvous, so what was a mother to do?"

"Mama loves to contradict herself," I said to Andy, "but she's not a racist; she has a ruminate for a daughter-in-law."

"Excuse me?" he said.

"Ignore her," Mama told him, "she's just trying to get my goat. My name is Mozella Wiggins, by the way. And yes I am Abigail's mother, but I was a child bride."

Andy took Mama's outstretched hand and kissed it as he bowed deeply. "I am very pleased to meet you Senora Wiggins," he said, adopting a slight accent. "My name is Andre Garcia Corrales Reynoso Delarosa Escobar Salcido Fuentes Sosa Hidalgo Vallejo Iglesias Zambrano Lucero Viera Tamayo Barajas."

Mama giggled. "My, what a mouthful. Although I suppose Hatshepsut isn't much easier."

"What did you say, Mama?"

"Hatshepsut. She was the most powerful queen in all of ancient Egypt."

"Yes, I know, but what does that have to do with you?"

"Because that's my middle name."

"No, it's not."

"Then what is it?"

"The letter H. You always told us it didn't stand for anything—except maybe for *handsome*. In the old sense of the word."

"That's because I didn't want to put on airs."

"So here in the mall, in front of a complete stranger, you reveal that you're named after the most powerful woman in all of ancient history?"

"Abigail Louise, there is a time and place for everything, and I do think that a pouting episode is quite inappropriate at the moment. Might I suggest that we move on down to the food court, find ourselves a table, and then over some lunch we could interview this very attractive young man."

"Who is young enough to be your *grandson*. Excellent idea about the food, though." Mama's picnic could wait.

Andy agreed, so we headed for the food court. He and I both got the teriyaki chicken from the Japanese vendor, and Mama, who only eats what she calls American, had a slice of pepperoni pizza—with extra cheese.

"So," Andy said, taking care to swallow before speaking, "Fig said I can trust you."

"Likewise," I said. I may not have been quite as considerate about what I did with my food, but at least it was all pushed into one cheek.

"How can I help you ladies?" he asked.

"I don't know if Fig told you this, but I'm primarily an antiques dealer. It's my suspicion that Magic Genie Carpet Cleaners is involved in a racket whereby folks turn over their genuine antique Oriental rugs for cleaning, but in return get machine-made copies worth a fraction as much."

Andy groaned. "That doesn't surprise me. But I don't think it's the counter people or the drivers who are in on the scam. Don't get me wrong—they're mean as snakes, but—oh man, this is going to bring on the bad karma for sure—they're just not that bright."

"How would you describe them?" I asked.

"Country people through and through. But from the Upstate."

"How do you know that?"

"You can always tell those people by their accents."

Intrigued, I pressed on. "How do you mean?"

"Imagine trying to quack with your mouth full of marbles."

Although born and reared in the Upstate, I found this immensely funny. Fortunately, before I broke into loud guffaws and started slapping bruise marks on my thighs, I noticed Mama's lips disappear into a thin straight line. Her Wigginsness was not amused.

"Hmm," I said. "An interesting observation, Mr. Garcia Corrales Reynoso Delarosa Escobar Salcido Fuentes—"

It was Andy who laughed. "Please, Mrs. Washburn, call me Andy. Now how in the world did you memorize my name so fast?"

"Whew! I didn't; that's as far as I've gotten. Thank goodness you stopped me there. And please, call me Abby."

"Is this little love fest going to last as long as his name?" Mama asked.

"Mama, how rude!"

"Rude of *me*? Abby, he just said we speak with marbles in our mouths."

Poor Andy turned the color of ricotta cheese. "Uh . . . I'm so sorry, Mrs. Wiggins. Abby. I didn't realize—I mean, how wrong that was of me. I apologize."

"And just so you know," Mama said, scooting up an inch taller in her seat, "we're not country folk."

"Maybe we shouldn't dis country folk either," I said. "Believe me, it's always easier for me to get off my high horse than to get on it in the first place. I might as well just stay off the dang thing."

"Actually," Andy said, "I'm originally from just outside Fort Lawn, South Carolina. Do you know where that is?"

Mama and I exchanged glances. "*That* place is smaller than a speck on a gnat's navel," Mama said. "How can there be an 'outside' to a place that has no 'inside'?"

"Touché. My parents were actually *legal* immigrants from Mexico City. They picked Fort Lawn because they thought it sounded nice—lots of grass and stuff. They stuck it out until I was three. So who am I to talk, right? I could just as easily end up speaking like those women at the cleaners."

"Do you think they were from Fort Lawn?"

He shrugged. "I don't know. Maybe. Sometimes friends of parents come to visit, and they sound sort of like that."

"Did only women work at Magic Genie Cleaners? Can you describe anyone or anything that might be distinctive?"

He laid down his chopsticks. "I go to church regularly," he said, "so I'd take my dress shirts in there to have them laundered. And yes, as far as I could tell, only women worked inside, and the drivers and loaders were always men. As far as anything distinctive— well, there was Big Tina."

Mama slurped up a string of cheese that was dangling from her chin. Her eyes flashed like a pair of warning lights.

"Was that a truck name?" I asked.

Andy laughed. "Nah, but it sounds like one, doesn't it?"

"That isn't kind," Mama snapped. "Abigail, I'm especially ashamed of you. When you were a little girl other children called you 'elf' and 'Barbie Doll' and even 'Dinky Toy.'"

"Go on, Andy," I said, feeling properly chastised.

"I swear, Abby, I've never seen a bigger woman in my life. I'd say about six-five and three hundred pounds. A real giantess. All the other women were afraid of Big Tina, and I didn't blame them. All she had to do was say a word or two and they got cracking, but I'm telling you, if those women hadn't obeyed, Big Tina could have ripped their heads off using just her pinkies."

"Do you think she was a transvestment?" Mama asked.

"No Mama, I'm pretty sure she wasn't."

"How do you know, Abby? You didn't see her."

"Mrs. Wiggins," Andy said, "when I first saw Big Tina she was four or five months pregnant. When I last saw her she was carrying Little Larry around on her hip. Tell me, has either of you ladies ever heard of a baby weighing thirteen pounds at birth? That's what he weighed. And when he was one-year-old he looked like a four-year-old child. It even occurred to me that the government might be up to something—you know, like a secret breeding program of some kind."

Lacking Andy's good manners, I licked the tips of my chopsticks before setting them aside. "Mama, where did you *really* meet Big Larry?"

I could see Andy start out of the corner of my eye. As for Mama, if she drew back in her chair any farther, she was going to become one with the hard plastic.

"You can't hide inside yourself, Mama. You're not a turtle, for crying out loud. And don't tell me you met Big Larry at the Senior Center, or the Shepherd's Center, because I know that those answers aren't true."

"All right, all right, you don't have to get your knickers in a knot," Mama said, patting her pearls. "It's possible that I met Larry on my doorstep."

Remain calm, I ordered myself. Flying off the handle only works for axe heads, and then they have logistics problems.

"*When,* Mama?"

"It might have been the day we went to Pasha's Palace and you bought that carpet as a wedding present for Toy and C.J."

"And what was he doing there?" Even though my voice was an octave higher, I believe it still registered as calm.

"He might have been distributing coupons to use at Magic Genie Cleaners."

"And just how likely are these 'mights'?"

"Pretty probable. Abby, don't be angry with me. I'm just a poor old widder woman with very few friends. What am I supposed to do when the Almighty drops a big old bear of a man on my doorstep? I have needs too."

"Euw!"

"TMI," Andy muttered as he looked away.

"Mama, you didn't!"

"Are you saying I'm undesirable, Abby?"

"No, I'm saying no such thing." Then I remembered how long it took to dissuade Mama of that notion the last time it took hold of her. "Tell her how desirable she is, Andy."

"*What?*"

I mouthed the words *sweet nothings.*

Euw, he mouthed back.

A picture may be worth a thousand words, but a pair of Wiggins-Washburn eyes is worth an entire novel. The poor lad didn't stand a chance.

"Mrs. Wiggins," he said, "for, uh, a woman of your age, you are—uh—very nice looking. And your hair is very attractive."

Mama pushed her greasy paper plate aside, laid her head on her arms and proceeded to wail. It sounded as if she was mourning an entire village of closely related dead relatives, Middle Eastern style. It was certainly an inappropriate response from an elderly woman, just because a virile young man had been somewhat guarded with his praise. Clearly there was more to the situation than met my eardrums.

I put my arm around Mama's heaving shoulders, while trying my best to be oblivious to the mounting stares of the lunchtime shoppers. "Mama, shall we go someplace else and talk about this?"

Her wails spiraled higher as she achieved notes that only seven-year-old girls and mezzo sopranos are supposed to reach. "No," she managed to say at the same time.

"Here comes a mall security guard," Andy said. He practically had to shout to be heard. "I'll try to head him off."

I used Andy's absence as an excuse to get the conversation started. "Andy's gone," I said, "so let's talk quickly." Of course this was all spoken directly into Mama's left ear, which works better than her right.

Immediately she ceased wailing and began to blow her nose into the pile of paper napkins we'd brought to the table. It was not entirely pleasant sitting that close to her. Even worse than the sound effects was the sight of her red swollen face, and bags under her eyes so huge that I could pack for a weekend getaway in just one of them. Finally she announced that the job was done.

"So then talk to me, Mama." Meanwhile I kept an eye out for Andy and the mall cop, as well as nosy shoppers.

"It has nothing to do with that boy, Abby—although he is awfully cute. It's all about me; what an old fool I've been. When Big Larry showed up at my door with that million dollar grin of his and that Mississippi accent, why I was just putty to his charms."

"I think the correct expression is—oh never mind. Let's not go there again, okay? Unless you need to see a doctor. Do you?"

Mama shook her head, flinging fresh tears in all directions.

"Okay. My gut instinct tells me that Big Larry is related to Little Larry and Big Tina. I know I'm basing this on circumstantial evidence, but Big Larry's appearance in both our lives is just too coincidental. Do you agree?"

Mama nodded. "And Abby, afterward, when he was—uh—showering, I peeked in his wallet."

"You didn't!" I said proudly.

"Of course, dear. Isn't that what they do in the movies?"

"Yes, but they also usually get caught. Maybe even get strangled with a silk stocking."

"Do you want to hear what I found, or not?"

22

"Of course I want to hear what you found in his wallet!"

"Well—" Mama dabbed dramatically at her eyes with what remained of the napkins. "—Big Larry is *not* from Mississippi after all; he's from South Carolina."

"Aha!"

"*And* he wears contacts. Or at least he has to wear some kind of vision correction when he drives."

"Mama," I growled through clenched teeth, "pertinent facts only, please."

"Well you never know, dear. Next time we see him he could be wearing glasses instead of contacts, and we might not recognize him."

"Point taken. Anything else?"

"He has a wife and son."

My jaw dropped. I hate when that happens in someplace as unsanitary as the food court at the mall.

"Mama, you slept with a married man?"

My mother's mandible ended up on the table alongside mine. I'd never seen her remain speechless for so long. Before she found her tongue, however, she slapped me across the face. This was the first time, and the only time, my petite progenitress has ever gotten physically violent with me.

"You take that back, Abby, if not for my sake, then your daddy's! I have *never*, and I *will* never, allow another man to take those same liberties that I allowed your dear, sweet father. I am shocked—appalled is more like it—that you could even think those words, much less say them. What a wicked, vile woman you must take me to be, to suppose that I would share this body with another man while the memory of your father yet flickers through my brain."

"But you said—I'm sure you said you had *needs*."

"Dry cleaning needs, silly. These pleated skirts I wear are a pain to iron, so I invited him in and served him coffee and cake."

"Then when did he shower? And *why*?"

"Oh, that. Well, I served him chocolate ice cream along with the cake—a nice yellow pound cake that I baked. He asked me a lot of questions—you know, about Charleston: did I like it here, whom did I know—so many, in fact, that my ice cream melted before I could eat half of it. That's when he asked me to dribble a little bit of melted ice cream on his shirt, and then he would bring it back the next day to show me what a good job his company did. When I said I would rather not, he grabbed my wrist and the bowl went flying. And I do mean flying, dear. The melted ice cream landed everywhere: on his face, in his eyes, in his hair, everywhere, but on me. It was the funniest thing."

"Let me guess. You had him go shower while you

threw his clothes in the washing machine. I bet you got them as clean as Magic Genie Cleaners would have done."

"You can bet your bottom dollar, Abby."

"What did he wear in the meantime?"

"Nothing!" Mama started laughing. "Of course he didn't have the nerve to leave the bathroom without his clothes—I gave him only one itty bitty towel—so he was stuck." Her volume rose as she resumed laughing.

I knew I had to work fast to head off hysteria. "But you took him with you to Kitty Bohring's command performance and you two acted like it was a date and—"

"Hush your mouth, Abby. Big Larry had his own invitation. And I just pretended like we were dating so you didn't think your old mama was such a pitiful character."

"I don't think that, Mama."

"Are you willing to swear on your daddy's memory, Abby?"

Andy returned then, having successfully deflected the mall Gestapo. "Whassup?" he whispered.

"Deus ex machina," I whispered back.

"*Es esto sobre su madre?*"

I nodded.

"What did he say?" Mama asked.

"Just that the mall cop said we need to keep our voices down."

Mama must have been satisfied with his answer, because she'd already tuned us out. I made Andy swear an oath of confidentiality and filled him in on the so-called pertinent details while my mother enjoyed her peaceful respite off in la-la land. I was almost done talking when she turned so suddenly I let out a little yelp of surprise.

"Calm down, dear," Mama said in all seriousness. "It isn't seemly to carry on so in public—especially in a shopping mall."

"I'll try to behave better, I promise."

"Good. I just wanted to tell you that I remembered something else that might be useful in your investigation."

"Yes?"

"Big Larry had a library card."

"That's nice, Mama. I think everyone should have one. Reading is fundamental, and if more fundamentalists read, there might be fewer of them."

"Honestly, Abby, sometimes you make no sense at all. On his card was his full name and address."

Why is it that having a conversation with Mama feels like building a pyramid from the top down? "What *is* his name, Mama? Where does he live? Did you even bother to write that stuff down?"

The dear woman who taught me that ladies must always sit with their legs crossed at the ankles, their knees together, and that stealing was breaking one of God's ten big laws, opened her taupe handbag, withdrew her color-coordinated wallet, and removed a library card that very clearly was not hers.

"Dear Abby," she said with a smile, "when are you ever going to learn to trust your mama?"

I took the card from Mama. YORK COUNTY PUBLIC LIBRARY, ROCK HILL, S.C. "We know where that is," I said.

"Now look at his name."

"'Lively Lawrence Tupperman,'" I read aloud.

"What kind of person names their child Lively?" Andy asked.

"It's undoubtedly a family name," Mama said, "and it's probably his mother's maiden name, although I think I like your custom better."

I nodded in agreement. So many Northerners have commented to me on the strangeness of Southern first names, I've concluded that it must be a regional custom. I'm still not sure exactly what the issue is, but it's supposed to be something about our first names not sounding particularly gender friendly.

For instance, I know a girl named Grazier, which sounds masculine to some ears, and I know a man named Lynn, which sounds feminine to others. Since I know families by both those names, it never would have occurred to me, on my own, that these names would sound odd to newcomers. Then again, my mother is named Mozella Hatshepsut and I have a brother named Toy.

"So," I said, as I gathered up my detritus, "where do we go from here?"

"Abby, the MSG in your teriyaki sauce has already affected your thinking."

"I think not. Hmm—you must be right!"

"Ha ha, very funny. The next thing we do, dear, is hop in the car and drive up Interstate 26 to Columbia, switch over to Interstate 77, and don't stop until we've found Lively Larry's house—except for powder room breaks, of course."

"Mama, interstate toilet facilities are hardly considered powder rooms. That's like calling eating at Mc-Donald's a fine dining experience. Anyway, we can't just bop up the interstate on the spur of the moment. What are we supposed to do when we get there, look in Big Larry's windows?"

"You wouldn't need to look in his windows," Andy said, "because I'd go with you, and I'd think of an excuse to talk to him face-to-face. He doesn't know me."

"No, but his big wife does."

"That's right, Abby," Mama said, "keep thinking up the excuses: anything to keep from having to ask Greg's permission to go." She turned to Andy. "My son-in-law is the salt of the earth, but he keeps my daughter on a short leash."

I snatched up Andy's trash—but not Mama's—and stomped off to the nearest receptacle. If Greg is the salt of the earth, then Mama is the pepper. While I love her dearly, she is best taken in small doses.

"I am *not* on a leash," I said upon returning. "And I most certainly do *not* have to ask permission to go anywhere. And just to make things clear, I know what psychological BS you're trying to pull here. Well, it's not going to work." I growled as I grabbed her trash as well. "So there." I took the long way getting back to them, which means I circled around so I passed the DQ stand, where I got a dipped cone. I had just finished licking the last of it from my lips when I returned to our table.

By then Mama and Andy were standing. "Abby," Mama said softly, "I'm really sorry. I shouldn't have pushed your buttons like that. You can't go; I appreciate that. But Mr. Garcia and I *can*, and so we shall. He's agreed to drive, and I've graciously consented to chip in for mileage and, of course, to navigate. Now if you'll excuse us, dear, we have miles to go before we cheap."

"I think the word is 'sleep,' Mama."

"In the poem, yes. But 'cheap' refers to a healthy young man who lets a little old lady on a fixed income pay for gas."

"Andy went bankrupt, Mama, and besides, your fixed income has been bolstered considerably by the fact that Greg and I share our house with you. And it's not like Daddy left you penniless in the first place."

"I swan, dear," Mama said, her dander rising, "sometimes you approach life with such dreary literalism that it isn't any wonder that— Oh, just you never mind."

"Spit it out, Mama. Whatever it is, I can take it."

"I most certainly will not," she said with the stamp of a petite taupe pump, "and you can't make me. No matter how hard you try." She placed her right hand on Andy's left arm, as if she were the mother-of-the-bride about to be escorted to her seat. "Please forgive our little family tiff, darling. But I guess families everywhere do the same thing, right?"

"I don't know, ma'am."

"Well, like you and your mother, for instance. Surely the two of you have had a few, knockdown, drag-out fights—in a civilized way, of course."

Andy shook his head. "No ma'am. I respect my mama; I would never talk back to her. And if I did— whoa, I think that would be the last of me."

"Did you hear *that*, Abby?"

"Different cultures, different ways of discourse, Mama. The Hispanic culture tends to revere the mother figure."

"I am an American," Andy said. "My culture *is* American."

"Don't misunderstand me, please," I said. "I wasn't disputing that. Please, can we just drop this conversation?"

"Gladly," Mama said. Although she didn't remove the hand that was resting on Andy's arm, I could see her chalk up a point on the message board in my mind's eye. "Well," she said as we approached the doors to the outside, "what would they say in your country, Andy, at a time like this? Vamoose?"

"This *is* my country."

"You know what I mean."

"Unfortunately, I do. What if I was to ask you the same question, Mrs. Wiggins?"

"Well—we'd say something like, 'Let's get a move on it,' or 'Let's get this show on the road.'"

"We'd say the same thing."

"They speak English in your country?"

I'd heard enough. As the oldest responsible person there, I couldn't very well let the two of them drive off into the arms of danger.

"Okay," I practically shouted, "I'll come. Just let me call Greg first." I proceeded to dig in my purse for my ever elusive cell phone.

"Nothing doing," Mama said. "Greg will forbid you, and you know that."

"I'm a grown woman, Mama; I can do what I want."

"Right."

"Then I'll call the Rob-Bobs."

"Ditto."

"That's just being stupid. We can't be driving up to York County with a complete stranger—especially a man—along. We could become those sidebars you read in true crime books: two women, one middle age, the other elderly; both headless; found in a hunter's blind a mile from their car. No motive or suspect ever identified."

"*That* does it," Andy said. "I'm going back home."

Mama was so angry that I swear her voluminous skirt puffed an inch fuller than usual. "You see what you've done? Your racial profiling has injured poor Mr. Garcia to the quick."

"Poor Andy is the same race as you and I—white. But yes, I was profiling; I was stranger profiling. Andy, I'm sorry that I hurt your feelings, but I doubt if I would drive up to York County with Tom Cruise without knowing him for a while first." That wasn't quite true, because even though I find some of Tom's beliefs somewhat odd, I'd quite possibly follow him on a two-person expedition to the South Pole (in anticipation of a lot of innocent cuddling to conserve lifesaving body warmth).

"Abby," Mama said, shaking her head, "I don't know when I've ever been more ashamed of you. Didn't Fig have nice things to say about Mr. Garcia?"

"Yes, but how well do you really know Fig, Mama? How many years has it been since the two of you have really talked? People change; you've said so yourself a million times. And please don't think for a minute that

I'm putting Fig down or calling him a criminal; I'm just saying that as women, we have to be very cautious, and for you and me to ride up to Rock Hill with a stranger is just too much."

"Your daughter's right," Andy said.

"*What?*" Mama looked like she wanted to slap the very man she'd been defending.

"I've been thinking," Andy said, his voice as calm as that of a funeral director. "If it were my mama and my sister we were discussing, there is no way I would be comfortable with them driving that far—or any distance—with a man they'd met only minutes before. I don't care how many Figs gave him the stamp of approval."

"You see?" I said to Mama. I turned to Andy. "I'm really sorry. I really didn't mean to offend you."

He backed away even as he flung his arms to show it was no big deal. "No, we're cool now. I meant what I said. But hey, I really do have to go. I forgot about ball practice. I'm in a church league."

"Soccer?" I asked.

"Softball," Andy said, and took off almost at a run.

"Well, look at that," I said.

"Can't say as I blame him," Mama said. "Soccer indeed. When are you going to stop stereotyping, Abby?"

"Not that, Mama. Look who walked in."

23

No, don't look!"

That was exactly the wrong thing to say. A card laid might be a card played to a serious participant in the game, but a "don't" to Mama is just so much doo-doo. Immediately she turned and stared.

"It's their graces," she said in a voice loud enough to get even Daddy's attention. You can be sure, by the way, that he spends his days playing celestial golf.

There was no question that the fake nobles heard her. They stopped short, glanced around the crowded court, but then seemed to miss us on the first pass.

"Crouch," I whispered to Mama.

"I most certainly will *not*," she said. Having been issued an order, she had no choice but to disregard it.

This was not my intention, mind you, but the MSG in the teriyaki sauce *had* indeed muddied my thinking. "Mama, please," I begged, "don't make a scene—I mean, go ahead and make one. I dare you to."

Unfortunately, the signal had long since been sent to Mama's brain. She responded to my dare by whipping out a flowered hankie from between her bosoms, standing on her tiptoes and waving the brightly colored cloth about like a lure. "Over here, dears," she called. "Yoo-hoo, Your Royal Highnies."

Laughter ignited around us like spontaneous brushfires and I wanted to crawl into the nearest crack in the floor. But since I shun clichés, and even I would have a hard time fitting into most floor cracks, I just closed my eyes and waited for the awful moment to pass. It's at times like that when one needs to retreat inwardly to that "special place," a concept popularized by self-help gurus. My special place is the old pavilion at Myrtle Beach, on a starry summer night, watching Mama and Daddy shag.

"What's the matter, dear? Why are your eyes closed? Did that cheap mascara you use flake again?"

I opened my peepers. Nobody was looking at me except Mama.

"Where did their graces go?"

"As soon as they saw it was us, they high-tailed it out of here like ducks after June bugs. The looks on their faces were priceless. Too bad you were blinded by flakes of cheap mascara."

In retrospect I think it was frustration more than anything that caused me to behave so irresponsibly. I'm not a control freak—really, I'm not—but this was my investigation, and Mama was supposed to be along only for the ride. Why was it, then, that half the time I felt like she was doing the driving? I don't mean just driving me crazy either.

"Mama," I said sternly, "if you want to go home now, say the word and I'll drive you. Better yet, I'll put you in a cab."

That's when the woman who'd endured an undetermined number of painful hours to bring me into the world tucked her exquisite hankie back into the safety offered by her breasts. "I know what you're thinking, dear, and you just try and leave me behind."

The stretch of Interstate 26 between Upchuck and I-95 is one long monument to mankind's need to get ahead. I do mean that literally. Although this four-lane highway is as flat as a ten-year-old boy's chest, with a woodsy median that divides it in half, judging by the number of wooden crosses planted along this stretch, the fatality rate is staggering. When I figure out why it is that so many people have needlessly died along such a benign strip of land, I'll set about to bringing peace to the Middle East. Sadly, Greg and I have taken to calling this eerie thoroughfare Death Row.

It is only a three hour drive to Rock Hill from North Charleston if one doesn't stop *and* follows the unwritten *nine miles above the speed limit* rule. However, I am a law abiding woman with a bladder the size of a walnut; I set my cruise control on exactly the speed limit and avail myself of every official restroom I come across. Suppose we should encounter the vestiges of a terrible accident and can't get to the next facility for hours. Then what?

As it happens, I also get the munchies when I drive, so even though we only recently had lunch, when we got to Orangeburg, Mama and I both voted to stop at McDonald's and get milk shakes. Suppose we encountered the vestiges of a terrible accident—well, you get the picture. I mean, just in case Mama's picnic had gone bad.

At any rate, Mama is a firm vanilla devotee, and I'm an aspiring chocoholic. So busy were we defending our favorite flavors that we missed the turn into McDonald's. Without even tapping the brake, I made a split-second decision to whip into the adjacent parking lot, that of Day's Inn. It was, perhaps, a rather sharp turn, and Mama did squeal a little, but neither the car nor our persons were injured. Nor anyone else for that matter.

"Abby!"

"Mama, please. I know I shouldn't have done that. I'm sorry. If you like, you can make a citizen's arrest and haul me off to the slammer. But then you'd have to drive back to Charleston alone. And since I'm almost out of gas, you'd have to pump that as well, and you know how much you hate that. Betty Anderson *never* pumped gas."

"It's not that, dear—"

"I know; we're in the wrong parking lot. But how much farther do we have to walk? Ten feet—if we cut across the grass. Look, I'll even carry you piggyback if that will make you happy. Better yet, why don't you just stay here with the AC running? Do you need a book to read? I think there's an old paperback under the seat."

"*Listen* to me!"

The Mama that roared certainly had my attention. "Yes, ma'am."

"I think that was their graces behind us."

"Where?"

"They just zoomed past us. There! They went through that light."

217

Now what was I supposed to do? Chase after a car I hadn't seen in hopes of catching up to it, then somehow convincing the driver to pull over so I could ask a pair of fake aristocrats—assuming that was indeed them—if they were, in fact, following us? I wasn't questioning Mama's powers of recognition, but that old adage about a bird in the hand seemed to make a heck of a lot more sense, especially since the bird—at least in my case—was an ice cold chocolate milk shake.

"Hmm," I said, pretending to think, even though I'd already made up my mind, "they could be really dangerous people—you know, like spies or something. The best thing we can do is to go get our shakes and then hit the road. Preferably before they have a chance to turn around."

Although she had to traverse both hot gravelly tarmac and turf in her pumps, I'd never seen Mama move so fast. Donna Reed, Betty Anderson, and June Cleaver would all have been proud of the way she handled her pumps.

What should have been a three and a half hour drive (including our stops) took an additional three hours, due to an overturned truck about ten miles south of Columbia. The cab was nose down in the left-hand-side drainage ditch, while the long cargo bed lay on its side, sprawling across both lanes. Upside down in the right-hand drainage ditch was an SUV limousine. Clearly the two vehicles had an unpleasant encounter.

We were the eighteenth to arrive on the scene. By then someone had called 911 and the sheriff, a fire truck, and two ambulances had already been dispatched—at least that's what I heard from driver number sixteen, a young man about to report to Fort Jackson for military training. Driver number seventeen, a woman in her fifties, remained locked in her car, staring straight ahead.

"There's a nurse up there," the new recruit panted. "She's says the truck driver might have broken his back. Them folks in the SUV limo are all shook up. Can't say as how I blame them, but still, they ain't acting very decent about it. Ain't none of them asking about the truck driver. They say they ain't getting out of their limo until their lawyer comes and takes some pictures, on account of it was the truck driver's fault. Trouble is, their lawyer is all the way over in Atlanta."

"Lord have mercy!" Mama said. I hadn't heard her get out of the car, but if there was a story to be heard, and of course embellished and repeated, you can bet that my minimadre would find her way there.

"Yes, ma'am, I agree; it ain't very neighborly, if you ask me. But even if their lawyer was to fly here in one of them helicopters (he pronounced it *hee*-licopters), this here accident is gonna take one heck of a long time to get cleaned up. I reckon that—"

Mama gasped. "Guts and blood everywhere?"

"Yes' ma'am, but—"

"Come on, Abby," Mama said, and grabbed my arm. "Let's get there before the cops do and seal everything off."

"*What?*"

"Don't be such a prude, dear. How many chances do we get to see real gore?"

"Mama!" I said. Perhaps I said it too sharply, but I was genuinely shocked by her callousness.

"I'm supposed to report by six," the young man said. "I don't know what to do."

I checked my watch. "It's not even three o'clock, and Fort Jackson is fifteen minutes away. I'm sure you'll make it."

"Maybe—maybe not. The last time I was behind an overturned livestock truck, it took them seven hours to clean up the highway enough to let us through. But them being pigs is probably why it took so long."

"*Livestock?*" Mama and I asked in unison.

He nodded. "Chickens. Hundreds of them—could be thousands. They're everywhere. Look out, here comes one now."

Sure enough, a big white chicken came flying past us right at my ear level, only to crash-land into the windshield of the next car. With a great deal of fuss it hopped to the ground, but apart from rumpled feathers, it appeared otherwise unhurt.

"I didn't know chickens could fly," I said.

"Sure they can," Mama said just as calmly as could be. "At my great Uncle Harlan and Aunt Ida's farm the chickens used to roost in the trees come nightfall. It kept them safe from foxes and raccoons."

"What about the cute little chicks? The ones with no feathers, just fuzz?"

"They weren't so lucky. Abby, now quit asking questions and let's help this young man figure out what he's going to do."

As it turned out there wasn't much we could do except help the state troopers round up the live chickens. They refused to let anyone pass until every single known escapee was apprehended, on the grounds that confused chickens crisscrossing the highway could pose a danger to future motorists. You can be certain, therefore, that a lot of us got into the act of bird-catching. When we were through, we'd rounded up just over twelve hundred potential fryers. Using her full circle skirt as a corral, Mama managed to capture three of them all by herself. The part that boggles my mind is that every single one of them, even the health-iest looking chicken, had to be destroyed, in keeping with the Department of Health requirements.

Blood can be deceiving, so I was surprised to learn that there probably weren't more than three hundred dead fowl on the highway. As for the truck driver, he was unconscious by the time the ambulance arrived, and even though I bought a copy of *The State* the next day, I never learned his fate. We were, however, still chasing chickens when the lawyer from Atlanta ar-rived, and sure enough, he did arrive in a helicopter. Whatever chickens remained on the loose were blown to kingdom come, ensuring that some foxes were going to eat well that night.

Mama and I got to witness a dramatic confrontation between tired troopers and a dandy in a three-piece seersucker suit, white buckskin shoes, and a polka dot bow tie. From what we could see and hear, law en-forcement at least temporarily won the standoff. When the occupants of the limo stumbled out into the dwin-dling daylight, they appeared unharmed, but most an-noyed to see us and the rest of the rubberneckers who'd gathered around to watch the free show.

"Oh my gawd!" shouted a girl, whose family car sported New York plates. "It's really him!"

"And her!" shouted the younger brother.

"*Who?*" Mama demanded.

"Them," the girl said, her lips pulling back into a sneer of derision. "Don't you know anything?" She edged away, trying to get closer to the limo. By then our fellow travelers, tired and covered in feathers and chicken poop, had begun to perk up as they took notice as well.

Meanwhile the brother, a boy about ten, held his hands to his chest, palms up. "Sorry," he said. "I can't take Lynne anywhere; she's such a groupie."

"That's all right," Mama said. "But who are these people?"

"That's Sister Nash, the rock star," the boy said. "Don't tell me you've never heard of him?"

"Nope," said Mama, "I haven't."

"Or me either," I said.

"But he's the best. At his last concert in New York he swallowed a live frog. When he got to Dallas he started peeing little tadpoles. He did it right on stage. It was in all those magazine you see at the supermarket."

"I don't read them," I said quite honestly.

"I missed that issue," Mama wailed.

"Why is he called 'sister' if he is a man?" I asked.

The boy shrugged. "Why do I call my priest 'father' when he's not my dad? Maybe it's the same thing."

It was my turn to shrug. "So then who is the woman?"

"That's Baby Nash."

"But she looks old enough to be his mother," Mama said.

"She is. Didn't you see that video, *Baby Gonna Rock Sister House Bleeds*?"

"Celebrities," Mama muttered.

"Hey, these just aren't *any* celebrities, lady. These are, like, bigger stars than Brittney or Paris. I mean like, they're really huge."

"But you're only te—Abby." It sounded like Mama was calling me a striped cat. I could see, however, that something, or someone, had caught her attention on the fringe of the group.

"Hey," he said. "Why does your mama call you that?"

I glanced around.

24

I saw them for a split second. No more. And I could
have been wrong.

"It was them," Mama hollered in my ear. "I swear
on Nanny's chin hairs."

"What'll we do?"

"You tell *me*—you're the detective!"

I pulled her to the shoulder of the road, hoping for a
better view of the vehicle lineup. It was a waste of
energy. Although there were plenty of bright lights to
the rear of us—rescue vehicles, squad cars, the helicopter—every one of the waiting cars, for as far as I
could see, had its motor turned off in order to conserve
gas. At that hour of the day the receding line of cars
resembled a chain of dominoes, their black backs
turned in our direction.

"No, I'm not a detective. I'm just a pint-size antiques
dealer with a penchant for biting off a gallon's worth
of trouble far too often."

"Boy, I'll say."

"Mama, you're supposed to disagree! Besides, this
is an all volunteer mission."

"Harrumph. Do I at least get combat pay?"

"Uhm—maybe. What seems fair to you? Aside from a free trip to the fabulous Upstate region of South Carolina, otherwise known as the Olde English District? For starters, I can promise you enough adventure to last a lifetime."

"You can keep the adventure, Abby, but I've had my eye on this teensy weensy little emerald ring, of miserable quality, that you have locked up in your estate jewelry case. I know that must be a mistake, because it really belongs on the costume rack up by the register. At any rate, I thought that would make a very nice Labor Day present."

"*Labor Day* present? Mama, who the heck gives Labor Day presents?"

"Children who appreciate the fact that their mama labored for sixty-five hours to bring them into this world."

"Children with no math skills, I presume. And anyway, Mama, that teensy weensy emerald is really a five carat gem quality tsavorite."

"Is it valuable?"

"Quite."

"Okay, that's fine then too."

"Can we drop the stones for a minute, Mama? What shall we do about their graces? Shall we tell the sheriff—although he doesn't look very happy, considering he won his battle to evict Sister Nash and Baby from their limo."

In the last of nature's light I could see Mama's hand fly up to her pearls. "And what will we tell them, Abby? Shall we begin by saying that we're being followed by fake nobility, which we—more specifically I—*may*, or may *not*, be seeing?"

"What do you mean by '*may*, or may *not* be seeing'?"

Mama looked around before cupping her hands to my ear. "Do you know how old I am, Abby?"

"Only God and the IRS know for sure, Mama, but I have a pretty good idea."

"And you know that I don't wear glasses, right?"

"Not unless you want to read, or do needlework, or do your nails, or write letters, or—"

"You know what I mean, dear."

"No, which is why we're having this conversation."

Mama sniffed. "Exactly, so then listen and stop arguing. I went to see my optimist last week and she said I'm getting a cataract on my left eye."

"Oh my. It's a good thing she isn't a pessimist then, or else you might be getting them on both eyes."

I could hear, but not see, Mama pat her pearls. "Was that a cruel joke at my expense, Abby?"

"Uh—no ma'am, and yes, ma'am. That is to say, I was trying to be clever, not cruel, and I'm sorry, and I totally take it back. Totally. Mama, how awful. What are you going to do?"

"Do? I'm going to have it removed, of course. This isn't the Dark Ages, dear. Anyway, my point is that I can't be one hundred percent sure it was them, but I'm pretty darn sure nonetheless."

"How sure? Wager a guess."

"Eighty-seven and a quarter percent."

A quarter percent? Gotta love the woman who bore me; at least she never bores me.

All at once it happened: people began running for their cars; headlights flashed, horns honked, scumbags swore.

"We're moving on out, Mama."

But she was already running as fast as her size five pumps could carry her.

I will reluctantly admit that we had been too very irresponsible women. No matter how you parsed our ages, adding them together should have amounted to a hundred years of accumulated wisdom, not stupidity. For starters, what the heck were we going to do in the Upcountry now that it was dark? As for poor Greg, I realized that he must have been frantic, about to go out of his mind with worry. I wouldn't have blamed him if he'd already reported me missing to the Charleston police.

As if the gods were mocking me and my childish behavior, not five miles up the road from the overturned poultry truck there was an official rest area. Even though I had just barely gotten back up to the speed limit, I braked just in time and slipped into what was undoubtedly going to be a very crowded parking lot.

"Hallelujah!" Mama sang. "My bladder thanks you!"

"Then you better scoot on in and find a stall. I have a feeling there are a hundred other bladders waiting to be just as thankful."

I jumped out and searched for a phone signal. Mama had wrestled her skirts out of the car and was traipsing after me.

"Who are you calling?"

"Mama, run! Here comes a high school activities bus. You know how noisy and messy those kids can be."

"Yes, and speaking of which, I'm sticking to you like stupid to a teenager until you tell me who it is."

"Mama, that was rude."

"As a matter of fact it was, and so is lying to your mama. I don't see a bus in sight."

I pressed the Send button on my phone. The party on the other end picked up immediately.

"Abby, I was just fixing to call you."

"Greg! Listen, dear—"

"No, you listen. Hon, I lied to you; Booger Boy's boat didn't break down. I've been playing golf for the last— uh, coupla days."

"Would you repeat that please? I think we have a bad connection."

"I said that I've been playing golf for the last coupla days."

I was careful to breathe in through my nose and out through my mouth. "That's what I thought you said."

"What did he say?" Mama demanded.

"Greg, dearest," I said, trying to keep him off guard by the lightness of my tone, "what exactly does 'coupla' mean? Two, three? As in, 'I drank a coupla beers last night'?"

"Is he drunk?" Mama said. "I knew it! The first time I met him I could smell mouthwash on his breath. That's never a good sign, you know. And once I could smell *too* much deodorant. That's got to mean something bad, Abby; I just don't know what yet."

"Well, not exactly a *couple*," Greg said in the meantime, although I could barely hear him with Mama yammering on. Then again, his volume had dropped to almost a whisper. "Maybe more like two weeks. But hey, that is a coupla weeks, isn't it?" The volume increased, as did his confidence, stoked as it was by his convoluted reasoning.

Mercifully I remembered that I had not tried the phone reception while still in the car. By then I was about a hundred yards from my vehicle, and although I was wearing strappy sandals, at least they had low heels.

"Look over there, Mama!" I screamed, pointing toward the nearest light pole. "Isn't that a wallet lying on the ground?"

It was no contest; I got there long before Mama did. Of course I locked the doors behind me and put the child safety on.

"What was that all about?" Greg asked. "Where are you?"

Someone once said—it's probably been said by hundreds of someones over the course of history—that if you're going to lie, at least keep it close to the truth. That way it will be easier for you—the liar—to remember.

"Mama got it in her head to go to Rock Hill and visit her cousin Imogene. We're at the rest area just south of Columbia. What you heard was me doing an evasive maneuver."

"Trying to get some privacy out of the earshot of Donna Reed?"

"Bingo."

"How long will you be up there?"

"We're coming back tomorrow—we better! You know how impetuous she is. I didn't even pack a tooth-brush."

"Abby, you don't sound pissed at all. Why is that? And how come no third degree?"

"Of course I'm pissed. And you better believe you're getting the third degree; all the way home I'll be think-ing up ways to torture you. But seriously, dear, I figure that you must have a good reason for doing what you did, and an even better one for not telling me. At least you better have. Taking early retirement without tell-ing your spouse is . . . well, it's kind of serious stuff. Like maybe we need to see a marriage counselor."

"Geez, Abby, I knew you were going to say that, and that's exactly why I didn't tell you any sooner."

"Yeah, right," I said through clenched teeth. "I'm sure that was the only reason."

"What the hell is that supposed to mean?"

I leaned on the horn with my elbow. "Gotta go; some maniac really wants my parking space in the worst way."

Before seeing Mama again I managed to make my way to the ladies' room through a veil of tears, do my business, wash my face, and regain my composure. At least I thought I had. But when I exited the restroom into the lobby that separates the women's from the men's, and saw Mama busy studying a highway map, I dissolved into tears again. I knew she was faking it, just trying to be kind.

Finally I went up to her. "Is there any chance we can stay with Cousin Imogene tonight? I told Greg that's where we'd be, and knowing him, he'll check up on us."

"Do you mean *my* Cousin Imogene? The one who breeds rats for a living?"

"Do you have another?"

"But you hate rats, Abby. The first time I took you to see her, you screamed so long and so hard, it brought on a full-blown case of tonsillitis."

"Yes, but I was only six years old. Besides, she made me hold one."

"Okay, Abby, if that's what you think you want to do, I'll give her a call. You go wait in the car, dear, I'll be back in a few minutes." That was it, no first, second, or third degree.

As usual, the woman who'd suffered an undetermined number of agonizing hours to bring me into this world—at whose breast I fed, and reportedly gnawed; who comforted me when my daddy died and pulled double duty as a single mother to rear and support Toy and me; who was there for me when my own children were born; who propped me up when Buford Timberlake, the timber snake, cheated on me with Tweetie, a woman half my age, and then left me penniless—was there for me at the drop of a gumball. She didn't even ask me for details—not *yet* at any rate. She just went off looking for the pay phone so she could call Cousin Imogene and get directions to her house (Mama does not believe in using cell phones when land lines will suffice).

I waited inside the car at first, while I listened to a CD of Russell Watson music. He's my favorite male vocalist and he usually sends my spirits soaring. But there are times when beauty can be so intense that it hurts; this, apparently, was one of those times. It was either turn Russell off or bawl my eyes out. Since I'd already shed enough cheap mascara for one day, I chose not to cry anymore.

As the evening air in the Piedmont can be somewhat cooler than on the coast, I decided to wait outside the car on the grass. Sure enough, a gentle breeze was blowing, and despite the bright lights over the parking lot, I could see hundreds of stars. Except for the carnage on the interstate, and Greg's disturbing news, it had the makings of a fine night. For a moment the smell of loblolly pines made me homesick.

"Abby? *Abby!* Where are you?"

"Over here, Mama. I'm up on the pet walk area."

"Get down from there, dear, before you step in doodoo."

"I can see fine, Mama." I got down anyway and walked back to my car.

"I did what you asked, dear."

"Thank you, Mama."

"Think nothing of it; that's what mamas are for. And do you know what else we're for?"

If Mama had been shouting through a bullhorn, she still could not have been heard any better. At this point the parking lot was filled and everyone in it, along with their mama, was beginning to look our way.

"Later," I mumbled. "Let's get in first."

"*What*? You hit a *gator* with your *fist*?"

I zapped the keyless entry button and slid in behind the wheel just in time. Dozens of eyes were already trained on my fists. It always takes Mama more time to get in and settled, thanks to her layers of starched crinolines, so I will confess to having backed out of the parking space, and maybe even to have shot halfway up the ramp, before she was securely buckled in.

"Abby, what are you trying to do? Kill me?"

"Not this time, Mama."

"Are you going to tell me what's wrong?"

"I'm not sure, Mama.

25

Cousin Imogene was delighted to "receive" us. She hadn't had overnight guests in thirteen years, which seemed like an auspicious number to me, until Mama reminded me that was how long it was since Cousin Cadaveat's death. In the meantime she'd been using the guest room as a breeding facility, so she put Mama and me up on the pull-out couch.

"I hope you don't mind sleeping on the Murphy bed," she squeaked. She always did have a voice that registered an octave higher than the average woman's, but now it seemed to need a little oil.

"Absolutely not, dear," Mama said graciously. "We've slept on much worse, haven't we, Abby?"

I certainly hadn't. I remembered the couch from when I was six, and some of Cousin Cadaveat's food stains (he loved to eat in front of the "boob tube") seemed to remember me. As for the springs, they'd given up all memory years ago.

"We're very grateful, Cousin Imogene," I said. "We should be ashamed of ourselves for barging in on you without any warning like this, but you being family and all, we thought you'd be insulted if we didn't give you first dibs. And don't worry about the bed, I'm sure it's very comfortable."

"Oh it is. It's a *de*luxe; says it right here on the mattress. See? No, it isn't the bed that I was concerned about in the first place. It's just that some folks have strange ideas about sleeping where someone has gone to meet the Lord—if you know what I mean."

I processed that bit of information for a nanosecond—or maybe ten. After all, I was exhausted.

"Are you saying that Cousin Cadaveat passed away on this couch?"

"You mean you didn't hear?"

"Hear what?" Mama said. I knew for a fact that she was a bit squeamish about that sort of thing.

"Well you see, your cousin—strictly speaking that would be your mama's cousin by marriage, Abby—went to his celestial home while I was enjoying myself out in Vegas with my girlfriends. I suppose that was the Lord's way of punishing me."

"I'm an Episcopalian," Mama said, "remember? I don't believe God zaps us for playing the slot machines."

"Believe whatever you like, Mozella, but when I left for Sin City my husband was as healthy as a plow horse, and when I returned home I found him lying dead on this very couch. According to the coroner, my dear sweet Cadaveat may have suffered a heart attack, and who knows, he might even have had it the very moment I sat down to my first nickel machine."

"I'm so sorry," I said. "I didn't know the details." I paused for ten more respectful nanoseconds. "Why wasn't the coroner able to pinpoint the exact cause of death—if you don't mind my asking?"

"Well, shoot a monkey! I bribed Coroner Stokes ten thousand dollars—only he called it a political contribution—if he didn't breathe a word to anyone about how, or where, your cousin died. But I just assumed that folks found out somehow, because everywhere I go they look at me kinda funny."

"To be honest, cousin," Mama said gently, "perhaps you carry with you a certain eau de rat. You might consider housing the little dears in a separate facility altogether, or better yet, get yourself some new digs. Maybe a new wardrobe as well."

"It could be fun," I said. "I'll help you shop. But if you don't mind, for now, can we go back to the coroner and the secrets he kept?"

Tears filled the poor woman's eyes. "The rat business was really Cadaveat's idea in the first place. And there is money to be made, especially by breeding the fancy varieties. We ship to laboratories, pet stores—" She took a deep breath. "Anyway, it might have been a heart attack. All we really know for sure is that it happened during the time period when my husband usually cleans the cages, and so the rats were running loose—they're very tame, you see. These aren't wild rats."

"Go on."

"So when I stepped into the house that day and saw a skeleton lying on my couch, I thought my eyes were playing tricks on me."

"You're kidding!" I backed away from the couch. "Oh my heavens, you're *not* kidding, are you?"

"Achoo!" I'd never heard such a loud sneeze come from Mama.

"Bless you, Mama. Did you hear what Cousin Imogene just said?"

"Achoo! Achoo!"

"Mama, are you coming down with a cold?"

"Mercy me, I think it's worse than that. Do you remember last winter when I was diagnosed with reoccurring galloping pneumonia?"

"Oh yes, that particularly virulent strain. Didn't your doctor say it could show up at a moment's notice, and probably would if you were subjected to stress?"

"Stress?" Cousin Imogene appeared to take umbrage at the word. "Mozella, do you find my company stressful? Why we used to play naked together in the bathtub."

"Ah, that's so cute when baby cousins do that," I said, forgetting for a moment that Mama was on a tear of some kind.

"We weren't babies," Imogene said. "We were thirteen, if we were a day."

"We were late bloomers," Mama said. "Lordy, I think I'm about to pass out. Abby, you need to take me to Piedmont Medical Center. Tell them what I have, and warn them that if they have any laboratory animals, they better remove them from the premises pronto. Tell them what happened to the white mice in the lab at Medical University of South Carolina in Charleston."

Imogene was all ears, and they were right in front of Mama. "What happened?"

"They died within twenty-four hours. Every last one

of them. It turns out that reoccurring leaping pneumonia is an airborne disease that is easily caught by rodents and always fatal. In fact, I shouldn't even be here."

Imogene cocked her ears, and along with them, her head. "Just a second ago you said it was *galloping*, not *leaping.*"

"Huh?"

"That's one of its symptoms for sure," I said. I stepped between Imogene and Mama and felt Mama's forehead. "Yowza! It feels like a steam iron."

"Let me feel," Imogene said. The woman was as stubborn as a brace of Georgia mules.

"No! You'll infect your vermin—I mean your rats!" I gave Mama a mighty push in the direction of the front door.

Thank heavens she didn't need more of a start than that to overcome the resistance of her skirts. All that material tends to act like a parachute, so that watching her go from zero to a flat out run is like watching water run uphill. Sometimes, on gusty days, I've observed her move backward for as far as a block before making any headway.

I heard someone shout, but I don't have a clue as to whether dear Cousin Imogene tried to chase after us. I wouldn't have blamed her. She was undoubtedly lonely, living as a pariah in her hometown, and all because her business took her husband to lunch.

Rock Hill is home to beautiful Winthrop University, and there are a number of historical treasures scattered about town. What a shame then that one of the main entrances to the city is nothing more than one long strip mall. As Cherry Road begins on the north end of the town (in a location choked with motels), a cynic might postulate that the powers that be wish to discourage Yankee visitors from plumbing the city's riches and settle down for a spell.

Mama and I needed only a roof over our heads and a hot meal, nothing else. And anonymity, of course; it wouldn't do if word got out that Mozella Wiggins and her entrepreneur daughter from Charleston were staying at the Princess and the Pea out by the interstate. Just think of the rumors that could result from such a sighting. Since we were both too old to be hookers— well, at least Mama was—folks might speculate that we'd become drug runners, or worse yet, we were sneaking Buckeyes and Hoosiers into the pretty parts of Rock Hill. It was decided that I would leave Mama in the car while I ventured in to see if there was a room available.

When you're my height, the only way to go unnoticed is to walk fast and pray that folks don't look down. My subterfuge was wasted, however, by the total indifference of the teenage desk clerk, who was on the phone. And by the smile on her young face, interrupted by the occasional riff of giggles, it was clear that she was not on a business call. After five toe-tapping minutes I'd had enough and decided to *really* listen to what was going on. After another minute I couldn't stand it anymore.

"Hey Ayden, I'll leave my panties home if that's what you want."

"You most certainly will not, Jennifer," I said, having noticed her name badge.

Jennifer made eye contact with me for the first time. "Huh?"

"Tell Ayden to get his butt to work like he's supposed to—I mean like he said McDonald's is shorthanded tonight—and then you come wait on me. Please."

"Hey, you can't tell me what to do."

"Yes I can; I'm the customer. The first rule in any successful business is that the customer is always right."

"Yeah? Well, my boss ain't here, so I'm saying you ain't right." I could hear Ayden's tinny voice in the background, and Jennifer addressed him next. "Just some old lady who's trying to give me a hard time," she said. "What? Hell no, Sean's not here, which means I'm covering for his ass too. Oh, and get this, she said I should tell you to get your butt over to McDonald's. Can you believe that?"

"Jennifer, *sweetie*," I said, "I'm going to go now, but just so you know, I'm going to call Grayson Xavier Hollingsworth, specifically to tell him that Jennifer Latrobe Hollingsworth was rude, crude, and utterly inattentive. I will strongly urge him to terminate your employment here at the Princess and the Pea and not give you a favorable reference for any job—unless it involves pulling the wings off flies."

"Gotta go, Ayden." The phone slammed into its cradle. "Ma'am," Jennifer said, but I was already halfway to the door.

"Yes?"

"Ma'am, I need to talk to you. It ain't like you think."

"Then tell me how it is, Jennifer."

I'd stopped, but I hadn't turned around. That forced her to leave the security of her counter and come around until she faced me. Shame on me for laying such a power trip on a teenager, but I was doing it for her mother, after all; I was doing it for mothers everywhere whose teenage daughters go on after-work dates and leave their panties at home.

"Ma'am," Jennifer said, when we were face-to-face, but of course not eye-to-eye, "how did you know my—I mean, the owner's name? Like even his middle name?"

"Well, while you were busy flapping your gums to Ayden I had plenty of time to look around the lobby, and one of the things I noticed is that immense bowling trophy over the fireplace. Is that a working fireplace, by the way?"

"Yes, ma'am. But like only in the winter, on account of it can get real hot in here at other times."

"I understand. At any rate, the name engraved on the trophy is Grayson X. Hollingsworth. As it so happens, I graduated from Rock Hill High School with a boy by that name. The Grayson I knew was also a champion bowler *and* said he was going to be a businessman someday. Now throw in the X. I'm willing to bet that not many people have X for a middle initial, and how many Grayson X. Hollingsworths can there be?"

"Wow, you're really good. You a detective or something?"

"Something is more like it."

"But how'd you know my middle name? Or my last name? My badge just says 'Jennifer'?"

"Again, while you were making promises to run

around town à la Brittany Spears, I was looking at the work schedule, laying there on the counter. I'm assuming the J. Hollings is meant to be you."

"Yeah, there's another Jennifer—Jennifer Montgomery. She's J. Mont."

"As for your middle name, that was just a guess. But your dad was dating Denise Latrobe when last I knew him. So he married her?"

"Yeah, but she died when I was only three. She was killed in a car accident. She was beheaded." She paused. "I was with her."

"I'm so sorry."

"Don't be; I can't remember nothing. Hey, you want a room or something?"

"That is why I'm here. Do you have a quiet one— away from the elevator, maybe two-thirds down a hallway? Top floor is preferable."

"Hey, the whole place is yours. We ain't got but one other couple staying here. You alone, or with someone?" She had the nerve to smirk.

"My mother is waiting in the car."

"Two beds, or one?" The smirk was still in place.

"Two."

"I'm going to need your driver's license and a major credit card."

I promptly handed her the documents. She glanced at the photo and then back at me.

"You oughta sue them," she said. "I heard it can be done. Hey, you're from Mount Pleasant. That's down by Charleston, isn't it?"

"Yes, it is. On the pleasant side of the harbor, as we like to say."

"Well, ain't that funny, because that other couple that's here, they're from Charleston too."

For the umpteenth time that day tiredness drained from my body as adrenaline seemed to flow in from nowhere. I imagined that the exchange of energy was akin to the fluid exchange in the embalming process.

"Would it be possible to ask their names? Please."

"Yes, ma'am."

I waited patiently while she jotted down the information on my documents and handed them back. "Jennifer?" I prompted her at last.

"Abigail," she said, looking me straight in the eye, "I'm still waiting for you to ask."

"What?"

"You know; you wanted to know if it was possible to ask their names?"

I wanted to wring her neck, that's what I wanted to do. Figuratively, of course.

"What are their names?" I tried—oh how I tried—to keep the sarcasm to a minimum.

"They registered as Mr. and Mrs. Smith," she said without even looking at the sheet in front of her. "Don't you think that's odd?"

"Not especially," I said, trying to play it cool. "Do you?"

"Trust me, they seemed suspicious to me. They asked all kinds of questions: like were there any other guests from Charleston. They were looking for two petite women, they said. So your mama must be like, really short too, huh?"

"You know, on second thought, I think I've changed my mind about staying here—"

"No, don't go! You don't squeal on me, and I won't squeal on you. I swear! And I'll be like your under-cover spy. I'll call and let you know every time they leave, or enter, the building. Or even just ask about you. And if you want food brought to your room—there's a Denny's right across the street. I can run over there and get whatever you want."

I was too tired to think straight, and she seemed so eager to play James Bond that I let my guard down. "Fine," I said.

An alert Abby would have seen the figure lurking in the hallway to the left. As I passed, on my way to the front door, it ducked behind the ice machine.

26

I found Mama fast asleep, slumped low in the front seat. Her lips were parted slightly and she didn't stir until I touched her shoulder.

"B sixteen," she blurted. "Bingo!"

I gave her a moment to enjoy her dreamland win and then helped her upstairs. By then she was fully awake and ravenous. Fortunately, Jennifer was true to her word, and within a reasonable length of time delivered two Grand Slams and a pair of diet colas right to the door. Along with the food came an espionage update: the weirdoes from Charleston had inquired again about their vertically challenged friends.

Jennifer called three more times before I told her we were turning in for the night. The news, by the way, was always the same: the couple was anxious for our arrival.

Thank goodness Mama is an early riser, and by five-thirty the next morning we were ready to hit the road. I'd arranged it with Jennifer so that our room account was already settled; all Mama and I had to do was walk out the side door. By six we were seated in the

245

IHOP opposite the PetSmart, still working on putting a game plan in place. I was already on my second cup of coffee.

"Well, we screwed up," I said. "Today is Sunday, so the library doesn't open until this afternoon, and there aren't any Tuppermans in the phone book. What do we do now?"

"Abby, I hate it when you use that word. It is so—so uncouth."

"Sorry, Mama. From now I'll say 'that man.'"

Mama sighed and patted her pearls. They were a gift from Daddy shortly before he died. Real pearls, either cultured or natural, are essentially an irritant coated with layers of nacre, a substance secreted by the oyster. Generally, the more layers of nacre, the larger and more expensive the pearl. That Mama's pearls suffer so much abuse at her hands yet retain so much of their nacre is truly a mystery worthy of the Discovery Channel.

"You *know* what I mean, dear. Just for that, I think we should go to church."

"The Episcopal Church of Our Savior?"

"What other church is there?"

"And how would we explain our presence in Rock Hill, not to mention yesterday's clothes, our unbrushed teeth, etcetera, etcetera, etcetera?"

"Why Abby, you sound like Yul Brynner in the *King and I*. Anyway, dear, are you saying that we should go home as soon as we're done eating? By the way, where *are* my pecan pancakes? I'm starving."

Of course I didn't have any answers. Rock Hill, South Carolina, where I grew up, is often considered part of the Greater Charlotte Metropolitan Area, but culturally it is light-years away. Scratch a Charlottean and you have a fifty-fifty chance of hearing a New Yorker yelp in pain. Scratch a Rock Hillian and he or she will apologize to *you* for having gotten too close to your fingernails. Rock Hill, being a much smaller city, also observes Sunday Blue Laws, which meant that we would be unable to obtain a clean change of clothes until after one-thirty P.M.

"No, I'm *not* throwing in the towel." My mind wandered for a few seconds to towels and linens and the fact that Rock Hill was smack dab in what used to be cotton producing country. Later, as the technology developed, textile mills became a major source of employment for the Piedmont, including Charlotte. But those halcyon days were gone, the millwork having long since been outsourced to China and other Asian countries.

Although the jobs are gone, many of the brick fortresslike buildings were left standing. Some have been turned into warehouses or outlet stores, while others were left empty. During the ensuing years, the abandoned mills have become overgrown by the kudzu vine, which is a native of China and Japan. Now these former mills rise ghostlike from the imported jungle in the Carolina mists that precede and follow the rising and setting of the sun, and are every bit as intriguing as Angkor Wat.

Who owned these vine-covered castles, and why hadn't they been replaced with tract housing or golf courses? Not that I wanted them to fall prey to developers! No siree, Bob! I was thinking how lovely it would be to turn one of them into an antiques emporium.

Some of those mills had great bones, as they say in the trade. Many of them still have usable parts; when my friends James and Gretchen Werrell refurbished a house, they were able to purchase old-growth maple flooring that had once been used in a mill.

At any rate, there are a great collection of dealers up at Metrolina, just north of Charlotte, and it opens its doors once a month. Then in the spring and fall it hosts antiques extravaganzas that draw vendors from all over the Southeast. But why not have a similar operation in South Carolina, built, of course, in an abandoned mill? You could bet that my shop, the Den of Antiquity, would be well-represented.

As for the kudzu, it can be eaten as a vegetable—by both humans and livestock—turned into soaps, jellies, woven into baskets, and most appropriately, processed into a powder that is used as a thickening agent for cooking and is very popular in Asian food markets. Perhaps by figuring out a way to keep overhead down, I could send kudzu back to China and Japan from whence it came.

"Mama, what mills do you remember around here that were not torn down after the great exodus of the textile industry?"

"Well, there's that one over by the *Rock Hill Herald* that's now a linen store."

"Pledges? I heard it's been converted into high-end condos."

Mama frowned; she hates it when I know something about our old stomping grounds that she doesn't.

"Then there's the old Putrid Mill out on Dead Man's Lane."

"*Excuse me?*"

"You heard me, dear. It's too disgusting to repeat in a place of fine dining."

"This is the IHOP for goodness sake, and except for that priest sitting by his lonesome, we're the only ones here."

"All right, calm down. But you *do* know where Dead Man's Lane is, don't you, dear?"

"No, and I was born and raised here."

"It's just a dirt road south of town, out in the country a good ways. Just stay on Cherry Road until it becomes McConnells Highway, follow it all the way to the town of McConnells, where the road changes names and becomes West McConnells Highway. Keep going straight. Then it will be nothing but country, so keep a sharp lookout for an immense oak on the left—Lordy, I don't know if it even exists anymore. Anyway, I have no idea how Dead Man's Lane got its name, but when I was growing up we called it the Putrid Mill because—why shoot a monkey, Abby, I can't recall that either."

"It's okay, Mama."

"Easy for you to say; it's not your brain that's turning into fish flakes. Now there was something else—oh yes, the Putrid Mill was one of the very first to close, if not the first. I remember because Uncle Benny used to work there until he was called up to serve in the Pacific. One day Aunt Connie came over, her eyes all red, and said that instead of hiring women workers to replace the men, like the mill had promised, they were going to shut down instead. Back then a lot of factories that made nonessential products—for the war effort, I mean—were converting to munitions or, in some cases, melting down their machinery and shipping the metal off to where it was needed.

"But the company that owned the Putrid Mill was more interested in profit than in patriotism, and after letting its employees go, hunkered down to wait out the war in a kudzu patch off of a dirt road. After the war, however, the men of Rock Hill remembered the broken promises made to their wives and looked for other jobs. Can you blame them, Abby?"

"No, ma'am."

"You know, of course, that your Uncle Benny never came back from Iwo Jima, but if he had, he wouldn't have wanted his old job back either. So anyway, one day, when you were just a baby, your daddy and I and Aunt Connie were taking a Sunday ride in the country and we found ourselves driving past Dead Man's Lane. It was your Aunt Connie's idea, otherwise I would never have agreed to it; you do understand, don't you?"

"No, Mama, as I have no earthly idea what it is that you agreed to do."

"To drive down the lane, of course, and take a look around the old mill. By then the lane was rutted and somewhat overgrown because nobody used it except for spooning couples." She paused to savor the shock on my face, and when none was forthcoming, she sighed heavily. "You do know what to spoon means, don't you, Abby?"

"I'm not rightly sure, ma'am," I said in my best

Gomer Pyle voice (which is pretty darn awful), "but is that why some children are born with silver spoons in their mouths?"

"Abby, be serious! Now where was I? Oh yes, well, the surprising thing was that the mill itself was untouched: no broken windows, no forced doors. Your daddy said he thought it was because the people were afraid of the owners and didn't want trouble. That made your Aunt Connie so mad she said she could spit cotton and we all laughed. After that we peeked in some of the windows, and do you know what? All the looms and such were still in there. I swan, Abby, anyone who knew how to operate that machinery could have waltzed right in there and woven chenille spreads—that's what the Putrid Mill was particularly famous for—well, not famous, but you know what I mean. That, and beach towels."

"Holy guacamole!" I shouted as the light of a thousand days dawned in my pea size brain. I jumped to my feet, knocking over my chair, just as Tamika, our waitress, arrived with a tray loaded down with our breakfast.

"Ab—" was all Mama could say as she watched her much anticipated pecan pancakes sail over her head and into the booth behind her. My poached eggs didn't even get airborne, and had to be scraped from the floor.

"I am so sorry, ladies," Tamika said.

Do you see what I mean about Rock Hillians? I'd tipped the chair directly into her path, for crying out loud. Fifty percent of Charlotteans would be excavating me a new anus, not apologizing to me.

I dug two twenty dollar bills from my purse and slapped them into our waitress's hand. "This should more than cover our meal, and you keep the change. Have a great day, Tamika." Next I grabbed Mama's arm and all but dragged her out the front door.

"But I didn't get my pecan cakes," she wailed.

"We'll get something to go from Bojangles," I said.

To be sure, I wasn't about to take a left turn on Dead Man's Lane on an empty stomach. My hunch was that together Mama and I had just solved the mystery of Charleston's counterfeit carpets. While I intended to confirm that hunch, I had no intention of getting caught. Yet on the outside chance that a dead woman showed up anywhere near Dead Man's Lane, I wanted her to have met her Maker on a full stomach, and for a Southern gal like me, a sausage biscuit would do just fine.

I explained my eureka moment to Mama and then briefed her on her assignment. Upon arriving at Dead Man's Lane—assuming we could find it—she was to wait in the car, on the driver's side, while I walked surreptitiously down the road. With any luck, she would be shaded by the immense water oak that she remembered. We would both have our cell phones on. Once I was able to get confirmation that the old mill was used clandestinely to manufacture fake antique rugs, I would immediately turn around and head back for the car. In the meantime, should another vehicle turn down Dead Man's Lane, Mama was to call and warn me of its approach. If questioned by anyone, she was to say that she'd gotten drowsy and pulled over for a nap.

With a few notable exceptions, most folks are still very kind to the elderly.

Unfortunately the word "unfortunately" must be used far too often to describe my life. We drove up and down West McConnells Highway, almost as far as the Cherokee and Union County lines, without spotting a massive water oak that stood alone by the highway. Although we came across a number of small lanes on the left-hand side of the road that otherwise appeared promising, they either bore numbers or had no signs at all.

On our sixth pass, about an hour and a half later, Mama stomped at the floor with her little taupe pump. "Stop, Abby, stop!"

"Why here? That's a new subdivision. I can see only one tree, and its trunk isn't any thicker than Paris Hilton's legs."

"Stop anyway!"

I pulled into the nearest driveway. Several dozen houses had recently been erected along a cluster of treeless streets, yet each street was named after a tree. I could see two home styles: ugly and uglier. I shuddered thinking of the children who would be reared in this place, which was neither a town nor true country.

"Look at that street to your right," Mama said. "It's named 'Water Oak.' And look at the lawn on this side, right up by the corner. You see that depression in the grass?"

"The one with the standing water? Otherwise known as Mosquitoville, South Carolina?"

"That's where the water oak was. When they dug

out the stump, they didn't fill it back in properly. I bet you anything that Putrid Mill is down this road."

"But it's paved, Mama."

"I think that's called progress, dear. Believe me, bumping down Dead Man's Lane in your granddaddy's old Ford was no picnic for the kidneys."

"I remember that rust bucket! He kept it out behind the garage, right?"

"Speak kindly of that car, Abigail, seeing as how that's where you got your start."

If the windows hadn't been closed, it would have taken me much longer to catch my breath. "I was conceived in a car?"

"And right here on Dead Man's Lane too. I know, that's an awful place to begin a life, but it wasn't like we planned it—in fact, your daddy swore up and down that it wouldn't happen, just so long as I stood on my head for half an hour afterward while saying the Lord's Prayer over and over again."

"Mama, I can't *believe* we're having this conversation." I looked up to the sunny heavens beyond the shoddy roofs of the prefabricated houses. "Obviously that was not a reliable method of birth control."

"Who knows," Mama said, sounding wistful. "All the blood rushed to my head and I fainted after only nine minutes. I sure miss your daddy something awful, even though he did have some odd ways about him."

"We're being watched," I said.

"Of course, dear. I know folks think I'm a cashew short of a bridge mix because I dress the way I do. But Abby, I'm telling you, all your daddy has to do is glance down from Heaven and he can spot me right off, because I haven't changed a thing since the day he died. Well, my hair—"

"No, Mama, she's coming out on the porch. What should I do?"

Mama gave a little gasp when she returned to earth and realized that the homeowner was now a broom length away from my car, but she recovered mighty fast. She leaned over my way, all smiles, while her manicured fingers slid under my right butt cheek and pinched hard. That was Mama's way of telling me to hold my tongue for the meanwhile.

I lowered the window on my side.

"Good morning," Mama drawled, each word dripping in fine, Upstate honey (to heck with the marbles). "Are you by any chance Cora Beth's daughter?"

"No ma'am."

"Are you sure? You look so much like her. It's the cheekbones, you know. Not many women are blessed like you. Sophia Loren comes to mind, and Angelina Jolie, but nobody else."

"Why bless your heart. You know, you remind me of somebody as well: Mozella Wiggins. You wouldn't by any chance be her, would you?"

"*Her*? Oh my, whatever gave you that idea?"

"No, of course not, you couldn't be her. She was in Junior League with me, eons ago. A psychopath in the making, if you ask me."

"A nutcase in the cracking," Mama said.

"A teapot in the breaking," I said.

Mama pinched me hard. "How could anyone forget her?" she asked. "I wasn't in Junior League—seeing as how it was out of my league—but everyone in Rock

Hill knew that wacko. By the way, I'm Miranda Sue Coldcutz—that's with a Z—and this is my daughter, Prunella Rae Washburn. Prunella has been living in Seattle for the last fifteen or so years, and I live in Charleston now in a retirement home. Last week she decided to pay her lonesome old mama a visit, and let me tell you, it's been wonderful! Then last night, on the spur of the moment, we decided to drive up here so I could show her some of the places I used to frequent when I was a girl, but everything has changed. I'm telling you, I've only been gone ten years myself, and I don't recognize anything anymore."

The homeowner, who had every right to be suspicious, smiled. "I couldn't agree with you more, and I've been here the entire time. I'm Cynthia LaBec Whitely, by the way. Is there anything specific you're looking for, Miranda?"

"Prunella Rae," Mama said, "close your ears. Cynthia," she said behind her hand, while affecting a loud whisper, "didn't there used to be a large tree there and a dirt road—"

"Dead Man's Lane," Cynthia said, and giggled. "But there was nothing dead about it on a Saturday night, was there? I swan, Miranda Sue. Half the war babies in Rock Hill were conceived there—including my very own Missy Kaye." Cynthia, who was Mama's age, and thus quite beyond the age of innocence, blushed and giggled again.

"So I *was* at the right place!" Mama pinched me out of pure excitement. "What about that old textile mill—didn't we call it Putrid Mill, or something like that?"

The look on Cynthia's face said it all.

27

Indeed, we did call it that. Oh Miranda Sue, I can't tell you what a delight it is to talk to someone who remembers the old days. Wouldn't y'all like to come in and set a spell—maybe have some coffee and cinnamon rolls. They're not homemade, and I do apologize for that, but it's just me and the grandchildren. I'm babysitting for Silas and Marner, you see, while Missy Kaye and Bubba Jr. have themselves one last fling at the beach. Not that the kids wouldn't enjoy it, mind you, but we're talking about *Cancun*."

"Silas and *Marner*?" I said. "How utterly literary of Missy Kaye and Bubba the Younger."

"I beg your pardon?"

"Oh don't mind my Prunella Rae," Mama said. "She's suffering from the beginning stages of BAD, which is brain atrophy disease."

Cynthia scratched her holy-roller bun. "I never heard of that."

"It's a very rare condition, thought to be contacted by eating freshwater scallops from the Irrawaddy Delta. It starts with a headache, but by the time the sufferers seek help, it's usually too late; the brain has already begun to shrink. There is nothing doctors can do to stop it. Eventually Prunella Rae's brain will end up being the size of a walnut, at which point she'll change her political affiliation before toppling over dead."

"Shouldn't she at least be in a hospital?"

"Well, she certainly shouldn't be driving. I don't know what got over me that I allowed it."

"A full-blown case of BAD I reckon, Miranda Sue." I managed to say it without cracking a smile.

Mama pinched hard enough to make a tortoise yelp. "Unfortunately her condition brings on spells of rudeness, but it isn't dangerous." She glared at me as her talons tightened. "You amuse yourself, dear, by taking a little walk while I go in the house with this nice lady and have coffee. You don't like coffee, dear, remember?"

"Yes, Prunella Sue, coffee very bad. Bitter taste. Me no like. Me like walk; look at pretty houses. Me walk that road," I said, pointing to the unmarked road. "Other side nature. Me like nature very much better."

"I thought *her* name was Prunella," Cynthia said to Mama, signs of doubt flickering across her eyes.

"BAD is an awful disease. The heartbreak is worse than that of psoriasis."

"Why I declare: the things you learn every day. So how about it, Miranda Sue, are you coming in for coffee?"

"I don't mind if I do." Mama's sugary drawl had been replaced by a trill of delight. "But before I do that, just to make sure that Prunella Rae doesn't get lost, how far does that road go now?"

"All the way down to the new mill. And it's paved too, every bit of it."

"New mill?" Mama and I asked in unison.

"Yes, where my Missy Kaye and her husband work. It's still a textile mill, as a matter of fact, but from what I hear, very upscale. Miss Kaye says they make one-of-a-kind Oriental rugs for movie stars and the super rich. What we used to call the la-dee-da types."

"Like Felicity Shamming's family? She moved to Rock Hill from Greensborough in the fifth grade, I believe."

"Exactly," Cynthia said. "Gee, I haven't thought of her in at least thirty years."

"They were here only one year, weren't they? Two at the most. I heard they moved away because there was nobody here who could properly appreciate the quality of their home and its extraordinary furnishings. Honestly, it put these modern-day McMansions all to shame."

"Good one, Mama," I said. "I assume they took their fine furnishings with them when they left, but what happened to the house? I don't remember hearing about a Shamming house when I was growing up."

"Her lucidity comes and goes," Mama said quickly, her nails digging into a one-inch chunk of my buttocks.

Cynthia gave me a pitying glance. "The same thing happened to the Shamming house that happens to many mansions across the South, and probably across the country; it got turned into a funeral home."

"I don't remember that either," I said. "We had houses that had been turned into funeral homes, but nothing *that* spectacular."

"The disease," Mama muttered. "It breaks my heart."

"It must be just awful," Cynthia said.

"Yes, Mama's awful," I said, "just awful."

Cynthia took several long steps backward. "Miranda Sue, are you sure she'll be all right on her own out here?"

"She'll be fine as frog's hair split three ways. The doctors assure me that she has at least two months to go before she gets to the walnut stage."

Mama pinched me again before climbing out on the passenger side. If I'd have had a bean burrito for breakfast instead of sausages, I might have gotten revenge.

"Have fun with the boys," I said.

"Marner is a girl," Cynthia said, and turned quickly away. Mama, who was obviously enjoying her role to the hilt, followed closely behind.

In my opinion, roads are meant to be driven on, preferably in motorized vehicles, and as long as I kept my cell phone at the ready, it was probably a lot safer if I drove than walked. After all, a dachshund has longer legs that I do, and if I were to be chased on foot, I would undoubtedly end up having to dive into a thicket of brambles somewhere along the way.

But it was smooth sailing down that unmarked asphalt road. Halfway there I left the houses behind and drove through second growth mixed pine and hardwood forest. Although I thought I knew what to expect, upon turning the last bend I was so taken aback that the gum literally fell out of my mouth. I popped my sugar free Dentine back in and stared.

To both my left and right sprawled a parking lot

with dozens of empty spaces—possibly even hundreds. In fact, there was not a car in sight. This was exactly how it should have been in the Upstate region of South Carolina on a Sunday morning. Had Jesus himself reported for work, he'd have been given a stern lecture on the evils of desecrating the Sabbath and sent home.

At any rate, ahead of me loomed a typical turn-of-the-century mill building, with its castlelike brick facade, but this one sported a fresh coat of white paint. Its many windows were flanked with wooden shutters in good repair, their bright turquoise color perhaps hinting at the beauty contained within.

There were no signs of any kind: no arrows to direct incoming trucks; no proud company logo; not even any reserved parking spaces. It was this very omission of information, rather than anything that I *did* see, that set the alarm bells off in my head. Being my mama's daughter, however, has doomed me to a life of not taking anything at face value.

The first thing I had to decide was how to play this card. Should I park facing the exit and near the woods, or should I play it cool and pull right up to the front door? In the first scenario, I could practice my creeping and skulking skills, but in the second scenario, I was Miss Somebody: a dye or yarn saleswoman, perhaps one whose flight had gotten her in a day early and who decided to drive out to familiarize herself so she wouldn't feel so stressed come Monday morning. That was just the sort of thing folks did all the time to soothe their nerves and give themselves a leg up on the competition.

In the first scenario, if I were caught, I would pretend to be a curious Sunday driver—unless it was Big Larry doing the catching. In that case I would scream bloody murder and beg for mercy.

Scenario number two called for much better bluffing skills. What if the person—or persons—who stopped me called my bluff by stating that this mill produced its own dyes and all its yarn needs? I'd be much better off selling some obscure metal machine part named after George Eliot's Silas Marner, something that nobody in their right mind had ever heard of, because it didn't exist: such as a calibrated *renram* brace for metrically calibrated *salis* looms. If challenged, I'd have to act puzzled at first, and then angry, blaming my secretary for his incompetence in lining up this appointment.

After far too much deliberation, I chose to sell the very expensive and much needed renram brace (every commercial loom needs at least one). I parked my car directly in front of the entrance, left the engine running, and casually walked up and tested the doors. Of course they were locked. What a doofus I was—wait just one cotton-picking minute! The door on the left wasn't flush with the one on the right. That meant the mechanism hadn't latched properly when it was shut. And sure enough, with a jerk and a tug, it came right open!

The most astonishing thing of all was that no alarm deployed. Was this a trap? It had to be. Anyone bright enough to set up a successful counterfeit carpet business was not going to leave it unguarded and unlocked on a Sunday out of laziness or forgetfulness. I was already a goner and so was Mama: coffee with Miranda Sue, my hot cross buns! And here we thought we were being so clever, so droll. Oh well, life was a terminal illness, wasn't it? None of us got out of the experience alive; it all boiled down to when and how—not *if*—we croaked. Wasn't awareness of that little fact supposed to make impending death easier? Ha, if only I could believe that.

I stepped inside and shut the door behind me. As long I was up Dead Man's Creek without a paddle, I owed it to myself to see what sort of operation Magic Genie Cleaners was running up here in the old Putrid Mill building.

The foyer was well-lit because it was capped by a skylight, but a wise Abby would have taken a quick peek and then hightailed it out of there. But oh no, I just had to see what was on the other side of a pair of solid oak doors straight ahead that seemed to beckon me. The fact that they too were unlocked could only be a sign that for once fate was on my side.

I'm still not sure how it happened; I just know that the second set of doors closed behind me before I could find the light switch. I tried turning the knobs every which way but Sunday but finally had to concede that somehow the doors had become locked. Now there I was, in a space as dark as a well digger's shoe soles, without an exit strategy. Poor Greg was going to have to shop for a child-size coffin. Or maybe not. If I could stop panicking long enough to gather my wits—a darn hard thing to do in the dark—I might think of *something*.

The doomed Abby was debating with her Pollyanna

side when I heard the outer door close. The argument ended abruptly as instinct took over and I flattened myself against the nearest wall. Immediately I began to feel my way to a corner so that I had only to kick and bite in one direction, should I be attacked in the dark.

"I saw her come in here," a man's voice said. "And I assume, since that's her car outside—"

"Never assume anything," a woman snapped.

"Yes sir—I mean, ma'm."

"Just shut up and keep looking."

The voices were familiar. The man certainly wasn't Big Larry. Nor Andy. Nor Fig. I'd never heard Big Tina speak, so the female could be her. (I've known some very large women who had very small voices, and some tiny women with the vocal chords of a grizzly bear.) But not only were these voices familiar, I'd have been willing to swear on a night spent with Cousin Imogene's rat collection that I heard these two voices before and in conjunction with each other.

Why slap me up the side of the head and call me Charlie Brown! The voices in the dark belonged to the ducal dummies of some made-up European country. And here I thought we'd managed to give them the early bird slip; not a single car had driven past as we chatted with Miranda Sue. And while I don't have the eagle eyes Greg sometimes accuses me of having, surely I would have noticed a vehicle in the rear mirror as I drove down to the mill. Instead, it was as if this buffoonish pair had dropped from the ceiling in the outer lobby, and let me assure you, Tom Cruise they were not.

"Shall I cut on the lights?" the man asked, using our charming Carolina turn of phrase.

"You do," the woman growled, "and your ass is grass."

"Does that mean I'll be fired?"

"Let's put it this way—you're fired anyway, but I definitely won't take you back if you cut on the lights."

He said nothing in response. As a matter of fact I heard nothing for what seemed like many minutes. Perhaps they had heard me and were quietly, slowly, moving in my direction. At any second they might reach out and grab me. Just thinking about it made my skin crawl, and I was torn between the desire to scream and get it all over with or—and this I found very strange—to fall into a deep, all encompassing sleep.

The rational Abby, the one who, it might be argued, had been on a long summer vacation, fought hard to follow a third course of action, and that was to do as little as possible. I had to breathe, granted, and so I did. I also resolved to remain standing, as that took up less floor space than sitting and might make detection from above more difficult. Other than that, all I needed to do was remain alert and listen in the dark.

Remaining alert—ah, that was the hard part. I tried praying, which was a huge mistake; my consciousness began a rapid descent into Never Never Land. In order to put the brakes on the sand man's coach, I tried thinking about sex. Alas, that too was a total bust. In movies, not only can the heroines gyre and gimble with Wade, somehow they can manage to do so with broken ribs, and with bullets whizzing past their ears.

I, on the other hand, couldn't generate a spark of lust; George Clooney could have trotted by naked and I wouldn't have given a darn (assuming I'd seen him, of course).

Without any outside stimulus it was impossible to judge how much time had passed when I came to the conclusion that I had to do *something* or risk turning into a fossil. It seemed at least an hour had passed since I'd heard their graces' voices—if indeed I'd even heard them. Maybe the stress brought on by trespassing had caused me to hallucinate. I wasn't exactly your perfect buttoned-down coed in college, and on one or two occasions—okay, it was just one—I'd experienced a genuine, chemically induced hallucination, and let me tell you, hallucinations can seem awfully real. Perhaps Big Larry had managed to somehow taint our breakfasts.

Finally I couldn't stand feeling helpless anymore and began inching my way farther into the dark unknown. If their graces possessed a motion detector and suddenly pounced on me, so be it. The worst they could do was kill me—no, torture would be worse, and that's exactly what waiting in the dark was: torture.

My left hand felt its way along the wall like a giant fleshy spider, one equipped with five of the most complex sensors in the universe. Coupled with our large brains, human fingertips can coax music out of wood boxes with horse hair bows, cut up and safely stitch back together fellow humans, and weave intricate designs out of wool and caterpillar secretions. Without any other stimuli to divert attention from my hand, I felt every tiny imperfection on the surface of the wall, every pinprick-size bubble in the paint.

When my left hand pressed up against a doorjamb, I nearly jumped out of my sandals. I could swear that I gasped so loudly that Mama and Miranda Sue must have heard it. I froze for another eternity, waiting to feel the consequences of this involuntary action across my back—or maybe my head. In the movies it was usually a long-handled flashlight, or a shovel. After two minutes—or an hour—when nothing happened, I again threw caution to the wind and groped for the doorknob.

What were the chances that it too would be unlocked? Or that there would be a light switch inside, just to the right of the door, and that Abigail Wiggins Timberlake Washburn would be stupid enough, or curious enough, to cut it on? The chances were pretty good if it was a trap, and yes, yours truly is just that stupid.

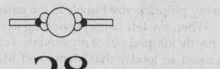

28

There were ten switches in all, and at least I wasn't stupid enough to flip them all on in rapid succession. The first fluorescent bulb to kick on was in the far right corner of the room, so that by the time all the lights were fully operational, my eyes had adjusted enough so I was no longer seeing floating images.

"Lord have mercy!" I said, no longer concerned about who heard me or from how far away.

Before me spread a vast room full of enormous looms, one that reached almost from the floor to the ceiling. Three-quarters of the looms were empty, but stretched across the remainder were Oriental carpets, or the beginnings of Oriental carpets. Immediately adjacent to each loom was a work station, each with its own computer and monitor, and an assortment of large, yarn-bearing spools overhead. A pile of carpets matching the one on the loom or, it could be reasonably supposed, the space for such a pile, was on the floor beside each work station.

I am not the quickest study, but even I was able to

put two and two together and get sixteen. Or even twenty. The folks who owned Magic Genie Cleaners couldn't care less about cleaning and preserving carpets. Somewhere in this vast building they had scanned the "borrowed" carpets into computers and were feeding the images into the individual computers that operated these. I already knew that the quality of good bogus antiques could fool the general public, so depending on their distribution system . . .

"So what do you think?"

It was a woman's voice, and it seemed to be coming from above; had I been as religious as Mama, I might have thought it was God. I was fairly certain it did not belong to the same woman I'd heard in the blackened hallway.

"You must be tired, Abby. Wasn't your bed at the Princess and the Pea comfortable?"

I scanned the upper reaches of the towering space for a balcony but had no success. "Who are you?" I demanded. "And where are you, damn it?"

"I'm speaking to you from Charleston, Abby, but you can look at any of the television monitors."

I strode indignantly—yet with dignity—to the nearest work station. "Heavens to Betsy," I exclaimed. "I can't believe it's you."

"I wish I could say the same about you, Abby. I was rather fond of you in the beginning. I actually thought we might grow to be friends. This woman is different, I told myself. She isn't stuck up like the other Charleston folks. But no matter how many breaks I cut you— and believe me, I cut you plenty—you just couldn't seem to mind your own business."

"For example? I mean really, what did I ever do to you?"

"You mean besides dump shrimp cocktail sauce on my Savonnerie carpet and then announce to the world that it was a copy? Oh of course you do. You had to begin a whole new career running all over Charleston and Timbuktu—" She laughed bitterly. "Timbuktu, now that's a good one! I'll bet you'd find some pretty decent carpets there. Anyway, what business was it of yours if people were too stupid to figure out that they'd been scammed?"

"Would the death of a young woman make it my business? Because I do believe that a very nice young saleswoman named Gwen, who worked for Pasha's Palace, was trying to warn me that she'd figured out your scam, on account of at least one if not more rather costly originals slipped through your quality control procedures."

I had the distinct displeasure of watching Kitty Bohring react on a half-dozen monitors simultaneously. The way she threw back her head, her throaty laugh—Vincent Price couldn't have done a better job.

"It was such a shame getting rid of that rug, but by the time we got that *nice* young woman ready to swim with the fishes, it was beyond repair. Really, Abby, you might consider giving your friends etiquette classes; my people had to put six bullets in her at close range before she quit struggling."

"You want me to teach courses on how to be murdered peacefully?"

"You're spunky, Abby, I like that; I could use you in

this business. Your mother, on the other hand, is downright annoying."

"*Mama*? What have you done with Mama?"

"Relax, Abby. Cynthia is serving her coffee and cake, just as she promised, so that you and I could visit. By the way, dear, there are no grandchildren named Marner and Silas. I was hoping you were educated enough to catch that, and I see that you were. However, your mother's story about you suffering from brain atrophy disease was a little over the top. You see what I mean?"

I nodded vigorously. "Yes, ma'am. In addition to my Manners for Victims class you want me to train my mama to lie better."

"In a nutshell, yes. And next time—should there even be a next time—I don't want her tagging along. That's extremely annoying for everyone involved, and I dare say, it has absolutely ruined a perfectly good Sunday for a great many folks—including that poor demented cousin of yours."

My mind raced through my family tree. Cousin Willard over in Florence had been falsely accused of flashing, but his reputation was forever ruined; Aunt Marilyn down in Savannah had long since crossed the divide that separates eccentric from peculiar, but she had yet to slide into full-blown dementia; and Uncle Norbitt from up in Kannapolis pretended to be crackers to get out of Korea, but since then his only odd habit was that he preferred to walk on his hands instead of his feet. Once you got used to that, and didn't try to make him clap while standing on a stairs, he was a perfectly ordinary man. That was pretty much it except for . . .

"You didn't!" I shouted, my voice echoing in the cavernous room.

"But I did. I thought the tale she told you last night provided the perfect means of disposal."

"You were there? At Cousin Imogene's?"

"Don't be silly, dear—you don't mind if I call you dear, do you, dear? It's such a Southern thing to do, and I'm trying so hard to lose my brittle Yankee ways. Anyway, I wasn't there in Rock Hill in *person*, of course; that's what a staff is for. That's why I'm hoping to hire you. By the way, please thank your mother—or should I say your mama—for calling your auntie from a pay phone and repeating the directions in a voice so loud I almost heard it down here. They were good directions too: much better than Mapquest's. My people had no trouble getting in place before you all showed up."

"That's *y'all*, Kitty."

"Right."

"And whatever you do, only use it in a plural context."

"Will do. So Abby, here's the deal: I understand that your business at the Den of Iniquity is doing well—"

"Antiquity," I grunted through clenched teeth. *"Iniquity* would be your cup of tea."

"Good one. Now where was I? Oh yes, I figure, now that you have some employees to help out, you are free to delegate some of that responsibility and take on a job that would be a lot more challenging."

"Such as strangling the Devil with a spool of white yarn?"

"Good luck. That spool weighs in the neighborhood of two hundred pounds. Now where was I? Oh yes,

your duties would involve a fair amount of traveling—
since you no longer have children at home, I don't see
that as a problem. You'll be establishing markets for
our—uh, higher end products."

"You mean, fencing the *real* antique carpets?"

"How crudely, yet delightfully, put. Abby, I've no
doubt that you and I will get along famously."

I seethed with hatred for the woman who wanted so
badly to be loved by Charleston. "*This* is no way to
make friends, Kitty."

"Oh, I know that. But do try your best, darling, otherwise your poor mama might suffer an early stroke.
As advanced as medicine is these days, we still have
far too many cases of people dying from causes that
are never properly explained. My own sister's death
was a bit of a mystery."

"You killed her?" I asked the question not out of
shock, or because I was morbidly curious, but because
I needed to know if there were limits to the things
Kitty Bohring would do.

"You better believe it. She didn't want to move to the
South. Can you imagine that? She thought y'alls were
all a bunch of uneducated rednecks who talk like
Larry the Cable Guy. Do you know, he's not even from
down here?"

"I do, and *y'all's* is a possessive."

"*What?*"

"Never mind." What kind of fool was I, anyway?
Not that it would ever happen, but did I ever want
Kitty Bohring to blend seamlessly into Charleston society? I delivered a quick mental whipping to my mind
with a couple of stalks of sweetgrass. "Seriously Kitty,

speaking as your new best friend, don't you think our relationship would work better if one of us wasn't always under the gun—so to speak."

"You'll be handsomely paid, Abby—not that you need it. I know that you enjoy your work, making the sale, and not only will this job constantly give you such opportunities, but you will be moving amongst the crème de la crème of society. And don't forget that I've had the distinct pleasure of watching you interact with society—even fake aristocracy—and I know you can more than hold your own."

I pirouetted so Kitty Bohring and her evil minions could see the mocking smile on my petite mug from all angles. "Kitty, *dear*, a padded cell is far too good for you. You belong in a regular state penitentiary where you can make lots of close friends. And although I don't approve of the death penalty, there is a part of me that almost wishes that you've killed someone in Texas and you'll get extradited there. I hear they have a special rehabilitation program for convicted murderers, but you have to be dead first to apply."

"Tsk tsk, Abby," the would-be grand dame said, shaking her head on a dozen or more screens, "is that any way to speak to your employer?"

"You stupid, social-climbing bitch," I hissed. "You are not *now* nor will you ever *be* my employer."

"I've had enough of your impertinence for now," Kitty Bohring said, "but don't think that this is the last you've seen of me. Miss Kitty gets what Miss Kitty wants, and she wants you, Abby."

The screens blackened, and before I could gather

my thoughts, a single door to my right opened and in strode the giant himself, Big Larry.

"There's no use running, little lady. All the outside doors are locked, and I got me a gun, see?" He waved an automatic weapon of some kind. Then again, it could have been one of those superduper water pistols available at Wal-Mart. My nerves were stretched as tight as a gnat's ass over a steel drum—pardon my vulgarity—so my powers of observation were not at their keenest.

"You can't get away with this," I said. The second my lips closed I realized how stupid that must have sounded; that was a line straight out of a very grade B movie.

"I'm not going to argue with you, Abby." The wicked giant had long legs, so he was approaching rapidly. "But you must admit, it's really rather a clever racket. We literally pull the rug out from beneath the customer"—he laughed diabolically—"make dozens of exact copies, which we sell all over the globe; then we sell the original to some idiot with too much money to spend. Meanwhile, we've replaced the original with a cheap knockoff and everyone's happy. Well, that was the case until you came along."

"I doubt if you'll be very happy where you're going, Big Lar—"

From somewhere to the left of the nearest work station two people, dressed all in black, including ski masks, popped out of nowhere and positioned themselves between Big Larry and me. One of them was pointing a gun at Big Larry, while the other began to approach me, frantically waving her hands.

"Freeze! FBI," I heard her partner shout. He sounded remarkably like the ding-dong duke who'd been tailing us for the last day.

"Mrs. Washburn," the female purred, "don't worry, we really are FBI." Somehow, despite the fact that she was wearing gloves, she managed to flip open a badge.

"Why I'll be hog-tied and dippity-doodled," I said. "So you *are*! But you're faux nobility, aren't you?"

"Very faux. You really make a much better queen of a make-believe country than I do the Duchess of Malberry. Although, in my defense, my feeble attempt at portraying her grace has met with better results before."

It suddenly occurred to me—much to my extreme horror—that the humongous weapon Big Larry was carrying might shoot more rounds than the smaller guns the FBI agents held. If so, then I was playing right into his hands by making small talk with her daffiness.

"Shouldn't you get back to work, sweetie?" I tried to keep my tone light, but there was a heck of a lot of commotion happening behind her, none of which I was able to see. Whichever direction I leaned to get a gander, the female FBI agent leaned as well. It was as if she was purposely blocking my vision.

I felt and heard a thud simultaneously. It didn't take a genius to know that Goliath had fallen, even though I hadn't heard a shot being fired. My agent must have received a message through an earpiece because shortly after that she nodded and stepped aside.

"The FBI always gets its man, Mrs. Washburn. Its

woman too; although I am sorry to say that Miss Kitty Bohring took her own life rather than surrender to our agents in Charleston. For your sake I hope that she really wasn't a personal friend of yours."

"I could take umbrage with you for even asking that, Agent, uh, Agent Whatever-your-name-is."

She whipped off her mask but kept on her black kidskin gloves. "Whew, that thing is hot! Agent Krukowski—Elizabeth Krukowski. Since I don't even know what the word 'umbrage' means, I'll choose to interpret your answer as a no. By the way," she said, shaking her long brown hair, "you would have made one heck of an agent—with the proper training of course."

I barely heard her last comment. There were at least two other Zorrolike creatures in the room, and they were standing next to the immense spread-eagled body of Big Larry. The pretend duke was with them, and that's precisely where I wanted to be as well.

29

Although I do realize that humanity is somehow connected, and that the death of even just one of us diminishes all mankind, nonetheless, I approached the scene before me with a mixture of awe and revulsion. Spread out on the floor, without even his personality to contain him, Big Larry seemed to take up twice as much space in death as he did in life.

I read somewhere that nowadays funeral homes are stocking plus-size coffins in order to accommodate the helpless victims of fast food chains, but I doubted if even one of those would be adequate to see Big Larry into the ground. Since Charleston is a port city, stacked to the gills with containers, it would make more sense to pick up the deceased in one of those, seal it, and use that as his final home. The only downside in my opinion is that metal containers are generally fireproof. The Devil's flunkies were going to have their work cut for them.

"I didn't see him go down," I said. "What happened?"

"You shouldn't be here, Mrs. Washburn," the fake duke said. "Agent Krukowski," he bellowed, "take her outside!"

"Agent Nadel," she said calmly, "we owe a lot to Mrs. Washburn, not the least of which is an explanation."

Agent Nadel grunted and pointed to one of the other Zorros with his chin

"I shot six rounds into him," said the third Zorro. To his credit, he sounded sad. "I used a silencer; that's why you didn't hear anything, that and the fact that Agent Krukowski kept you occupied. Plus, all this machinery humming makes a lot of ambient noise."

Agent Nadel grunted again, but with less hostility. "We can't have civilians watching people die—not if we can help it."

"Thanks—although to be entirely honest," I said, "it would have been interesting."

The fourth Zorro snickered, but stopped abruptly when Agent Nadel whipped off his mask and glared at him. "How about some professionalism, Agent Newman?"

Suddenly I felt like throwing up. One minute I'd been fascinated by the corpse of a killer, the next I saw a *man* lying dead on the floor at my feet. No doubt Big Larry would have happily killed me, had perhaps killed others, but he was a husband and a father, as well as somebody's son. At some point he had even been an innocent child brimming with potential. What a waste of life, what certain heartbreak for others.

I felt Agent Krukowski's arm across my shoulder. "Mrs. Washburn, are you going to be alright?"

"Yes—just not anytime soon. I feel like it's some-how—I know it doesn't make any sense, but—"

"That it's your fault?"

"Yes! How did you know?"

"Because you're a kind, caring human being, who unfortunately got mixed up in this awful mess. But you have to understand, Lively Tupperman's death had nothing to do with you. He was going to take out Agent Nadel; that's why we brought him down."

"Come again?"

"Big Larry."

"Ah yes, of course. I remember now. Mama read that off his library card— Mama! We have to save Mama!"

"Where is she?"

"What do you *mean* where is she? I was beginning to think you spooks lived inside our underwear. How come you don't know where Mama is?"

"Mrs. Washburn—"

"You have your arm around my shoulder; you may as well call me Abby."

"Thank you. Abby, as you've probably guessed by now, we've been keeping close tabs on you."

"You stayed at the Princess and the Pea, didn't you?"

"Don't you think that with a name like that, they should have provided better mattresses?"

"For real—hey, we don't have time to compare motel amenities."

"Right. As I was about to say, we knew you were headed out here, so when you stopped at Bojangles we went on ahead and got into place. Security was abso-lutely appalling—although easy on us. We took everyone out, except for Mr. Tupperman. Sorry, Abby, but we needed to keep him in the game in hopes of getting a confession out of him. But thanks to you, we did better than that! Your conversation with the Rug Lord herself was brilliant."

I shook off her arm. "But Mama! We have to get back to Mama!"

"Yes, certainly. Where is she?"

"She's having coffee with a killer named Cynthia," I wailed.

They used to say that death and taxes were the only two inevitable things (although the very wealthy get closer each year to avoiding both). Now they've added a third exception to this rule: Abigail Louise Washburn cannot be kept from her beloved Mama.

Short of pistol-whipping me into submission and tying me up with yarn, I left the FBI no choice. In fact, so intently (and perhaps eloquently) did I plead my case that they let me pick my own team; I picked Agents Elizabeth Krukowski and Clyde Dilworth Standingwater. Agent Standingwater was the man who'd brought Big Larry down. He was also a member of the Cheyenne Nation.

We all got into Agent Krukowski's car, which is the same car that had trailed us up from Charleston. Upon sighting Cynthia's house, Agent Krukowski pulled over and cut the engine.

"Who's that child on the porch?" Agent Standingwater asked.

"That's no child—that's my mother!"

Although the agents may have muttered words of

admonishment, neither of them made an effort to stop me from jumping from the car. I took off running so fast that I plumb left my shadow behind (it made an embarrassed appearance a nanosecond later).

"Mama," I screamed. "Mama!"

My minimadre was both tapping her feet and spinning her pearls. In her free hand she held her cell phone.

"It's about time, Abigail Louise. I was fixing to come look for you, and in my brand new Naturalizers too. I could have gotten these new pumps all scuffed up."

"Are you all right, Mama? Where's Cynthia?"

"She's taking a nap, dear." She stiffened when she noticed my trailing entourage. "Who, pray tell, are these people? Oh Lordy, they look like Lithuanian acrobats to me; I saw some once on the Ed Sullivan show who dressed just like that. Abby, are you being held hostage by insurgents from the Baltics?"

"No Mama, they're FBI agents. It turns out that Kitty Bohring was the mastermind behind an international distribution ring of stolen and counterfeit carpets. She's dead now, by the way. She committed suicide just a few minutes ago, rather than be taken into custody."

"Oh, my." She let go of her pearls and scooped me into her arms. "You poor, poor baby."

"I didn't see it, Mama; it happened in Charleston. But I was there when Lively Larry Tupperman went to meet his Maker—although again I was spared the sight. Agent Krukowski, here, kept me distracted during the actual event."

Like it or not, both agents got a dose of "Mama love." While she fussed over them, holding their heads to her bosom, each in turn, and giving them memorable whiffs of her very expensive French perfume called Eau de Pan, commingled with the odors one might expect to pick up on a stress-filled trip sans deodorant, I sneaked into the house. Just inside the back door, mere inches from where Mama was marking the FBI with her scent, Cynthia sat slumped in a dinette chair, her head resting on a Formica-topped table. The drool seeping from her mouth was frothy in places.

I dashed back out. "Mama, that's no mere nap. What have you *done* to her?"

Mama reluctantly released the very handsome Agent Standingwater, who likewise seemed somewhat reluctant to stand on his own. "I made her some coffee, dear, and then we chatted. It's as simple as that."

"Details, Mama!"

"Well, you know that she lied about the grandchildren. How evil can one person get? One minute those two little darlings were happy and healthy, and just as cute as buttons, and the next minute—poof!" Mama snapped her fingers. "She killed them! Just like that she killed them by saying they never existed."

"Listen to yourself, Mama; she couldn't have killed them if they never existed in the first place."

"Abigail, this is no time for logic. Now where was I? Oh yes, so she's trying to keep me occupied, and she has a gun, but she's Southern too, you see, so she asks me if I want coffee. Of *course* I want coffee; it's Sunday morning, for goodness sake. Does a hoppy toad want a nice moist spot in the garden? Anyway, then she confesses that she doesn't know *how* to make a good cup of coffee on account of she grew up in a culture in which caffeine was forbidden and has never developed a taste for the stuff—did I tell y'all that this isn't even her house?"

"No ma'am," Agent Krukowski said.

"It belongs—I guess belong*ed* is the word—to Kitty Bohring. This whole development does. It has no official name, because they don't want it on a map, but some of the folks call it—in fun, they say—Stepford Acres. My, but I do seem to prattle on."

"Prattle, please," Agent Standingwater said. "I insist."

Mama beamed. "Very well then, just for you. At any rate, as I was going to say, I managed to convince Cynthia that she might like coffee the way I fix it: with lots and lots of sugar and milk, and just a pinch of cinnamon. Then when she was helping me hunt for the cinnamon, I emptied the contents of my pill case into her mug. The rest, as they say, is his—"

Much to my surprise, Mama didn't seem the least bit surprised to have her story cut short by the arrival of two squad cars and an ambulance.

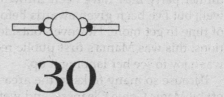

30

And what *was* in your pill case?" Rob's mother, Sandra Goldburg, is capable of conducting interrogations in the most charming of Southern accents, while at the same time not moving a single facial muscle. One gets the impression that her face has been freeze-dried with disapproval, and that just one wrong word from you will cause the facade to crumble into the salad serving bowl, where it will disappear amidst the croutons and bacon bits.

"Oh just about everything," Mama said. She was thoroughly enjoying her moment in the spotlight, and was oblivious to the existence of the anti-pill-popping, but wine-swigging, contingent of contemporary society, or else she didn't give her proverbial gnat's ass.

"Be more specific."

"Mama, please," Rob begged.

"Yes, Mother Goldburg," Bob pleaded even more strongly.

My dear friends had every right to demand that Sandra toe the line tonight. The occasion was, after all, a dinner to celebrate Mama's heroism. Okay, so the dinner party may have been thrown in my honor as well, but I've been given awards before, and have lots of time to get more. However, outside of church functions, this was Mama's first public recognition, and it was a joy to see her lapping it up.

Because so many folks in the area had been ripped off by Magic Genie Cleaners, and were glad to see the counterfeit ring exposed, pressure was brought on City Hall to throw Mama an official parade. Since parades are expensive—there is always a huge amount of cleanup—so Mama's route was very short, just once around the Battery in a horse and carriage, but afterward she said it was the high point of her life. Personally, I think it was well worth the $25,000 I donated toward the city's new sewer system.

That evening, because Mama's head was still in the clouds, she stepped right up to Sandra's challenge. "Let's see. I've had that pill case for a very long time, so there was a birth control pill in it, two acetaminophen, a thyroid pill, a muscle relaxer, three tranquilizers, and two prescription sleeping pills. The timed release kind."

Sandra's face thawed instantaneously. "You could have killed that poor woman with your drugs! You're not a doctor. Shame on you, Mozella. *Shame on you!*"

Unfortunately, the two women had been seated next to each other, and I could see Mama wince with each word Mrs. Goldburg practically spat in her face.

"There wasn't a chance I could have killed her with my drugs," Mama said. "She hated my coffee; she took just three sips, and then only because I dared her. If I hadn't tapped her on the head— Oops, did I say that?"

We all gasped, but I gasped the loudest. "Mama, you *didn't*," I wailed.

"It was only a light tap, dear. Like this." Mama picked up her salad plate and gave Sandra a rather solid thwack on the noggin.

Well, at least from my perspective it looked that way, but Sandra just snorted in derision. "I'm sure it was harder than that. But just so you know, Mozella, if you weren't the mother of my son's best friend, I would sue you."

Too bad Bob had gone to so much trouble to make such a lovely gourmet dinner, because at that point no one was eating. The musk-oxen scrotums stuffed with lichens were getting cold on the serving platter, and the side dish of thrice boiled dandelion leaves cooked in a reduction of farm-raised caribou broth had developed a sheen that didn't appear to be what the cook intended. It was time to move the show along, for the best was yet to come. But first I needed an answer to a very important question.

"Mama, did you tell the paramedics what you did? Because I certainly did not hear you mention it to them."

Mama gave me the evil eye. "I did; you can ask Greg."

"What?"

Greg cleared his throat. "While Mozella was waiting for you to return from reconnoitering, she called and told me everything. I *am* a retired police officer, remember? You see, she was afraid that if she called 911, their arrival might put you in danger. I talked to the York County sheriff on her behalf, and a couple of squad cars and an ambulance were waiting just about a mile down the road. Did you notice how quickly they arrived on the scene, Abby?"

"Uh—sorry, Mama."

"Apology accepted, dear." Dang it, it just wasn't right that Greg and Mama had kept me out of the loop. It's not like I would have disapproved of Mama conking a criminal on the bean with a frying pan. Okay, I might have disapproved a little; it *was* assault, after all.

"Well, no matter how you slice and dice it," Sandra said, her face beginning to refreeze around the edges, "it's still assault. That poor woman has every right to press charges."

Although Bob rolled his eyes, he was careful to do it in a way that neither Rob nor his mother could see. I pitied my friend. Our experiment with Aunt Nanny had come to naught, as she had fled the Rob-Bobs' house bleating in despair and exasperation. Sandra Goldburg had repeatedly thrown out Aunt Nanny's stash of timothy hay, and had, on more than one occasion, served mutton for dinner when it was her turn to cook.

Unless our surprise, due to arrive any minute—it was past due, in fact—worked, it looked as if Rob's mother was going to be a permanent part of my friends' household. Without as much as asking, she had declared her intention of taking over two of the six bedrooms, the butler's pantry, and the maid's room, gutting all of them and turning them into one grand mother-in-law suite. In fact, the first of many designers was scheduled to arrive on the morrow. One of them had even been on HGTV.

Sadly, my respect for Rob had eroded a great deal since his mother's arrival in Charleston. Not only had she taken over the house, which was only half his, but she'd practically taken over his half of The Finer Things as well. The woman was insidious, like an algae bloom on an ornamental pond; one didn't really notice how much she'd taken over until it was too late.

Unless something drastic happened, the Rob-Bobs were bound to split up, and become just ordinary singles named Bob and Rob, names that, frankly, had no cachet. More importantly, I might be forced to take sides and choose one of the two with whom to remain friends, which was the last thing I wanted to do; although I've known Rob much longer than Bob, and I *do* consider him my best friend, I could never just throw Bob's friendship away.

"A penny for your thoughts," Rob said. The man is a mind reader, but fortunately he has become myopic in recent years.

"A penny?" I said in mock indignation. "I'll have you know that my thoughts are worth at least a dollar now because—"

The doorbell rang just then, a fact for which I'll be eternally grateful. Bob and I jumped up simultaneously, both knocking back our chairs. Silly us; we were like children who believed Santa Claus was waiting on the other side of a couple of stained wooden planks.

"What the heck?" Rob said.

"I bet that's the flowers I ordered," Sandra said. "They were supposed to arrive three hours ago. In

Charlotte they would have arrived on time. Not only is this guy *not* getting a tip, but I'm not paying for the damn things."

But by then the door was wide open and there were no flowers to be seen, only Cousin Imogene and an oversized handbag. Her eyes lit up when she saw me, and she was practically ecstatic to see Mama. After the requisite hugs and kisses, I introduced her all around. To be sure, I saved the best for last.

"Now," I whispered.

"Everyone," Bob boomed in his marvelous basso profundo, "Abby and I have an announcement to make."

"And what would that be, darling?" Sandra said. "Will she be inviting that woman to this so-called dinner of yours?"

"Mama!" Rob's jaw twitched with anger.

"Why that *is* a lovely idea, Mrs. Goldberg," I said. "Cousin Imogene, seeing as how this *is* my celebratory dinner, I feel as if I have a right to ask you: would you care to have dinner with us? We've hardly begun."

"I'd love to, thank you very much."

Sandra Goldburg, who'd always been a class act in my eyes, turned her back on the new arrival and addressed the ceiling in low but quite audible tones. "What's next? Are y'all going to ask her to move in?"

"Thank you, Mother Goldburg, for *yet* another wonderful suggestion!" Bob slipped a scrawny arm around Imogene's scrawny shoulders. Funny, but the two of them looked as related as it is possible to be.

Rob looked stunned. "You're not serious—I mean, if you are, that's great, but—well, shouldn't we have talked it over first?"

"I think it's a fabulous idea," Mama said. "We're going to have such fun together, Imogene."

Bob had managed to maneuver Imogene around the dining room so he could put his other scrawny arm around his partner. "Hey Rob," he said, "Abby is your best friend, and you're terribly fond of Mozella. I thought you'd be pleased if I invited their cousin to stay with us for a while."

"With *us*? What does that mean?" Rob's beautiful, and very wealthy, mother was far too much of a control freak to raise her voice outside of the bedroom (I doubt if she'd ever done so, even in there), but it was exceedingly clear that she'd already had all four of her burners lit. When not speaking, her lips totally disappeared in a thin hard line.

Bob smiled. He'd rehearsed a casual, slightly condescending smile, but the one that appeared on his lips was as twisted as a stick of red licorice. Clearly the man was nervous as a long-tailed cat on a porch full of rocking chairs.

"It *means*," he said, "that Cousin Imogene can be my guest here for as long as she wishes to be."

Sandra gasped, despite her intentions. "You can't do that! It's my house too. Rob, darling, say something to these dear people."

At least Rob had the courtesy to look us each in the eye for a second or two before responding. "Mama," he said quietly, "Bob does have a right to have guests."

"Why I never!" Her voice had risen three notes, so great was her agitation.

"But speaking of guests," I said, trying my best not to gloat, "Rob, do you like pets?"

"Pets?"

"*No* pets," Sandra said. She closed her eyes and shivered. "Absolutely *no* pets! The shedding, the smell—it's unthinkable."

"Abby," Rob said, "you know that I love cats, but we can't have any because of Bob's allergies."

"Do you like even smaller pets?"

"You mean like hamsters?"

"Sort of. Cousin Imogene brought along Willard and Ben. They're very quiet, so you won't even know they're here."

Sandra opened one eye and fixed it on me. "That's completely out of the question. We haven't even said yes to that woman, much less her rodents."

Rob squared his shoulders and, I swear, grew three inches in height at the same time, even though he was already fifty years old. "Cousin Imogene," he said, gallantly kissing her hand, "you are welcome to stay here as long as you like."

Cousin Imogene blushed and giggled like a nine-year-old. "Abby, you didn't tell me how cute he was."

"That's because he's spoken for," I whispered.

"Oh you naughty, naughty boy," she said before giggling again. "Well, I suppose a fellow can always have two girlfriends, can't he?"

"Uh-uh," Bob stammered, "you see, Cousin Imogene—"

"Are Ben and Willard in the car?" I asked.

"Oh no, dear," she said, her attention quite diverted for the moment, "they're right here."

She hefted the oversized handbag up on the nearest chair and held the wooden handles about an inch apart. Immediately two very whiskered snouts poked out and commenced twitching.

"What the hell?" Rob said.

"Lord have mercy," Sandra and Mama said simultaneously.

"Come on out boys," Cousin Imogene said. She tore the bag open the rest of the way and out clambered two of the biggest and ugliest rodents I've ever seen, and that includes everyone in my ex-husband's family.

Mama, who'd raised a son who kept white mice as pets, was green around the gills, but still a step or two away from fainting. She grabbed her purse from the console by the door.

"It's been a lovely evening everyone," she said, speaking faster than a Southern woman ought to. "Good night y'all."

"Good night," we chorused.

Perhaps it was the door shutting hard behind Mama, but something definitely spooked one of the rats. It took off like greased lightning and disappeared in the direction of Sandra's bedroom.

"Oh my," Cousin Imogene said, "Willard's always been a bit rambunctious. But don't you worry, he'll come out when he's hungry."

"That could be days," I said, "because rats will eat just about anything—if you know what I mean."

"Oops," Cousin Imogene said as she unsuccessfully

lunged at Ben, who proved himself the less intelligent of the two by jumping on the table and heading straight for the stuffed musk-oxen scrotums.

"That does it," Sandra said, her voice a full octave above normal. "I'm moving back to Charlotte, *tonight*, and there's nothing you can do to stop me."

Nor did we even try.

Welcome to the
Den of Antiquity

*Home to rare antiques, priceless artwork—
and murder!*

Celebrated author Tamar Myers invites you to enjoy
her hilarious mystery series featuring Charleston's
favorite shopkeeper-turned-detective,
Abigail Timberlake.

"A very funny mystery series . . . a hilarious hero-
ine."

Charleston Post & Courier

"Professionally plotted and developed, and fun
to read."

San Francisco Valley Times

"Rollicking!"

The Washington Post

"Who do you read after Sue Grafton or Margaret
Moron or Patricia Cornwell? . . . Tamar Myers!"
Greensboro News & Record

Step into the world of Tamar Myers, and see what
mysteries the Den of Antiquity has in
store for you . . .

Larceny and Old Lace
For whom the bell pull tolls . . .

As owner of the Den of Antiquity, recently divorced (but *never* bitter!) Abigail Timberlake is accustomed to delving into the past, searching for lost treasures, and navigating the cutthroat world of rival dealers at flea markets and auctions. Still, she never thought she'd be putting her expertise in mayhem and detection to other use—until a crotchety "junque" dealer, Abby's aunt Eulonia Wiggins, was found murdered!

Although Abigail is puzzled by the instrument of death—an exquisite antique bell pull that Aunt Eulonia *never* would have had the taste to acquire—she's willing to let the authorities find the culprit. But now, Auntie's prized lace collection is missing, and sombody's threatened Abby's most priceless possession: her son, Charlie. It's up to Abby to put the murderer "on the block."

Gilt by Association
A closetful of corpse . . .

Abigail Timberlake parlayed her savvy about exquisite
old things into a thriving antiques enterprise: the Den
of Antiquity. Now she's a force to be reckoned with in
Charlotte's close-knit world of mavens and eccentrics.
But a superb, gilt-edged eighteenth-century French ar-
moire she purchased for a song at an estate auction has
just arrived along with something she didn't pay for: a
dead body.

Suddenly her shop is a crime scene—and closed to the
public during the busiest shopping season of the year—
so Abigail is determined to speed the lumbering police
investigation along. But amateur sleuthing is leading
the feisty antiques expert into a murderous mess of
dysfunctional family secrets. And the next cadaver
found stuffed into fine old furniture could wind up being Abigail's own.

The Ming and I

Rattling old family skeletons . . .

North Carolina native Abigail Timberlake is quick to dismiss the seller of a hideous old vase—until the poor lady comes hurtling back through the shop window minutes later, the victim of a fatal hit-and-run. Tall, dark, and handsome homicide investigator Greg Washburn—who just happens to be Abby's boyfriend—is frustrated by conflicting accounts from eyewitnesses. And he's just short of furious when he learns that the vase was a valuable Ming, and Abby let it vanish from the crime scene. Abby decides she had better find out for herself what happened to the treasure—and to the lady who was dying to get rid of it.

As it turns out, the victim had a lineage that would make a Daughter of the Confederacy green with envy, and her connection with the historic old Roselawn Plantation makes that a good place to start sleuthing. Thanks to her own mama's impeccable Southern credentials, Abby is granted an appointment with the board members—but no one gives her the right to snoop. And digging into the long-festering secrets of a proud family of the Old South turns out to be a breach of good manners that could land Abby six feet under in the family plot.

So Faux, So Good
Every shroud has a silver lining . . .

Abigail Timberlake has never been happier. She is about to marry the man of her dreams AND has just outbid all other Charlotte antiques dealers for an exquisite English tea service. But an early wedding present rains on Abby's parade. The one-of-a-kind tea service Abby paid big bucks for has a twin. A frazzled Abby finds more trouble on her doorstep—literally—when a local auctioneer mysteriously collapses outside her shop and a press clipping of her engagement announcement turns up in the wallet of a dead man. (Obviously she won't be getting a wedding present from him.)

Tracing the deceased to a small town in the Pennsylvania Dutch country, Abby heads above the Mason-Dixon Line to search for clues. Accompanied by a trio of eccentric dealers and her beloved but stressed-out cat, she longs for her Southern homeland as she confronts a menagerie of dubious characters. Digging for answers, Abby realizes that she might just be digging her own grave in—horrors!—Yankeeland.

Baroque and Desperate

Good help is hard to keep—alive . . .

Unflappable and resourceful, Abigail Timberlake relies on her knowledge and savvy to authenticate the facts from the fakes when it comes to either curios *or* people. Her expertise makes Abby invaluable to exceptionally handsome Tradd Maxwell Burton, wealthy scion of the renowned Latham family. He needs her to determine the most priceless item in the Latham mansion. A treasure hunt in an antique-filled manor? All Abby can say is "Let the games begin!"

But when Abby, accompanied by her best friend C.J., arrives at the estate she receives a less than warm welcome from the Latham clan. Trying to fulfill Tradd's request, Abby finds she could cut the household tension with a knife. Only someone has beaten her to it by stabbing a maid to death with an ancient kris. Suddenly all eyes are on C.J., whose fingerprints just happen to be all over the murder weapon. Now Abby must use her knack for detecting forgeries to expose the fake alibi of the genuine killer.

Estate of Mind

A faux van Gogh that's to die for . . .

When Abigail Timberlake makes a bid of $150.99 on a truly awful copy of van Gogh's *Starry Night*, she's just trying to support the church auction. Hopefully she'll make her money back on the beautiful gold antique frame. Little does she expect she's bought herself a fortune . . . and a ton of trouble.

Hidden behind the faux van Gogh canvas is a multi-million-dollar lost art treasure. Suddenly she's a popular lady in her old hometown, and her first visit is from Gilbert Sweeny, her schoolyard sweetie who claims the family's painting was donated by mistake. But social calls quickly turn from nice to nasty as it's revealed that the mysterious masterpiece conceals a dark and deadly past and some modern-day misconduct that threatens to rock the Rock Hill social structure to its core. Someone apparently thinks the art is worth killing for, and Abby knows she better get to the bottom of the secret scandal and multiple murders before she ends up buried six feet under a starry night.

A Penny Urned
Pickled, then potted . . .

All that remains of Lula Mae Wiggins—who drowned in a bathtub of cheap champagne on New Year's Eve—now sits in an alleged Etruscan urn in Savannah, Georgia. Farther north, in Charleston, South Carolina, Abigail Timberlake is astonished to learn that she is the sole inheritor of the Wiggins estate. Late Aunt Lula was, after all, as distant a relative as kin can get.

Arriving in Savannah, Abby makes a couple of startling discoveries. First, that Lula Mae's final resting place is more American cheap than Italian antique. And second, that there was a very valuable 1793 one-cent piece taped to the inside lid. Perhaps a coin collection worth millions is hidden among the deceased's worldly possessions—making Lula's passing more suspicious than originally surmised. With the strange appearance of a voodoo priestess coupled with the disturbing disappearance of a loved one—and with nasty family skeletons tumbling from the trees like acorns—Abby needs to find her penny auntie's killer or she'll be up to her ashes in serious trouble.

Nightmare in Shining Armor
The corpse is in the mail . . .

Abigail Timberlake's Halloween costume party is a roaring success—until an unexpected fire sends the panicked guests fleeing from Abby's emporium. One exiting reveler she is only too happy to see the back of is Tweetie "Little Bo Peep" Timberlake—unfaithful wife of Abby's faithless ex, Buford. But not long after the fire is brought under control, the former Mrs. T discovers an unfamiliar suit of armor in her house. And stuffed inside is the heavily siliconed, no-longer-living body of the current Mrs. T.

Certainly some enraged collector of medieval chain mail has sent Abby this deadly delivery. But diving into their eccentric ranks could prove a lethal proposition for the plucky antiques dealer turned amateur sleuth. And even a metal suit may not be enough to protect Abby from the vicious and vindictive attention of a crazed killer.

Splendor in the Glass
Murder is a glass act . . .

Antiques dealer Abby Timberlake is thrilled when *the* Ms. Amelia Shadbark—doyenne of Charleston society—invites her to broker a pricey collection of Lalique glass sculpture. These treasures will certainly boost business at the Den of Antiquity, and maybe hoist Abby into the upper crust—which would please her class-conscious mom, Mozella, to no end. Alas, Abby's fragile dream is soon shattered when Mrs. Shadbark meets a foul, untimely end. And as the last known visitor to the victim's palatial abode, Abby's being pegged by the local law as suspect Numero Uno.

Of course, there are other possible killers—including several dysfunctional offspring and a handyman who may have been doing more for the late Mrs. S than fixing her leaky faucets. But Abby's the one who'll have to piece the shards of this deadly puzzle together—or else face a fate far worse than a mere seven years of bad luck!

Tiles and Tribulations

Supernatural born killer . . .

Abigail Timberlake would rather be anywhere else on a muggy Charleston summer evening—even putting in extra hours at her antiques shop—than at a séance. But her best friend, "Calamity Jane," thinks a spirit—or "Apparition American," as ectoplasmically correct Abby puts it—lurks in the eighteenth-century Georgian mansion, complete with priceless, seventeenth-century Portuguese kitchen tiles, that C.J. just bought as a fixer-upper. Luckily, Abby's mama located a psychic in the yellow pages—a certain Madame Woo-Woo—and, together with a motley group of feisty retirees know as the "Heavenly Hustlers," they all get down to give an unwanted spook the heave-ho.

But, for all her extrasensory abilities, the Madame didn't foresee that she, herself, would be forced over to the other side prematurely. Suddenly Abby fears there's more than a specter haunting C.J. And they'd better exorcise a flesh-and-blood killer fast before the recently departed Woo-Woo gets company.

Statue of Limitations
Death by David . . .

Abigail Timberlake, petite but feisty proprietor of Charleston's Den of Antiquity antiques shop, stopped speaking to best friend and temporary decorating partner Wynnell Crawford a month ago—after questioning her choice of a cheap, three-foot-high replica of Michelangelo's David to adorn the garden of a local bed-and-breakfast. But now Wynnell has broken the silence with one phone call . . . *from prison!*

It seems the B and B owner has been fatally beaten—allegedly by the same tacky statue—and Wynnell's been fingered by the cops for the bashing. But Abby suspects there's more to this well-sculpted slaying than initially meets the eye, and she wants to take a closer look at the not-so-bereaved widower and the two very odd couples presently guesting at the hostelry. Because if bad taste was a capital crime, Wynnell would be guilty as sin—but she's certainly no killer!

Monet Talks

Birds of a feather die together . . .

Abigail Timberlake is thrilled to purchase an elaborate Victorian birdcage that is a miniature replica of the Taj Mahal. However she's less excited by the cage's surprise occupant—a loud, talkative myna bird named Monet. But Monet soon becomes a favorite with Abby's customers—until one day he goes mysteriously missing. In his place is a stuffed bird and a ransom note demanding the real Monet painting in exchange for Abby's pet. "What Monet painting?" is Abby's only response.

Abby tries to put the bird-snatching out of her mind, dismissing it as a cruel joke—until Abby's mama, Mozella, is taken too. This time the kidnapper threatens to kill Mozella unless Abby produces the painting.

What do a talking bird, Mozella, and a painting hidden for hundreds of years have in common? Abby must figure it all out soon before the could-be killer flies the coop for good.

The Cane Mutiny

Abigail Timberlake Washburn understands the antiques game is a gamble—so she doesn't know what to expect when she wins the bidding for the contents of an old locker that has been sealed for years. It's a delightful surprise when she discovers inside a collection of exquisite old walking sticks—and a not-so-delightful one when she pulls out a decrepit gym bag containing . . . *a human skull!*

The last thing the diminutive South Carolina antiques dealer needs is to be suspected of foul play. So she grabs her chatty assistant (and future sister-in-law), C.J., and heads out to search for a killer they can stick it to. But this cane case will be no walk in the park—with its arcane clues hinting at poaching, counterfeiting, smuggling . . . and homicide, of course. And when a fresh corpse turns up, things are about to get *really* sticky for Abby and her staff of one.